IN PRAISE OF:
THE BUNKO BABES

"Too often here in the 21st Century, we become so busy making a living that we forget to create a life. In this book, Leah Starr Baker helps us all to discover, recognize, and strategically implement the elements of friendship, relationship, and true connection that can make our lives precious."

Jim Stovall
Author of *The Ultimate Gift*
President, *Narrative Television Network*

"*The Bunko Babes* is a great time and an utterly enjoyable read! The women are so much like those you already know and love (or want to know and love) it's like spending several hours with great friends! Enjoyable from front to back, it's great for a weekend alone or at the beach, just be sure to have chocolate handy!"

Marrianne White
Author of *Mommy Is Missing* and *Lost Child*

"Going Bunko for *The Bunko Babes!* Leah Starr Baker's first novel is an absolute winner—an entertaining read with deep implications. It's a book about faith lived out on the battlefields of everyday suburbia."

Max Davis
Author of *Luke's Passage*

D1418493

"What an incredible first novel! The characters are real, the story is poignant, encompassing the whole range of emotions, and it is full of wisdom. I can't wait for more."

Richard Exley
Author of *The Alabaster Cross* and *Encounters with Christ*

"This is a touching and honest story about a group of friends who help each other find joy, even as they struggle through some of life's toughest challenges."

Susan Breen
Author of *The Fiction Class*

"A rare book, which has the capacity to make the reader laugh on one page and be moved to tears on the next. Written in first person, *The Bunko Babes* is the account of a group of life-time friends who not only share fun, but also support each other through life-changing, hard times. Baker has a refreshing style which makes her first novel a rewarding read, capturing the essence of today's 30-somethings, and showing mature insight into human nature."

Evelyn Looper
Counselor, Educator, and Minister

THE BUNKO BABES

A NOVEL

LEAH STARR BAKER

Emerald Pointe Books

The Bunko Babes
A Novel
ISBN: 0-97851-375-4
Copyright © 2007 by Leah Starr Baker
P.O. 35327
Tulsa, Oklahoma 74153

Published by Emerald Pointe Books
P.O. Box 35327
Tulsa, Oklahoma 74153-0327

A friend

Celebrates your successes,

Shares in your sorrows,

Accepts your shortcomings,

And encourages you to never give up!

This book is dedicated to my closest girlfriends:

Susannah Gail Pogue

and

Karen "Renee" Dugger

My "Bunko Babes."

A NOTE FROM THE AUTHOR

Bunko, Bunco, or Bonco? Right up until sending my book to press, this seemed to be the glaring question. Back and forth the discussions volleyed till we were all ready to pull out our hair. Finally, my original spelling was agreed upon because in the end, it was determined that whether your group uses a "K" instead of a "C," or a "U" in place of an "O," none of that really matters.

The game of Bunko isn't about dice and door prizes. No, it's about fun, food, and fellowship, taking time out of our incredibly busy lives to come together, once a week or once a month, to reconnect with our community. Too often, we, as women especially, find ourselves overextended; so busy doing and proving that we completely forget about being and sharing.

As the author and as a woman, I want to encourage each one of you, if you haven't already, to join or begin a Bunko group of your own. Trust me, you won't regret it. I'll even go so far as to say, "You'll thank me," as your circle of confidantes expands and you find yourself looking forward to each time Bunko Night comes around. I don't doubt that you'll come to love and cherish the relationships you'll build in the process. So ladies, are you ready to ROLL?

Your Fellow Bunko Babe
Leah Starr Baker

THE BUNKO BABES

CHAPTER

ONE

MAY 2006

Picking up old newspapers and empty pizza boxes, I shove them haphazardly into the oven. It's 6:15 on a Thursday evening and I'm rushing around getting ready for my weekly Bunko night. Quickly, I brush the crumbs off the counter into the palm of my hand before tossing them in the sink. Glancing around, I peruse the kitchen looking for anything else that might give away my penchant for messiness.

Jessica Goldstein, my best friend since childhood, loves to tease me about my habit of hiding my messes as opposed to actually cleaning them up. You see, I'm a firm believer in the adage, "Out of sight, out of mind." As long as things look good on the surface, then that's all that matters to me. I've resigned myself to the fact that I will never win the Good Housekeeping Seal of Approval, and I'm okay with that. I figure Martha Stewart already has enough clones and one less won't be missed.

Taking a final sweep around the house, I stuff miscellaneous items into drawers and under the couch, before tossing Robert's smelly soccer shoes into the disaster he calls a bedroom and firmly close the door.

You guessed it! My children have inherited my cleaning habits or perhaps I should say the lack thereof. They've become quite adept at shoving things anywhere and everywhere as long as it is out of sight. In fact, they may even outdo me in that department. As a result, I dare not venture into their rooms, except on the rarest of occasions, for fear of what I might find. Their laundry, I leave stacked in the hallway outside their respective doors. More often than not, it remains there, slowly dwindling with each passing day, until I once again replenish the piles.

Brooklyn really isn't so bad but Robert...Ugh! I stopped straightening his room when I went to hang up a pair of jeans that were in the bottom of his closet and discovered they were stuffed full of shavings from the bottom of his hamster's cage. Instead of throwing the shavings away, he had simply hidden them. His hamster's cage *appeared to be clean* so I'd thought nothing of it. The truth was horrifying but not being the best example, I was in a quandary. How could I punish him when I'm constantly doing the same sort of thing myself? Still, something had to be done so I decided to consult my husband. He suggested that we ground Robert for a week, remove his X-Box 360 until his room passed inspection. We also require him to research the health hazards of animal excretions on the internet and write a three-page paper. Boy, did *we* learn a lot about germs.

I should probably take this moment to apologize to my future daughter-in-law. Whoever you are, sweetheart, I'm truly sorry. I never meant for things to get so out of hand. I got busy, I mean really busy. Raising twins isn't easy. Then, there was my father's funeral and the stress of relocating Mom from Tulsa to Fort Worth so she could be near her sister, not to mention Thomas' recent promotion. And lately, I've just been so incredibly tired...but enough of that. Robert's messiness is inexcusable. No thirteen-year-old should live in a room that looks the way his does. I pledge to you, for your sake and the sake of your marriage, that I will work to improve his cleaning habits (as well as my own). Of course, I've got plenty of time since I don't plan for him to marry for at least another ten years.

By the way, please forgive my rudeness. I don't believe that I've introduced myself. My name is Rebecca Thornton. My friends call me Becca. I'm thirty-seven years old, I've been married to Thomas for fifteen years and we have two children, twins no less. Robert and Brooklyn are thirteen. Robert is the oldest by two minutes and seventeen seconds and he never lets us forget it. Needless to say, those two keep me hopping.

Now, back to my story. I finally had to draw the line on allowing food in the bedrooms. Yep, you guessed it. The inevitable happened. One day last summer, a horrible smell began seeping out from under Robert's door and making its way throughout the rest of the house. It went unnoticed for several days because we had taken a spur-of-the-moment camping trip to Grand Lake and, par for the course, we had simply shoved things out of the way, turned up the thermostat of the air conditioner, and shut the door.

Upon our return, we were greeted by an appalling stench that caused us, one and all, to gag. The children refused to set foot inside the house. Thomas and I braved the smell, breathing primarily through our mouths, as we rushed to switch on ceiling fans and open windows. In our absence, the oppressive Oklahoma heat had served as an incubator for a half-eaten tuna fish sandwich Robert had shoved beneath his bed. Disgusting, I know. From that point on, the **No Food in the Bedrooms Rule** was established and strictly enforced.

Glancing at the clock, I realize I have a mere twenty minutes before my guests begin arriving. It's a good thing I'm adept at multitasking because I don't have much time to dress, put on a touch of makeup, and finish styling my hair. Grabbing my cordless straightener, I begin pulling it through my multicolored, choppy hair, all the while flipping through my closet for my favorite pair of jeans and new white blouse.

Last week, after years of futile searching, I finally stumbled upon that *perfect* white blouse. You know the one I'm talking about, ladies. The one you spend your whole life hoping to find. Well, I found it and I can't wait to wear it. Tossing aside the hot iron, I slip into my tastefully tattered baby blues but, before putting on my *perfect* blouse, I brush my cheeks with a dab of color, apply shimmery shadow to my lids, a quick coat of mascara, and finish with passion pink lip gloss.

Satisfied, I slip my arms into my blouse, slide my feet into my hot pink espadrilles, and grab my favorite silver hoops. Just in time, I might add, as the doorbell chimes announcing the first arrival. Without a doubt, it is Madison Monroe, one of my oldest and dearest friends. I smile to myself as I make my way to the door. Madison is always early and always perfect.

CHAPTER TWO

With great grandeur, I fling open the door. "Ms. Madison, what a surprise! You're the first to arrive."

She smiles graciously, accustomed to my constant teasing. "Hello, Becca. I brought the calamari."

Clapping my hands enthusiastically, I announce, "Ooh, my favorite." Taking the Zio's Restaurant bag from her, I head for the dining room inhaling the tantalizing aroma as I walk. Glancing over my shoulder, I lift my eyebrows crazily, give her my best Joey Tribiani look and say, "By the way, you look absolutely divine," all the while trying not to laugh.

Waving off my antics, she replies, "Thanks. I just got the belt today." Pausing, she does a little spin for my benefit and asks, "You don't think it's a little much, do you?"

Always dressed to the nines, tonight is no exception. Madison is head to toe Prada. Her long, tan legs are shown off to perfection by her classic white sundress, belted tightly at the waist by her "new" red, crocodile belt, which is wide, of course. She looks wonderful. Just do away with her ever-present, cashmere cardigan tossed casually over her shoulders and she would be absolute perfection.

I'm an attractive enough woman, tonight especially. I'm what you'd call the all-American girl next door. Truthfully, aside from a stubborn twenty pounds that refuse to come off without diet and exercise, I'm aging quite well. But next to Madison, I feel like Kansas in the shadow of the Rocky Mountains.

Ignoring my nagging insecurities, I assure her. "It's wonderful, Madison. I wouldn't change a thing...except...." I let the sentence hang, my eyes sparkling with fun.

Placing her coordinating clutch by the door, she trails me into the kitchen. "I know. You would lose the sweater. You've been telling me that since grade school."

Throwing my hands up in mock despair, I dramatically implore, "That's because you've been wearing them since grade school."

Madison's amazing lavender eyes meet mine across the kitchen cabinet before we break into girlish giggles. Bunko night always brings out our inner child.

At last, my *fashionista* friend takes notice of my most recent purchase and I glow as her kind words warm my heart. "I'm not the only one who's looking hot tonight, my dear. Is that a new blouse I see?" Taking a seat on one of my barstools, she crosses her ankles daintily before letting out a soft sigh.

After years of companionship, I am attuned to her nuances and tonight something is bothering her. "Tough day?" I ask, before reaching for a seldom-used crystal platter.

Madison doesn't respond and I can't help wondering what's troubling her. It's not like her to be so morose.

Not wanting to pry, I try to lighten the atmosphere. Holding up a beautiful lead crystal platter, I ask, "Do you ever wonder why people purchase such impractical gifts for newlyweds? I mean, how often do you break out the china? And who has actually ever used a soup tureen?" I chuckle, thinking of the one protectively wrapped and stored in the top of my very own pantry.

A simple lifting of one of Madison's perfectly arched eyebrows says it all and I can't help laughing at myself. "Duh...how silly of me," I say slapping my forehead. "I forgot who I was talking to."

Seeing I can't even coax a smile out of her I decide something is seriously wrong. Taking both of her hands in mine, I ask, "So what is it, girlfriend? What's troubling you?"

At my friend's continued silence, I study her, noticing for the first time, the dark circles under her eyes. She gives me a wane smile and I sense the weariness hidden just beneath the surface. She has never been one to talk about personal things and I can see this isn't easy for her. Sighing deeply, she finally says, "Do you ever feel...I don't know...tired? Overwhelmed?"

I can't help but laugh and Madison seems genuinely surprised and a little hurt by my reaction. I rush to explain. Placing my rarely groomed hand upon her perfectly manicured one, I say, "I'm sorry I laughed, my dear, sweet friend. I truly am. Your question just caught me off guard, that's all. But the answer is, yes! We all feel overwhelmed at one time or another; or, in my case, most of the time. In fact, the girls and I were beginning to wonder about you because you never seem to struggle like the rest of us."

Another deep sigh before Madison quietly admits, "Meredith still isn't sleeping through the night and it's wearing me out. I just don't know what to do."

Listening to my friend, I realize that beneath her perfectly composed persona she is struggling with the same feelings of inadequacy that so often haunt me. I shouldn't be surprised, sleep deprivation can make the best of us feel overwhelmed, but I am. It's just hard for me to imagine a situation Madison can't handle.

"Meredith is different from Mitchell. She doesn't listen and she refuses to adapt to a schedule."

Softly, I reply, "It sounds like she takes after her mother."

"What do you mean?" Madison asks, seeming genuinely puzzled. "You know I'm a stickler for schedules."

"She's got a mind of her own, like you. A child with her temperament can be a challenge for the best parent, but they usually grow up to be leaders. Consider yourself; you didn't turn out too bad, now did you?"

Not sure how to respond, she gives me a tentative smile, her full lips barely turning up. Madison is obviously out of her comfort zone. In her world, everything has its place and everything is in its place. Sometimes, I can only marvel that we've remained such close friends, seeing how different we are. Who knows, maybe she needs a little chaos in her life? The Lord knows I could use a little order in mine. Be that as it may, she's one of my dearest friends and my heart goes out to her.

Glancing at the clock, I head for the dining room to place the now-plated calamari dish on the buffet. The doorbell chimes and I turn toward the foyer, my best smile firmly in place. Within minutes, my house is bursting at the seams with my three childhood friends and our four newest comrades. The eight of us make up what we call "The Bunko Babes."

You've already met Madison, our blonde-haired beauty, so let me introduce you to the rest of the gang. Earlier I mentioned my best friend Jessica Goldstein. Jessica is a year younger than me and everything that I always wanted to be. But we'll get into all that later. We've been friends forever and we know each other inside and out. She's married to Jason, but unlike the rest of us, they still haven't been blessed with children, not from lack of trying I can assure you.

Kathleen Stone is Jessica's half sister and thirteen years her junior. We call her Kitty Kat (a nickname she tolerates). Adam, her husband, is an OU grad and a former football star who currently plays for the Tulsa Talons. They're newlyweds, having been married for less than a year, and she's already pregnant. We're all excited for her, but I can tell that it's hard for Jessica.

Autumn Levitt is the flower child of our group and I absolutely adore her. As my mom used to say, we've been thick as thieves since we were pollywogs making waves in the church nursery. She's the complete opposite of me and that's what makes her so much fun. We share the same birthday, having been born only hours apart, which is rather amazing considering we are so different. I'm a believer in all things modern and convenient, Autumn's into all things natural— organic foods, homeopathic medicines, and home births! Even after eight children, she has no plans of stopping and she homeschools them all. They eat only organic food or better yet that which is homegrown in their own garden. I think she's nuts but I love her to death.

Out of the corner of my eye, I glimpse Kitty Kat heading straight for the calamari and that just won't do. "Hey, stay away from the calamari! You know it's my favorite."

Grinning from ear to ear, she piles a heaping serving on her plate, daring me to interfere. With a roar, I plunge after her, scattering women like wild geese after a shotgun blast. Laughter and high-pitched squeals fill the evening air as she and I play cat and mouse around my seldom used mahogany table.

Always looking for an opportunity to tease her baby sis, Jessica sneaks up on Kat's blind side and catches her around her waist, giving me ample time to swoop in for the steal. Grabbing her plate, I flee with my prize, stuffing rapidly cooling calamari into my mouth.

"That's not fair!" Kitty Kat protests, trying desperately to spit out the dark hair stuck tenaciously in her raspberry lip gloss. Gasping for breath, she fights to speak through bouts of laughter, "Two against one!"

Patting her sister's tummy, Jessica replies, "Technically, that's not true."

Kat flushes slightly with embarrassment, her pale cheeks instantly brightening. "Jessica, please."

Smacking her soundly on her tush, Jessica says, "Oh, Kitty Kat! It's nothing to be embarrassed about." Her voice trailing off, Jessica's mouth turns down as her eyes begin to cloud.

Knowing immediately what is happening to my friend, I rush to her rescue. "Hey, ladies! Who's ready to gorge themselves on fattening foods, catch up on each other's lives, laugh a lot, share our secrets, and maybe, just maybe win some fabulous prizes?"

As they make their way to the buffet line, I catch Jessica's eye and she gives me her sweet, sassy smile. "Thank you," she mouths soundlessly. I give her my jaunty little wink and a goofy smile in return. She laughs and for the moment all is right with The Bunko Babes.

CHAPTER THREE

Grabbing our scorecards and pencils, we are ready for our table assignments. The evening's theme is "Under the Sea" (hence the calamari) and I've gone all out, as I usually do. The "High Table" is decked out in glittering arrays of turquoise, purple, coral, and lime green. Fish and Mermaids hang from the ceiling amongst a multitude of balloons. The table is covered in a sparkling sea blue cloth sprinkled with confetti in various shapes and colors befitting the theme. The dice are purple and the bell gleams brightly. The "Low Table" in the breakfast area is similarly decorated minus the bell. All is ready and we are giddy with excitement.

Now, before you seasoned Bunko Babes get upset, I am perfectly aware that normally Bunko is played with three tables but our group is a bit smaller, and trust me, it works out just fine. Sometimes, I think it actually works out better because we get to know each other even more.

As we pass by the coffee bar, we each reach into the red velvet bag and choose a chip. Those who select a blue chip head for the high table while those who draw a red chip are consigned to the low table for the first round of play. All around me, I hear shouts of glee and moans of artificial despair. As the evening's hostess, I am last to pick. Even though the result is obvious, I walk with a saucy flounce to the bag and make a big show of choosing the last lonely chip. It's blue, surprise! Yea! I bounce up and down on the balls of my feet giggling like a schoolgirl. The girls from the high table smack palms with me and off we go to begin the first round of competition.

"So where's your family this evening, Becca?" Karen Jones asks, her dark red hair bouncing about her shoulders as she walks. "I haven't seen hide nor hair of them."

Karen, an RN who works on the Labor and Delivery floor at St. Francis Hospital, gives me a sassy grin as she takes her seat at the table across from me. I can't help thinking that although she isn't really pretty, her infectious smile and the splash of freckles across her nose make her attractive in a tomboyish sort of way. Autumn has been trying, without much success, to convince her to become a midwife. I don't think it will ever happen. The one time she convinced

Karen to accompany her to a home birth, Karen was a nervous wreck.

Giving her a conspiratorial wink, I reply, "That's by design. I convinced Thomas to take the kids to see a movie." Taking a seat at the table, I continue, "What about you? Did you hire a sitter or is James on duty tonight?" Karen and James have three children under the age of four. They're adorable but incredibly rambunctious.

Pretending to be aghast, Karen replies, "James? Alone? With our girls? Are you kidding me? I have to place them in daycare during my shifts even if he is working at home for the day." Pausing, she shakes her head in disbelief, her "bobbed" do swaying with the rhythm of her mirth. "Do you know what happened the last time I left them with him?"

These are the kind of stories I live for and I lean forward in anticipation. It's my turn to roll so Mercedes Wallace, a recent transplant from Argentina and barely out of her teens, places the dice in my outstretched hand. I toss them absent-mindedly as Karen continues her story, her hazel eyes alight with merriment.

"It'd been a particularly stressful week at work and, with no help on the home front, I was nearly out of my mind. I simply had to have some time alone or I was going to go absolutely, positively insane. Taking care of three preschoolers might not be so overwhelming if I didn't have to work outside the home, but as it is I often feel like a piece of raw meat in a tank of piranhas. Everyone wants a piece of me, especially my girls."

Glancing at Madison, she says, "If anyone could handle it, I'm sure you could what with your genius for organizing." Karen pauses, clicking her tongue, before continuing, "But I'd bet that my three girls could give even you a run for your money."

Watching Madison closely, I see her flinch but I'm sure no one else notices. In their eyes, she is still the consummate mother and homemaker, the one we're all trying so desperately to emulate. My heart goes out to her as I recall our earlier conversation.

Karen continues, her round face flushed with animation. "There was absolutely no food in the house, except for what I was still providing." Glancing briefly down at her bust, she gives us a little wink.

Surprised laughter dances around the table and I am reminded, yet again, that there is much more to Karen than what meets the eye. Quiet and shy? Maybe at first but get to know her and she'll keep you in stitches. I tune back in...

"Given the circumstances, I decided that my time away could best be spent grocery shopping, I mean what choice did I have." Placing her hand to the side of her mouth as if sharing a secret, she whispers, "I've got to admit I've never enjoyed grocery shopping more. Unfortunately, my escape into the real world was short-lived. All too soon, the backseat was stacked with bags of groceries and I was headed home."

Although my points are adding up slowly, I'm so enthralled with Karen's story that I'm not even disappointed when I don't roll the required number. "Oh, well," I say, tossing the dice Madison's way. "Go on, Karen. I'm dying to know what happened."

Enjoying the moment, Karen draws out her story. I softly smile. Who can blame her? I too am a ham and I always prolong my time in the limelight as long as I can, never seeming to get too much attention. Mischief colors Karen's full face and I've never seen my friend look prettier. After additional coaxing from Madison and Mercedes, she at last concedes, "Okay, okay, I'd been gone no more than an hour-and-a-half, two hours, at the most." Sheepishly, she admits, "Okay, maybe it was closer to three hours. Whatever, it wasn't long enough I can tell you that."

Looking around the table, she measures our responses before continuing, "Your husbands may be good babysitters but James..." she fumbles for words trying hard not to sound disrespectful of her man. "James...well, the simple truth is he's clueless; absolutely clueless when it comes to taking care of three little girls. His idea of looking after the girls is turning them loose while he does his own thing. Don't get me wrong. James is a wonderful and devoted father, but let him start a video game and he's completely oblivious to the world around him."

"I was nervous, of course," Karen confides, "So once I was in the car and headed home, I tried calling just to reassure myself that everything was okay. To my dismay, the phone just rang and rang. Arriving home, I rushed into the house calling frantically, 'James! Girls! Where are you? Is everybody okay?'"

We're all hanging on Karen's every word, the Bunko game momentarily forgotten. After that buildup, I'm sure one of the girls has swallowed poison or poked out an eye or something equally traumatic.

"I found James kneeling in front of the playroom door, screwdriver in hand, sweat pouring off his brow. Nearly frantic, he was pounding on the door, while shouting at the girls. 'Unlock the door right this minute! Do you understand me? I'm not kidding! This is your last warning.'"

Smiling ruefully, she adds, "James will be the first to tell you, he's no 'Tim the Toolman.' Hammer, wrench, screwdriver? He doesn't know one from the other or even what they're used for. Hello? My man is even dangerous with a butter knife."

They say that in comedy, timing is everything and Karen's timing is perfect. After a beat, she resumes her story, a tender smile playing across her lips. "But give James a guitar and something magical happens."

"Well, enough about that," she waves off her comment. "If I hadn't been so frantic, I would have seen the humor in the situation. Especially since, unbeknownst to James, I keep a key above the door for situations just like this. Imagine his surprise when I reached up, located the key, and unlocked the door. His consternation, however, was nothing compared to the shock that awaited me."

She pauses dramatically, drawing us into the moment. By this time, I am ready to shake the story out of her. *This* is worse than the commercial break in the middle of Paul Harvey's "The Rest of the Story."

Suddenly, my cell phone emits the raucous sounds of "I Will Survive," alerting me to a call from my mother. Glancing at Karen, I groan. "We interrupt this program for a brief message," I quip, eliciting a few chuckles from around the table. Holding up my finger, I say, "Hold that thought. I'll be right back. It's my mother. If I don't answer it she might call 9-1-1."

Grabbing my cell off the kitchen counter, I head for the living room punching redial on the way. Mom's voice bursts in my ear as I plop onto the sofa. "Becca, you called back. Thank God."

Pulling the phone slightly away from my ear, I try to ask, "Is everything okay?" but as always, I am interrupted.

"Why didn't you answer the first time? I was starting to worry."

My mom, bless her heart, has never bothered to learn the art of cell phone etiquette. As a result, she talks too loud and as quickly as possible, barely pausing for air. This makes for an extremely difficult, often embarrassing, conversation. I've tried to explain this to her on any number of occasions but, obviously, my efforts have been lost on her.

Impatiently, I reply, "Mom, it's my Bunko night, remember?"

"Rebecca, what I have to share with you simply cannot wait. I have news, darling, exciting news."

Rubbing the bridge of my nose, I sigh before trying to inject a note of enthusiasm into my voice, "You sound happy so it must be good news." When she hesitates before sharing her "exciting news," I get the message. She is punishing me for suggesting her news could wait until a more convenient time. Restraining myself, I take a calming breath. "Please, Mom, the suspense is killing me."

Still, she hesitates and it's almost as if I can feel her sense of triumph bouncing from cell tower to cell tower. "Becca," she finally exclaims, "God has granted me a second chance at love."

Surely I misunderstood her. "What was that, Mom?"

Giggling like a schoolgirl, she says, "I'm in love, sweet girl. Can you believe it? Your mother is getting married! Isn't God good?"

Her news sucks the wind out of me and I feel like I've been slammed against the wall. *How can this be? Has my mother lost her mind? Dad hasn't even been dead a year.* In my head, these and a host of other thoughts spin crazily, leaving me more than a little disoriented. And beneath the confusion, like the relentless beating of a drum, I hear over and over the three words that have rocked my world— "I'm...in...love."

"Becca, darling," she says with just a hint of pleading in her voice, "I know this must come as a surprise to you, but I really need your support. I need to know that you're happy for me."

Like an automaton, I respond, "I'm happy for you, Mother." Determined not to cry, I manage to say, "I'll talk to you later. Gotta go, bye."

Snapping the cell phone shut, I allow it to slide harmlessly out of my hand and onto the sofa. Laughter drifts in from the other room and I know I should return to my guests, but I cannot make my limbs work. My mind is whirling, but I can't seem to make any sense of my thoughts. They are jumbled and confused, like pieces of a jigsaw puzzle spilled on the floor. *How could she do this? Has she no respect for Daddy's memory?*

Numbly, I stand, straighten my blouse, pinch my cheeks for color, and paste a smile upon my face before returning to the girls and my interrupted night of fun and fellowship.

CHAPTER FOUR

Turning the corner into the dining room, I hear the tell-tale ding of the bell and the cultured voice of Madison excitedly announcing, "Bunko!"

Catching my reflection in the mirror hanging just above the buffet, Mercedes adds, "We continued without you, Becca. I hope you don'ta minda."

"Of course not," I reply automatically, hardly noticing her Argentine accent. Picking up my score pad and pencil, I ask quietly, "Did my team win or lose?" My voice sounds strange in my ears, and I reach for my cup of coffee hoping no one has noticed my discomfiture.

Madison gives me a searching look and as I pass, she reaches out, catching my arm. Refusing to meet my intuitive friend's eyes, I stare at her elegant, tanned fingers against my stark white blouse. Squeezing my arm, she is trying desperately to get me to raise my gaze. At my stubborn refusal, Madison finally whispers, "Becca, is your mother all right? Did something happen?"

Her concern is nearly my undoing, but I manage to retain my composure. Now is not the time or place for an emotional breakdown. Exercising the determination I am known for, I force myself to smile. I will have fun. I will cut up with my girlfriends and forget about the insanity my mother is planning. I swallow hard against the lump crowding my throat before giving Madison's hand a gentle squeeze.

Nodding slightly, I hasten to reassure her. "Everything's fine."

I can tell she isn't convinced but she decides not to press the issue. On the way to the low table, I stop briefly in the powder room for a touch-up of my lipstick. A fresh coat of gloss, a few deep breathes, and I'm nearly ready to go. Giving myself a stern look, I repeat the infamous Scarlett O'Hara line, "Tomorrow, I'll think of it all tomorrow. After all, tomorrow is another day."

At the low table, I manage to greet my fellow "losers" with a measure of enthusiasm. If they realize that I'm not my usual gregarious self, no one lets on. The redhead on my left is Karen Jones. Her partner is Autumn Levitt, our displaced hippie and across from me is Michelle, whom I affectionately refer to as "my little mud-sucker."

Miss Michelle Black is the most recent addition to our group and the only single Babe. She's twenty-six, sharp as a whistle, and a fireball to boot. Cute and petite as a toy poodle, there's only one thing holding her back (besides maybe her "Marsha Brady" hair and slightly outdated sense of style). She's a first-class pessimist—what I call a "mud-sucker." She's also my pet project.

As it turns out, Michelle is my partner for the next round and Autumn smiles encouragingly knowing the soft spot I have for her. I give my lifelong friend a conspiratorial wink before turning to Michelle. "How's my little mud-sucker doing this evening?" I inquire, my voice sounding forced and hollow to me. I vow to try a little harder to put the situation with Mom out of my mind.

Pursing her thin lips, Michelle states, "Pretty good, actually."

My eyes widen with surprise. Dramatically, I throw my head back, my hand to my forehead as if in a faint, while Autumn rushes to my assistance, frantically fanning my face. Jessica hollers from the other room. "Hey, what's going on in there?"

"Nothing to worry about," Karen shouts back. "Michelle just said that she was doing pretty good. That's all."

Well aware of her nickname, the other girls break into applause. "Woohoo! Good for you, Michelle! We should throw a party."

Michelle's creamy complexion slowly reddens as a blush floods her youthful face. "Enough, ladies. If you're not careful, I'll never say anything positive again."

Immediately sitting up, I shoo Autumn in the direction of her seat and she quickly rushes to sit, lest our antics cause Michelle to revert to form.

Eyes burning with intensity, Michelle reaches for the dice and begins her Bunko ritual. Rolling the dice between her palms three times, she shakes them twice and blows once, before tossing them high into the air.

Watching her, I can hardly believe this is the same young woman who only months ago was so introverted that she seemed afraid of her own shadow. No matter how "happening" the party, she always remained in the background, observing but never really participating. Now here she is smiling, laughing, and carrying on with all of us. Shaking my head, I can only marvel as Michelle emits a high-pitched squeal before exchanging high fives with Karen.

"Two 2's, Michelle, that's awesome!" encourages Karen.

Giving her partner a piercing look, Autumn inquires, "Whose team are you on anyway?"

With an effort, I become my normal rambunctious self once more, inserting, "Pay her no mind, Michelle. Just keep doin' what you're doin'. With any luck, I just might actually win a round this week."

"This week?" interjects Autumn, "Don't you mean this year?"

Pointing my finger directly at her, I try not to laugh, "Touche!"

Forcing myself to be the gregarious hostess has enabled me to put my mother's situation out of my mind, at least for the time being. I will not allow her to spoil this time with my friends. Giving Autumn the "evil eye," I remind her that we have not yet exchanged birthday gifts.

"Oops!" replies Autumn, a slight grimace on her full face. Brightening slightly, she adds, "Haven't we cancelled that two or three times?"

Chuckling, I say, "You did."

"My bad," Autumn admits, running her fingers through her tousled hair. Assuming a melodramatic tone, she continues, "But, Becca, please, I'm begging you. Have mercy on your oldest, dearest, quirkiest friend."

Laughing at her antics, I let my friend off the hook once more, just like she knew I would.

Switching subjects, she says, "Rod is driving me crazy with this remodeling thing. I thought the house was just fine the way it was but nooooo.... He heard about somebody in Idaho who'd built their house out of nothing but natural fibers. So now, he's ripping out our walls and replacing the insulation with," she pauses here for dramatic effect, tossing her hair over her shoulder. Her eyes sparkling with humor, she continues, "Straw. Yep, that's right. You heard me. Straw. Right now, my house smells as bad as my barn!"

Shaking my head at the craziness of it all, I reply, "I don't know how you do it, Autumn. I really don't."

Embarrassed, she waves off my compliment. "Oh, come on, Becca."

Interrupting us, Michelle hands the dice to Autumn. "While you two characters were carrying on, I was racking up a ton of points."

Before Autumn has a chance to roll, we hear a loud "Bunko!" followed by the tell-tale ringing of the bell from the high table. Cackling gleefully, I high-five Michelle, give her a wink and say enthusiastically, "I guess mud-suckers are good for something." Before heading for the high table, I grab her in a bear hug.

Taking advantage of my vulnerability, Michelle playfully punches me in the stomach and I double over, pretending to gasp. "How can someone so small pack such a powerful punch?"

Dropping immediately into her Hulk Hogan pose, slender arms flexing and face tightening into a grimace, she retorts, "It's what I call my 'Body by Peeps.'"

I chuckle at the reference to our favorite marshmallow candy and follow Michelle as she sashays into the other room, her honey hair swishing wildly around her boyish hips.

"Look out, ladies, Mighty Mouse is on the warpath," I announce as we sit down and prepare for another round of Bunko.

CHAPTER FIVE

The night is drawing to a close and most of the girls have already gone. Only Jessica and Autumn remain. At the door, I give Autumn a tight squeeze and she whispers in my ear, "Is Jessica going to be okay?"

I shrug my shoulders before replying, "I hope so. I'm going to talk to her. You're welcome to stay if you like."

Glancing down at her watch, she shakes her head. "I wish I could but it's past eleven and Rod's had the kids by himself all evening long."

Grimacing at the thought, I shove her out the door calling after her, "Give me a call if anyone's hurt or the straw caught fire, okay?"

"Fire is the least of my worries," she exclaims with a sigh as she returns to the front porch. "Imagine the mess if little Carpenter decides to take his potty training cues from the cows instead of from his brothers."

Our laughter fills the night and I give my dear, sweet friend another tight squeeze. "I hadn't considered that."

Stepping out of my sisterly embrace, she replies, "Of course not, your children were potty trained years ago."

Suddenly nostalgic, I say in a rather husky voice, "It's hard to believe that both my babies are teenagers now and what...Israel is a junior this year?"

"Yes," she answers softly, her round face taking on a wistful look as she realizes how soon her firstborn will be leaving home. "He's seventeen, driving, and a junior. Can you believe that?"

I shake my head, words being unnecessary.

Jessica is on my mind and I really should get back to her, but Autumn is caught up in the moment and I can't excuse myself without seeming disinterested. I tell myself that Jess will understand, knowing well Autumn's penchant for chatting.

"Heather is almost sixteen and has her permit. God, help us all," she says, her eyes raised to the heavens. "She's a sophomore. Dustin is thirteen and in the eighth grade. In a couple of weeks, Summer will be a teenager as well." Almost as an afterthought, she adds, "I wish we could get the kids together more often like we used to."

I nod in agreement, but I know it's not practical. Her life is a zoo. Combine that with the craziness of Robert's football schedule and Brooklyn's drama rehearsals.... It's nearly impossible.

I try to refocus because my dear friend isn't done with her list of "blessings." "Michael's ten and precocious as ever. Oh, what was it he said the other day... give me a minute and I'll think of it. It was so cute."

Her button nose is crinkled in concentration as she sucks the left side of her lower lip, an old and all-too-familiar habit. Watching her now, the years and the few extra pounds simply melt away. It is easy to see the young, beautiful woman she used to be. Adorable, absolutely adorable, is what my friend Autumn is.

I let the memories take me back and for a moment the three of us and Madison are just girls again. Like so many other times, we are spending the night together, crowded into my bedroom, sharing secrets, heartbreaks, and youthful dreams. We nearly drove my mother "bonkos" with our antics. As a result, she christened us "The Bonko Babes." When Bunko became the national rage, we started a group of our own and it was a natural transition for us to become "The Bunko Babes."

Snapping her fingers, Autumn says excitedly, "I got it. One morning last week, Michael came into the kitchen, his red hair tousled with sleep, superman pajamas buttoned crooked, and one sock missing. Stretching his thin arms above his head, he said, 'Mmm, mmm, mmm, I do love the smell of bacon in the morning.'"

We share a smile, chuckling, and I feel a pang in my chest as I realize how quickly my children are growing up. My time with them is passing through my fingers like so much sand.

Continuing with her roll call, Autumn muses, putting a finger to her lips. I can see her mentally counting her children off, one by one, making sure she hasn't missed a single one. "Katrina's seven and as you know she's our artist. Her latest pencil drawing won first place at the county fair. Then, of course, there's Carpenter, who's three, and Olivia is almost one."

Leaning against the doorway for support, I am thunderstruck. "Every time you name them all, I nearly pass out." I hold up my hand in supplication. "Now don't get me wrong, I know that they're all wonderful, but I don't know how you do it. You're either a nominee for the Motherhood Hall of Fame or clinically insane. Either way, I'm impressed."

Laughing, she gives me one last hug, enveloping me in her comfortably abundant embrace. "I bet I know which way you're leaning," she says, as she heads toward the driveway. Pulling, what we lovingly refer to as her "mommy body" into her 1968 VW minibus, she drives off, blowing kisses my way.

I shake my head in amazement. Like almost everything else in her life, the VW is a work in progress.

Closing the front door snugly behind me, I lean against it mentally shifting gears. Thoughts of my mother's earlier phone call tug at me, but I refuse to go there. My closest friend is hurting and I want to console her, so I push my own troubled thoughts aside. Entering the kitchen, I watch as Jessica puts away the last of the party supplies. "Give me just a minute," she says, heading for the bathroom.

I can't help thinking how blessed I am to have not only one, but several truly wonderful friends. Grabbing a box of Kleenex, two cold Dr. Peppers, and our favorite comfort food—raw chocolate chip cookie dough straight from the package—I snip off the end and set it all on a wooden tray. In the living room, I set the spread on the coffee table and head down the hall to tell the kids goodnight and let Thomas know that I'm going to be a while.

When I return Jessica is settled on the couch with her head laid wearily against the back. Sorrow is etched in every line of her face and my heart goes out to her. Sensing my presence, she opens her eyes and gives me a tired smile. Indicating my quickly prepared spread, I say, "I've got everything we need for a heart to heart. Now shed your shoes and prepare to bare your soul."

I settle in beside her, grab a spoon, and squeeze off a portion of cookie dough, popping it into my mouth. Washing it down with a swig of D.P., I wait for Jessica to begin. Years of friendship make our relationship similar to that of a marriage. I know her nuances and her moods. You can't make Jessica talk. You just have to wait her out.

Another squeeze, pop, swig, and she still hasn't moved. Obviously, this is more serious than I thought.

Deciding that another approach may be needed, I reach for the box of Kleenex. Pulling a tissue from its floral domain, I offer it to her and the dam breaks. Grabbing the tissue, Jessica collapses into my arms sobbing. The intensity of her sorrow is unnerving. This has only happened one other time and I'm just as undone now as I was at sixteen.

Unable to understand a word she is saying, I simply rub her back, rocking her back and forth, praying. Desperately, I implore God to take her in His arms, to heal her aching heart, and to restore her life again. When I can think of nothing else to pray, I simply hold her.

My tears soak the shoulder of Jessica's blouse but she is oblivious to everything except her pain. With her head against my chest, I realize that her tears and mascara have surely stained my *perfect,* white blouse as well but it doesn't matter. Right now, all that matters is that my friend is hurting in a horribly frightening way and, as a result, so am I.

As her sobs finally begin to subside, I find myself humming one of the great old hymns of the church. From some half forgotten place in my childhood memory, the lyrics come back to me and I begin to sing softly, but with deep conviction. I sing of God's great faithfulness and His mercies that are new every morning. When I reach the chorus, Jessica joins me and together we softly sing in the face of our fears, in spite of our tears and pain.

After a time Jessica seems calmer, more in control. Spotting the black mascara on my white blouse, she hastens to apologize. Giving her a tight squeeze, I brush her concerns aside. "Jess, Sweetheart, it's nothing."

Looking down at the floor, she says, "Becca, I've got to talk to you. You're the only person who will understand."

Giving her hand a squeeze, I nod my encouragement. Taking a deep breath, she speaks in a voice I have to strain to hear. "You know that we've been seeing an infertility specialist, right?"

I nod.

"Well, last Tuesday they performed the test where they shoot the dye in your fallopian tubes and then X-ray your reproductive system to see if everything is functioning correctly." She pauses.

I nod again waiting for her to continue. She doesn't, and then it dawns on me. "What is it, Jess? What are you trying to tell me?"

She's sobbing again and she can't bring herself to look at me. "My fallopian tubes are damaged beyond repair. That's it. No babies for Jason and me. I'm a broken model."

Pulling her hand away, Jessica literally turns in upon herself, rolling her shoulders and drawing her legs up to her chest. Much like a turtle, she has entered her shell.

I scoot closer, placing my hand upon her back. My eyes swim with tears. I know how desperately Jess wants a child. This news is the death of a lifelong dream. I say the only thing I can think of…"Sweetheart, it isn't your fault."

Jessica shakes her head violently. "Yes, it is." Her words are barely audible, spoken with her mouth tucked tightly against her knees.

I'm at a loss. Rubbing my temples with my forefingers, I try to figure out why she's blaming herself. Tentatively I ask, "Surely, Jason can't think it's any fault of yours?"

The tiny voice again. "No, he says it's nobody's fault. But he doesn't know what I know. What we know."

I'm stumped. Truly. And I do mean, good and truly stumped. What is she talking about? Then, like a bolt of lightning it hits me, and in an instant I am carried back to a frantic midnight phone call more than twenty years ago.

CHAPTER

SIX

FEBRUARY 1986

Through the haze of a heavy sleep, I hear the ringing of a telephone. Groggily, I fumble for the receiver, knocking several things off my bedside table in the process.

"Hello?" I mumble, glancing at the clock radio's luminous dial. Obviously, it's a prank call. None of my friends would dare call at this late hour.

"Becca?" A shaky, yet vaguely familiar voice comes through the telephone receiver, jerking me awake.

I sit up, "Jess? Jess? Is that you? Talk to me!"

"Becca," barely audible and so weak, "help me, please."

"Where are you?" I implore, releasing a breath I didn't realize I was holding. "What's wrong? What can I do?" I know I'm rambling but that's what I do when I'm scared.

Crying softly, Jessica mumbles, "I'm down the block from Bobby Henthorn's house, at the convenience store."

Confused, I snap, "At this time of night? What do you think you're doing? Did you sneak out again?"

"Becca... Just come pick me up... please!"

Her voice cracks and I can hear her muffled sobs. In that instant, I realize that something is wrong, terribly wrong.

"Becca, please. I don't have anyone else. You know I can't call my mother."

Her words rip at my heart. She's never really had a relationship with her mother and since her mother remarried, it's been even worse. Although her mother insisted that she move back home, it was for appearance sake only. Jessica was never anything more than an afterthought to her, doubly so following the birth of Jessica's half sister Kathleen. As far as her mother is concerned, Jessica has always been more trouble than she's worth.

Torn between loyalty to my friend and obedience to my parents, I plead, "Jessica, it's past my curfew."

"I thought you were my friend."

Her words pierce my heart and I whisper, "I'm on my way."

"Hurry, please."

Trembling, I manage a choked, "Bet your beetles, Babe."

After an endless pause, she whispers, "Right as rain, alligator."

Hesitant to end the connection, I hold the receiver for a moment longer before replacing it carefully in its hot pink cradle.

JUNE 2006

That same timid voice, equally wounded now, nearly as scared, draws me back to the present and once more I am a middle-aged mom sharing a serious conversation with her best friend. "What am I gonna do, Becca?" Jessica begs, "Jason doesn't know."

Fearful and nervous, she shreds the Kleenex into tiny gossamer pieces that float like snowflakes onto her jeans. Lifting her sudden child-like eyes to mine, she admits, "He knows I wasn't a virgin but...not about the rest," shame causes her voice to trail off.

Placing my hand on her dampened cheek, I reply softly, "That's in the past, Jess. God has forgiven you. It's time you learn to forgive yourself."

She glances up and I see that her eyes are flooded with tears yet again. Choking with regret, she barely manages, "That's easier said than done."

Wrapping my arms around her trembling body, I whisper, "I know it is, Jessica. I know it is."

After a few moments, she slips out of my arms and across the room to the window. Staring out into the night, she asks, "What do I tell Jason? The truth about my past or simply what the doctor said?"

I'm not sure how to answer her so I say a quick prayer in my heart, seeking guidance from the Holy Spirit. "That's a decision only you can make," I say, choosing my words carefully. "Will telling him change anything or will it only cause him to question everything about your relationship? Will he begin to wonder what else you might not have told him?"

"I have no other secrets, Becca. You know that."

"I know that but Jason doesn't."

Walking up behind her, I gently turn her around. Placing my hands on her upper arms, I say, "Maybe we're getting ahead of ourselves here."

"What do you mean?"

"Are we really sure the abortion had anything to do with your infertility?"

"What are you talking about? Of course it did. You've seen the same studies I have documenting the connection between infertility and abortion."

I concede her point but I continue to press her, "Did the doctor say the infection caused by the abortion damaged your tubes or did you just assume that it did?"

Her brow furrows in concentration. Finally she concedes, "The doctor had no way of knowing about the abortion since I didn't include it in my medical history. So, I guess I just assumed it was the abortion."

"There you go," I say, "jumping to conclusions."

"You don't really believe that and neither do I."

Not willing to argue, I simply shrug my shoulders. In my heart, I believe she's right but I wanted to give her a way out. Unfortunately, she's not willing to let herself off the hook.

"What if I tell him and he divorces me, Becca? What will I do then?"

Finally, we are getting to the root of all of this: Jessica's own insecurities. "Listen to me, Jess." I lift her chin until her eyes are looking directly into mine. "Jason loves you, I love you, and most importantly, your Heavenly Father loves you. He will never leave you nor forsake you and I don't believe that Jason will either. Have a little faith, girlfriend."

On the mantel, my grandmother's antique clock chimes once, startling us with the lateness of the hour. Reaching for a new tissue, Jessica dries her eyes and begins gathering up her things. I walk her to the door where she gives me a hug. "Thanks, Becca. I don't know what I would do without you."

I watch until the taillights of her car disappear around the corner. Switching off the porch light, I close the door. Leaning against it, I review the evening, realizing for the first time how exhausted I am. There was plenty of good food, lots of laughter, some exciting Bunko games, and more than a few surprises. Not your ordinary Bunko night, that's for sure.

Against my will, I find my thoughts returning to my mother's telephone call. The thought of her getting married is nearly more than I can bear. *If she goes through with it, I don't know what I will do.* "God, help me," I pray, and soft as the brush of an angel's wing, I hear the whisper of my Heavenly Father's voice, *"Have a little faith, Becca. Have a little faith."*

CHAPTER SEVEN

Flipping the latch, I automatically begin my nighttime lockdown. Walking through the silent house checking doors, switching off lamps, and pulling shades, I mull over the night's events.

As soon as Jess got married, she started dreaming about becoming a mother. She didn't just dream of having one child either, she wanted children—lots of them, a whole houseful. And now, the determined words of that hopeful young bride come back to haunt me. How clearly I remember her saying, "Becca, I can't wait to be a mom and I'm going to be a great one. Just you watch and see."

Setting her chin in determination, she had concluded, "I won't follow in my mother's footsteps. That's for sure."

I grieve, for the "motherless" child Jessica once was and for the childless woman she has become. Silently I pray, *"God, help my dear friend. Comfort and sustain her in the hour of her grief."*

Padding down the hall towards the room I share with Thomas, I feel an overwhelming need to see my children—to gaze upon them, to bask in the wonder of their nearness.

Carefully, without a sound, I slip into Brooklyn's room. She is splayed comfortably across her bed, flaxen hair strewn upon her pillow. Her flawless face is peaceful in sleep, her tattered Winnie the Pooh stuffed under the crook of one arm. I smile softly as I spot the ever-present cords trailing from her ears. Music is her first love and she goes to sleep each night listening to her treasured iPod.

Shaking my head in wonder, I gently remove the lime-green earplugs, turn off the tiny contraption and place it securely on the bedside table. Watching her sleep, it's hard for me to believe, this is the same little girl, who at age two, used to dance across our living room floor. Once when we asked her to shake her booty, she stunned us all by replying innocently, "I can't. I've only got baby boobies." Well, she's almost grown now and developing quite nicely, but according to her, not nearly fast enough.

Unable to resist the urge, I bend over and give my nearly grown daughter a kiss on the cheek and turn to walk out.

Before reaching the door, I hear a mumbled, "Goodnight, Mommy. I love you."

My heart floods with a nearly overwhelming love and a tender smile spreads across my face. Huskily I reply, "I love you more than you could know, my precious Brooklyn Storm."

A tear slips silently down my cheek as I grieve for my dear friend who may never know the joy of a moment like this. Brushing it away, I go to check on Robert.

His bedroom is just down the hall and I now turn the handle opening his door just a crack, then further, watching intently as the soft light from the hall brings his sleeping profile into focus. He's certainly changed, especially over the past year, but I can still see hints of the little boy who used to rush into my room each morning. Dimples bursting, he would ask, "Mommy, do you know what time it is? It's morning time, time for chocolate milk, Cocoa Puffs in a bag, and my favorite cartoons!" Now he's thirteen, just shy of six feet tall, a hundred and fifty pounds, and a star running back on the Jenks junior-high football team.

His lithe frame is hanging halfway off the bed, sheets and blankets tangled about him, seemingly in a tug-of-war for the best position. Studying his handsome face, I can still see traces of the precocious little boy etched there, especially around his eyes.

Whereas Brooklyn sleeps with her iPod and Pooh, Robert is never without his football. A gift from his father when he was just seven, it is safely tucked between the headboard and his pillow. For an entire year, Thomas threw him passes each evening after work. It was a wonderful time of bonding for them and I find that I am smiling fondly at the memory. Suddenly, my eyes grow misty as I realize how swiftly his childhood is slipping away.

Leaning over, I brush his cheek with my lips, surprised at the course texture. *When,* I wonder, *did my baby boy start growing whiskers?*

Unlike Brooklyn, Robert is not awakened by my kiss. Yet, the mere sight of his sweet face and my own simple, motherly gesture somehow comfort me. Backing from the room, I watch him till the last vestiges of illumination fade gradually across his square jaw. At the last second possible, I close his door with a soft click and turn toward the master bedroom where my sleeping husband awaits...

CHAPTER EIGHT

Foregoing my normal bedtime routine, I silently shed my jeans and tear-soaked blouse, leaving them in a pile on the floor beside the four-poster bed. Careful not to disturb my slumbering husband, I slide under the covers, shivering slightly—bare skin unaccustomed, as of yet, to the silky coolness of the sheets. Despite my best efforts, Thomas shifts, mumbles, reaching instinctively for me. Gathering me against his chest, I snuggle deep into his comforting warmth. On this most difficult of nights, I am especially grateful for his embrace.

Time ticks relentlessly along and by now the hour is late, yet I am no closer to sleep. Willing my mind to shut off is impossible, and sleep is only an illusion dancing just beyond my reach, so I decide to get up. Carefully, so as not to wake the sleeping giant, I slither my way out from under his arm and scoot slowly off the bed. My Prince Charming groans deeply before rolling over but he does not wake.

I shiver as the coolness of the cherry wood floor works its way up my bare feet and into my legs. Grabbing Thomas' ever-present robe off the end of the bed, I slip it over my shoulders before exiting the bedroom and quietly closing the door behind me. Eyes gritty with exhaustion, I head to the kitchen.

Maybe a hot cup of chamomile tea will do the trick. Switching on the light above the stove, I carry the kettle to the sink and fill it with water. Returning to the stove, I turn on the burner, flipping up the whistle on the teapot before completing the rest of the preparations.

Reaching for my favorite mug, I run my finger over the emblem of a yellow taxicab, recalling the exact moment I'd purchased it. Jess and I had just taken our first ride in a New York City cab. I'd been terrified but Jessica, as always, was cool as a cucumber. After we'd reached our destination, we found an out-of-the-way curio shop and purchased matching mugs to commemorate the occasion.

Out of the corner of my eye, I see steam rising from the kettle. Turning off the burner, I place a tea bag in my mug, spoon in sugar, add the cream, and lastly, the water.

Wrapping my hands around the familiar mug, I comfort myself with memories of a happier time. In the living room, I turn on the lamp, carving a circle of light out of the darkness. Rummaging in the end table drawer, I eventually locate a coaster for my mug and collapse on the couch.

Finally situated, I take a sip of tea, savoring its warmth. Seeing the family Bible on the coffee table, I reach for it. It is heavy and awkward but I persevere. *How long has it been since our family has sat down and shared devotions?* My mind struggles to recall, shuffling through memories like so many slides in a PowerPoint presentation.

At last, I settle on one, only it is not Thomas' face I see but the face of my father. In his weathered hands, he holds the family Bible, his brow furrowed in concentration as he thumbs the well-worn pages searching for the evening's text. Mother, Jessica, and I have joined Daddy around the kitchen table for family devotions. Of course, Jessica and I are cutting up, but Daddy silences us with a stern look before he starts to read.

Blinking back my tears, I clasp the bulky Bible tightly to my chest and whisper, "I miss you, Daddy, so much."

Rubbing the sleep from his eyes, Thomas enters the living room and makes his way to me. Taking my face in his hands, he asks, "Sweetheart, what's wrong?" I choke back a sob but I cannot keep silent tears from staining my cheeks. Using his thumbs, he softly wipes them away, before touching his lips to mine. His kiss is gentle and for a moment his tenderness comforts me. Laying the Bible aside, I lean into him, resting my head against his shoulder, drawing strength from his nearness.

"What is it, Hon?" he asks again and I find myself searching for the words to explain my mother's betrayal. Sensing my struggle, he rubs the back of my shoulders while whispering comforting platitudes into the thickness of my hair. I'm not naïve enough to think he can fix what's troubling me; still I draw strength from his desire to do so.

Taking a deep breath, I begin, "My mother called this evening." I try to say more but I can't. The words stick in my throat.

Thomas gives me a squeeze for encouragement. "And..."

"She called in the middle of Bunko," I say, avoiding the real issue. "Can you believe that?"

"Your mother's lonely, Honey. I'm sure she just forgot it was your Bunko night."

Jumping up from the couch, I turn on Thomas, hurt and angry. "Why do you do that? Why do you always defend my mother?"

Unaccustomed to seeing me like this, he gives me a puzzled look. Before he can respond, a rush of words come tumbling out of me in a torrent of grief and anger. "For your information, dear husband, my 'saintly' mother, is 'in love' and even now she's planning the wedding." With my fingers, I indicate the quotation marks surrounding the phrase "in love."

Thomas is not easily rattled but I can see that this last piece of information has shaken him. He and my father were close, more like best friends than father-in-law and son-in-law. Not giving him time to digest this news, I press on. "She called to get my blessing and I've never even met the man. Not that it would make any difference. No one can take my father's place!"

I stand there, face flushed, blinking rapidly, as wave after wave of emotion breaks over me. Thomas doesn't try to comfort me with clichés, for which I am grateful. Instead, standing to his feet, he opens his arms to me and, like the little girl I once was, I run to him, desperate for the security found in his arms. For a long time, we simply hold each other, not speaking, for there is nothing to say. Finally, he leads me to our bed, where an exhausted but troubled sleep overtakes me at last.

CHAPTER

NINE

Seventy-two hours later, the knot in my stomach still remains and my mother's shocking announcement weighs heavily upon me. Not even the prospect of a relaxing vacation with my family and Jessica's in a majestic ski village in Colorado can lift my spirits. Although the plans have been months in the making, as the departure date approaches I am feeling less and less enthusiastic. Given everything that's happened, I simply can't muster much excitement but I'm determined to give it the old college try, lest I disappoint the twins.

For the moment, I am sitting propped against a slew of pillows piled high against our headboard while my normally reserved husband runs on about something. It's obvious he's unusually excited but I pay him no mind. Instead, I continue to fold the laundry while my mind grapples with weightier matters.

"Isn't that great, Honey?" he inquires looking to me for confirmation.

Staring blankly at Thomas, I mumble, "Yeah, Honey, it's wonderful. Sounds great," with as much enthusiasm as I can muster. The washcloth I am folding hangs forgotten in my hand as a vague uneasiness creeps into my mind. "Come again. We're going *where* on vacation? In *what?*"

Thomas is beaming, his smile splashed across his face like a toothpaste ad. I don't believe I've ever seen him this happy—except maybe when the twins were born. His chest swelling with pride, he announces, "We're going to the Colorado Rockies in our very own, brand-new fifth wheel."

Frozen in shock, I manage a single slow-motion blink. Hoping against hope it is all a dream. Surely, I'm mistaken. "Camping? We're going camping?" I choke.

Thomas shakes his head at my silliness and I am nearly giddy with relief. I knew I had misunderstood him. I mean, after fifteen years of marriage, there's no way the man could know so little about me.

Crossing the room, he sits on the edge of our bed. Taking my hands in his, he assures me, "Becca, sweetheart, we're not camping...we're RVing."

My eyes widen in horror. *Like that makes a difference.*

Thomas continues without interruption oblivious to my dismay. "Wait till you see our rig. You're gonna love it. Nothin' but the best for my baby." Brandishing the brochure from behind his back, he proudly states, "This is what I call getting back to nature in style. Whatdya think?"

Truth be known, I'm feeling a little nauseous right about now. My idea of experiencing the great outdoors is renting a luxurious condominium in an exclusive ski village, with a huge fireplace and a hot tub on the back deck. Don't get me wrong. I absolutely adore nature. I do. I just don't want to get up close and personal with it. After so many years of marriage, I was sure my Thomas understood this. Obviously, I was wrong.

Smiling weakly, I inquire, "Does Jessica know?"

Making himself comfortable, Thomas splays the brochure across our laps before answering. "Jason is telling her tonight."

Misery must love company because the thought almost makes me smile, as I recall the many misadventures Jessica endured while camping with my parents and me. Too soon, I remember that I too will be part of this ordeal and inwardly, I groan. Outwardly, I, "Ooh" and "Aaah," as

Thomas gives me a two dimensional, all too technical, tour of our rolling home.

The next two weeks pass in a frenzy of activity and almost before I know it, the day of departure has arrived. Sitting in the front seat preparing to drive off, I struggle to stay awake. Mentally, I excuse my unaccustomed exhaustion, chalking it up to high levels of stress (*Thank you, Mom*) and loads of laundry. Thomas' voice arouses me and I reach for my travel mug of cappuccino desperate for a dose of energy.

"First things first," he says, "we have to name her before we can take off."

Rolling my eyes, I toss Jessica a look that says, *Can you believe this?* via the passenger makeup mirror of our newly acquired Dodge Ram mega-cab. Seems the purchase of a fifth wheel also requires the purchase of Thomas' dream truck. *Convenient, hmmm?*

"Name who?" Jessica questions, feigning ignorance.

Jason jumps in, chest swelling with self-importance. "The fifth wheel, of course."

Thomas nods in agreement. "That's right. This vacation wouldn't be complete without a name. Does anyone have a suggestion?"

Playing along, Robert says, "How about 'Home on the Range'?"

"Real original, Robert," Brooklyn snorts in disdain.

"Do you have a better suggestion, Miss Smarty Pants?"

Nonchalantly, Brooklyn tosses out, "'Runaway Bride' sounds good to me. Fun for a time but nothing to get permanently hitched to."

"Cute, you two. Really cute," Jason teases.

"I like it," I pipe up.

"So do I," Jessica adds.

"Runaway Bride," Thomas repeats, "it does kind of grow on ya."

Lifting his hands, palms up, Jason quips good-naturedly, "'Runaway Bride' it is."

Putting the truck in gear, my husband prepares to drive off, doing all the necessary system checks, before finally taking his foot off the brake and placing it on the accelerator. The powerful truck lunges forward with a jolt. Checking both side mirrors, Thomas carefully turns the steering wheel.

Jessica and I try desperately not to laugh as he struggles to maneuver the nearly forty-foot attachment out of our cul-de-sac without taking any mailboxes or parked cars with us. A significant bump, one eyebrow arching screech, and we are finally free of our block and on our way to the majestic mountains of colorful Colorado. Snapping shut the mirror, I say deadpanned, "Don't worry, Honey. I'm sure the Rockies have nothing as harrowing as our cul-de-sac."

My words relieve the tension, freeing the flow of laughter. Even Thomas can't resist and after growling at me in mock anger, he breaks into a grin. "Laugh all you want, but I guarantee none of you can do any better."

Brooklyn pipes up, "That's not saying a lot, Daddy."

"She's right," I add mischievously. "The twins aren't driving yet and I'm a hazard every time I get behind a wheel. I'm dangerous just backing out of the driveway."

"Here, here," agrees Jason, lifting an imaginary champagne flute high in the air for a toast.

Coming to my defense, Jessica jabs him in the side with her elbow. "Now see here, Mister. You don't have any room to talk." Pursing her lips, she turns to the rest of us, "This guy's had more speeding tickets than Jeff Gordon. We'll be lucky if we don't have our car insurance cancelled."

"Well," Jason says defensively, "at least I didn't fail Driver's Ed."

"Is that true, Aunt Jessica?" Brooklyn asks. "Did you really fail Driver's Ed?"

Before Jessica can respond, Jason says, "Not once, but twice. She failed Driver's Ed two times."

Coming to my friend's rescue, I explain, "She's really not responsible. Being the prettiest girl in class the boys wouldn't give her a minute's peace. How can you learn to drive if you're always fighting the boys off?"

Looking at her "Aunt" Jessica with admiration, Brooklyn says, "You're the only person I know who can talk on her cell phone, apply mascara, fiddle with her iPod, and drive at the same time. If Mom tried that she would kill us all."

"Brooklyn," I say, a warning in my voice, "Don't go there."

Laughter again fills the cab and I begin to think this just might turn out to be a pretty good vacation after all.

Naive, wasn't I? Anyone who thinks four adults and two teenagers can co-exist in the same vehicle for two days without getting on each other's nerves probably hasn't tried it. Add a game boy, an iPod, and a DVD player and you have a recipe for conflict. The first couple of hours go okay but when we get back in the truck after stopping for breakfast the tension becomes almost unbearable.

Robert is playing some kind of war game on his game boy and every few seconds, we are subjected to another explosion. Being used to this kind of chaos, Thomas and I hardly notice but Jason glares at him. Trying to keep the peace, I hand Robert his earphones, motioning for him to use them. "Mom," he complains, "you know I hate those things. They make my ears hot."

I glare at him while he continues to ignore me. I am about ready to pinch his head off when he finally interrupts his game long enough to put them on. Jason just shakes his head and I find myself alternating between irritation and humiliation. I find I'm angry at Jason and humiliated by my son's disrespectful behavior. Did I mention ticked at Thomas? How he can ignore what's going on is beyond me, but he does.

Brooklyn is listening to her iPod, ear buds snuggly in place, but that doesn't keep her from belting out the words to her favorite "Little Big Town" song. I'm tempted to sing along with her, but one look at Jason and I think better of it.

I reach over and push the pause button on her iPod cutting off her song. Jerking out her ear buds, she demands, "Why didya do that?"

Ignoring her disrespectful tone, I ask her to please refrain from singing.

"But I want to," she whines, reverting to childish behavior in an attempt to manipulate me.

"If you can't listen without serenading us, I'll have to put your iPod away."

Jamming her ear buds back in her ears, she glares at me before deliberately turning her back to me. Trying to make light of the moment, I turn to Jessica, "I guess you can see why I gave them the initials R & B, hmm?"

Jessica chuckles but Jason just continues to stare out the side window. "Yeah," she replies. "Unfortunately, they've got the rhythm and we've got the blues."

I give her a wan smile, silently praying that she and Jason will still love the twins when this is over.

CHAPTER

TEN

Bits of gravel pepper the underside of the truck as we work our way up County Road 103. On either side of the narrow roadway, limestone peaks loom rugged and imposing, casting the valley in deep shadows even though the sun is still well up in the sky. Rounding a hairpin curve, we spot a Bull Moose standing knee deep in a pond, the blue of the Colorado sky breaking through his imposing crown. He gives us a look of warning before lowering his head to feed once more.

Jessica and I look at each other in amazement. As far as either one of us knew, there were no moose in Colorado. We spent many a vacation camping in the Rockies without ever seeing one or knowing of anyone else who had either. "Wow!" we say in unison, awe filling our voices.

Thomas gives me a smug look and I grin sheepishly. He tried to tell me that there were moose in this part of Colorado—Brown's Park Campground being located deep in the bowels of the Roosevelt National Forest, not far from the Colorado/Wyoming border—but I had argued vehemently. It appears I was wrong, the Colorado Game and Fish Department apparently reintroduced moose to this area. Although I hate being proven wrong, this is one time I'm glad Thomas was right.

Nearing the campground, several mule deer bolt across the road and through a meadow blanketed in splashes of royal blue, magenta, and gold. Reaching the tree line, they stop and look back at us before disappearing into the forest. I glance at the twins who are glued to their windows. "This is the best, Dad," Robert enthuses, his face flushed with excitement.

Returning his attention to the road, Thomas eases our rig forward. Directly ahead is a one-lane bridge leading into a rustic but picturesque campground. Surprising myself, I reach for the button to lower the window. Taking deep breaths of the pine-scented air, I can feel the tension draining out of me. Thomas was right. This is just what I needed— time away, sleeping in, relaxing around the campfire. Two weeks of this and I am sure I'll be rejuvenated.

At nearly 8,500 feet of elevation the mountain air is brisk, cutting through my cotton blouse causing me to shiver even though it is mid-June. Closing the window would probably be a good idea, but I can't bring myself to do so. Instead, I hug myself, breathing deeply, filling my lungs with the pure mountain air. Although the Front Range is shrouded in a layer of pollution, it has yet to infiltrate this pristine ecosystem, for which I am thankful.

"Isn't Colorado amazing?" Jessica asks, interrupting my thoughts.

Before I can reply, Thomas stops the truck to survey the campground. Being early in the season, not to mention the remoteness of the area, we are afforded our pick of camping spots. There's not a bad location in the entire campground, still we struggle with indecision debating the pros and cons of each one. Finally, we make a decision and Thomas eases the truck onto the one-lane bridge. To reach the spot we have selected, he must make a sharp right turn just after crossing the bridge. There is a more accessible location straight ahead, but I have insisted on the one that backs up to McIntyre Creek.

Given the cramped confines in which we must maneuver the big rig, Jason offers to get out and help direct us, but Thomas dismisses his suggestion as unnecessary. A decision he will soon come to regret. With trees lining both sides of the narrow drive Thomas must be careful not to damage our new fifth wheel trailer. Being nearly forty feet long, it was not designed for spots as tight as this. Cutting his eyes from mirror to mirror, he eases the truck forward. Turning the wheel sharply to the right, he inches ahead being ever mindful of the towering pines crowding his side of the road; the low-hanging branches a constant threat to the air-conditioning unit situated on the roof of the trailer. Concentrating on the trees, he fails to realize that he has cut the corner too tight. Suddenly, there is a loud thud followed by a horrible screeching, a sound like the pulling of rusty nails from an old board.

Piling out of the truck, we go to investigate and discover, to our dismay, that the back wheels of the trailer have gone off the gravel drive, bumped over one of the huge logs bordering the road and are firmly trapped between the log and a young Lodgepole pine. The trailer is setting on its rear axle, tilted slightly in the direction of the ditch. Raising his eyebrows, Jason turns to Thomas with a look that says, "You should have let me guide you."

I'm not about to say anything. I've lived with this man for fifteen years and I know when Thomas is about to go off. Glancing at Jessica, I nod toward a picnic table some distance away and we move toward it. Brooklyn follows but Robert stays with the men. They study the situation, walking around our rig to look at it from every angle. Thomas even gets down on his hands and knees to see what things look like from that vantage point.

It's nearly too much for me and I bury my face in my hands. Of late even the slightest bit of stress can send me into a tailspin and now I find myself on the verge of tears. Placing her hand on my arm, Jessica asks, "Are you okay?"

What can I say? We are literally in the middle of nowhere, hours from the nearest town, not another soul in sight, and our thirty-seven thousand dollar rig is stuck with little or no hope of getting it out without severely damaging it. Other than that I am fine. Just fine. Of course, I don't say this. Instead, I give my friend a tired smile and a reassuring nod.

Hearing another vehicle approaching, I look toward the bridge where a green, forest ranger pickup is crossing. Pulling to a stop behind our rig, the ranger climbs out and walks toward the guys. He looks to be in his mid-sixties, with a large red nose and overgrown eyebrows. Hitching up his pants, he walks around our rig, studying the situation. His hat is shoved snugly onto his head, making his too-large ears seem even bigger. In spite of myself, I can't help smiling.

Tugging at his pants once more, he turns to Thomas and announces, "Yep, it looks like you guys have got yourselves in quite a pickle."

His voice carries clearly to where we are seated and I tense involuntarily. Under circumstances like these, Thomas doesn't usually respond well to that tone. Surprisingly, he doesn't react. Instead, he says, "If you have any suggestions as to how we can get out of this mess, I'd sure appreciate it."

While they've been talking, I have come up with an idea. Carefully, I retrace my steps back to the road, my espadrilles making the footing precarious. "Why don't we gather rocks and build a ramp so we can pull the trailer back on the road?" I ask interrupting their discussion. "Of course, we would have to cut down that one pine tree but that shouldn't be any big deal; not if we can borrow a chain saw."

Looking at me as if I have asked him to sacrifice his first-born son, the Ranger informs me that it is illegal to cut down a tree in a national forest. "We take our trees seriously," he explains, "and it's up to all of us to protect this vanishing resource."

Surely, he can't be serious, can he? Giving him a disbelieving look, I make a show of surveying the thousands of trees covering these mountains, before asking, "You're kidding, of course?"

"Try cutting down that tree and you'll soon find out whether I'm kidding or not," he says without a hint of humor. "I seriously doubt that you can afford the fine the Federal Government would impose."

His tone is patronizing and I feel myself bristling. Before I can stop myself, I retort, "It's probably not nearly as costly as the thirty-seven thousand dollars my husband laid out for this beauty."

Sensing my rising anger, Thomas puts his arm around my shoulders protectively. I get the message. Biting my tongue, I don't say another word.

Turning back to the Ranger, Thomas asks, "What do you suggest?"

"If it was me, I'd drive into Walden and pick up some timbers, a heavy duty jack and some jack stands, plus some chain, and an electric winch." Noticing Thomas' puzzled expression, he explains, "Once you get the axle off the ground, you can put jack stands under it. Then you can use the winch to pull the trailer sideways. You may have to do it two or three times but you'll eventually get your rig back on the road. I've seen professional haulers do the same thing with seventy and eighty-foot mobile homes. It's back-breaking work and time-consuming but it can be done."

Glancing at his watch, Jason says, "We'd better get the trailer unhooked and head for town or we'll never get done before dark."

After thanking the Ranger for his help, such as it was, the men set about disconnecting the fifth wheel. I rejoin Jessica at the picnic table where we watch the Ranger drive away. *Good riddance,* I think, hoping to never see him again. I know that's not a very Christian attitude, but that's truly how I feel at this moment.

When the guys are ready to go they walk over to the table to bid us good-bye. Almost as an afterthought, Thomas asks, "Are you sure you don't want to ride into town with us? It may be three or four hours before we get back."

Answering for both of us, Jessica says, "After spending the last two-and-a-half days cooped up in that truck, I can't imagine wanting to spend another four hours in it." I nod in agreement as does Brooklyn.

"Staying or going, son?" Thomas asks, turning to Robert. "It's up to you."

For a moment, he looks undecided. It's obvious that he wants to go with the men but he also feels a certain responsibility for the three of us. "Are you sure you don't want me to stay and protect you?" He inquires with the self-importance only a thirteen-year-old can muster.

"We'll be just fine, sir," I drawl, doing my best southern bell impersonation, batting my eyelashes for good measure.

Jason and Thomas hoot with laughter and Robert flashes us his infectious grin, complete with dimples and perfect white teeth.

As if to prove my self-reliance, I make a show of stomping down the trail toward the river, nearly breaking my ankle as my espadrilles tip sideways on a loose rock. Catching myself, I continue on, head held high, as their laughter chases me toward the roaring river.

CHAPTER

ELEVEN

As the rumble of the diesel engine fades in the distance, I cease my silliness. Leaning against the nearest tree, I holler for my daughter's assistance. Under my breath, I bemoan my obstinacy regarding footwear and my insistence on fashionable shoes no matter where I am.

Watching Brooklyn picking her way precariously across the same rugged terrain, I am struck by the humor in our situation. Like me, she has insisted on wearing the latest platform shoes and they are now giving her fits, as well. Although my ankle is throbbing painfully, I cannot help laughing at our absurdity. Mistakenly, assuming that I am laughing at her, Brooklyn shoots me a look that could take down a Grizzly. "What? What is so funny, Mother?"

Surrendering to the moment, I toss up my hands, "I was just thinking that us girls make quite a team, don't we? The three of us, I mean." Glancing around, I ask, "By the way, where is Jess?"

Brooklyn gives a slight shrug before carefully making her way to me. "Dunno. Haven't seen her since the guys took off." Seemingly unconcerned, she inspects her nails, checking for snags or chips in the polish.

I quickly survey the area. With no idea where Jessica may have gone, I feel my apprehension rising and Brooklyn's attitude isn't helping. "Stop primping," I snap, "and help me back to the trailer so I can change my shoes. Then we'll look for Jessica."

"Chill out, Mom. Aunt Jessica knows how to take care of herself."

"Maybe, if she were in a mall or even New York City, but not out here in the wild. In case you haven't noticed, we have no cell phone service, no fast food restaurants, no 9-1-1, not even any indoor plumbing."

Her eyes widen in disbelief as I run down my list. Glancing around, she decides the scenic beauty of Roosevelt National Forest no longer seems so benign. Hurriedly, she places my arm across her narrow shoulders before putting her own arm around my waist. Being careful not to place too much of my weight on her, I allow her to help me hobble back to camp.

I am relieved to see Jessica standing at the rear of the trailer, involved in what appears to be a mostly one-sided conversation with a rather frumpy looking old woman. Seeing us limping out of the forest, she immediately excuses herself and hurries toward us. "Becca, what happened?" she inquires, wrapping my other arm around her shoulders.

As they help me toward our campsite, I notice that Jess has put three canvas camp chairs around the fire pit. "Not bad, Jess," I say, glancing at her with a newfound respect.

She winks. "Don't be too impressed." Helping me into one of the chairs, she nods toward the woman who is still standing at the rear of our trailer. "The Ranger's wife showed me how to get into the outer storage bins. You'll be happy to know I only broke off one key before she arrived to save the day."

I try to laugh but discover I don't have the energy. Every joint in my body is aching and I wonder if I'm coming down with the flu. "So that's the Ranger's wife?" I ask, cutting my eyes toward the woman who is now making her way toward us.

Smiling stiffly, Jess responds, without moving her lips. "The one and only. Beware, she reminds me of the Big Nurse in *"One Flew Over the Cuckoo's Nest."*

I giggle, enjoying her caustic humor. Glancing down, I notice that she has exchanged her bejeweled sling-backs for hiking boots. "Would you be a doll," I ask, smiling sweetly, "and grab me a pair of socks and my hiking boots out of the trailer?"

"Which ones?" she inquires rather sassily.

"Very funny," I return.

Leaving me to face the "Big Nurse" alone, she returns to the trailer to get my boots.

As the Ranger's wife takes the chair across from me, I study her. She is wearing a man's denim work shirt over a pair of faded jeans that she has tucked into knee-high rubber boots. Her gray hair is oily and pulled back in a limp ponytail. Too much sun has weathered her skin, leaving her with a permanent scowl. When she thrusts a bundle of papers at me, I can't help noticing that her fingers are nicotine stained.

"These are for you," she says, her voice gritty.

Unconsciously, I clear my throat hoping she'll do the same. "Thank you, I'll be sure to look them over."

It's a white lie and I know it. There's not a chance in the world that I'm going to spend my vacation reading a bunch of park regulations. I feel a twinge of guilt at my deception, but I'm sure no one else actually takes the time to read them either. Maybe, as a last resort, I can pawn them off on Jason.

Her stare is relentless and I find myself locked in a battle of wills. If she thinks I can be intimidated, she's got another thing coming. Deliberately, I toss the bundle on an empty chair and return her stare.

"If you had taken the time to read that," the Ranger's wife says, indicating the discarded pages, "you would know that there are bears in this area. All your trash must be stored in trash bags several feet off the ground or preferably in the outer compartments of your trailers...."

Bears, how cool, I muse as she rattles on.

Am I out of my mind? Bears aren't cool. They're dangerous. I've seen enough episodes of "I Shouldn't Be Alive" to know that they must be avoided. Reaching for the bundle of papers, I quickly scan them looking for whatever information I can find on the subject.

Preparing to leave, the Ranger's wife stands to her feet, unconsciously brushing a stray hair out of her face. Giving my shoulder a brief pat, she says patronizingly, "You city folks should be just fine out here. Just make sure you follow all the instructions right down to the letter."

Chuckling at my doleful expression, she is taken with a coughing spell. It comes from deep in her chest and is filled with phlegm. I look away in disgust, when after a few hacks, she reaches into her shirt pocket, extracts a stained hanky and spits into it, wiping her lips. Stuffing it back into her pocket, she again touches my shoulder. "I'll let you get back to your readin'. Don't you worry your pretty lil' head too much though," she tosses over her shoulder as she turns to leave, "because I'll be checkin' on you folks every night."

"Pardon?" I manage.

Her laughter, rough as gravel, grates on me as she walks away never looking back.

And so it begins, I think, and *so it begins.*

CHAPTER

TWELVE

The sky, over the towering peaks to the west, is a deep purple when Thomas finally backs the "Runaway Bride" into the campsite we have selected. Using flashlights, Jessica and I illuminate the work area as he and Jason position the built-in scissor jacks to stabilize the trailer, being careful to make sure it is level. The campfire and the table games we had planned for the evening will have to wait until another night. The guys are simply too tired to do more than gulp down a cold sandwich and fall into bed.

After they have turned in, Jessica and I drink steaming cups of tea while sitting in camp chairs under the stars. The clear air is surprisingly brisk, chilly to be truthful, and I wish for a blazing campfire but settle for a hooded sweatshirt and a wool blanket instead. Sipping her tea, Jessica studies the sky, softly quoting an ancient Psalm.

> *"When I consider your heavens,*
> *the work of your fingers,*
> *the moon and the stars,*
> *which you have set in place,*
> *what is man that you are mindful of him,*
> *the son of man that you care for him?"*

Exhausted, I doze off but jerk awake when my head nods. Tossing out the dregs of her tea, Jessica says, "We better get you to bed girl or you might end up spending the night in that uncomfortable camp chair. I'm not about to carry you into the trailer." All I can manage is a soft chuckle as I pull myself to my feet.

Once in bed, I pound my pillow, unable to find a comfortable position. Through the thin walls of the trailer, I hear the murmur of voices and I hope the twins aren't keeping Jessica and Jason awake. Thomas has opened the window above our bed and in the distance, I hear the sound of the creek as it rushes over the rocks and down the mountain. It reminds me of a camping trip Jessica and I took with my parents to Glacier National Park in Montana. We slept in sleeping bags, on air mattresses, in a tent Dad had pitched in a grove of trees just a few yards above the river. Even then, camping wasn't my thing but thinking about it now there is a certain nostalgia.

I remember the smell of wood smoke and the screech of magpies from high in the pines and playing backgammon on a flimsy aluminum folding table. One night, something awoke me and I remember crawling to the door of the tent and peering out. The clearing, all the way to the river, was awash with moonlight. In the distance, I could see Dad and Mom standing together on the river bank, his arm about her waist. As I watched, she turned toward him, lifting her face. He took her in his arms and kissed her with a tenderness that I found both mesmerizing and more than a little embarrassing. After a moment, they started up the bank toward camp, walking hand in hand. Hastily, I returned to my sleeping bag, pretending to be asleep when they slipped into the tent.

As I think about it now, a fresh wave of grief washes over me. Although Daddy has been gone nearly a year, my pain is as raw as it was the day of the funeral. Fifty-nine is too young to die and once more I'm tempted to ask *why*. According to my pastor, the valley of the shadow of death is a journey of hope, from grief to gratefulness. If that's so, I must have taken a wrong turn somewhere because I'm stuck. At times, my grief seems all-consuming.

A loud pounding on the trailer door jerks me from my melancholy thoughts and I sit up in bed reaching for my robe. Before I can tug it on, I hear Jason's voice, thick with sleep. "Just a minute," he calls, searching for his slippers.

I hear the door open, then a gravely voice. "You've gotta move your truck, unless you wanna pay for another campsite."

In an instant, my grief turns to anger and I can feel it throbbing in my head.

"The nerve of that woman," I fume, "pounding on our door at eleven o'clock at night. We're the only campers in the whole campground, so it's not like they need the site. What harm would it have done for her to wait until morning?"

Thomas is still dead to the world so I give him a sharp jab with my elbow. Groaning sleepily, he rolls over but doesn't wake, so I jab him again, harder this time. Pushing himself up on one elbow, he turns toward me. It is too dark for me to make out his features but I can feel him glaring at me. Before he can say anything, Jason calls through the bedroom door. "Hey, Thomas, where are the truck keys? I've got to move it."

"I think they're on the hook by the door."

"Nope. I've already checked there."

"I must have left them in my pant's pocket." Sitting up on the side of the bed, he reaches for his jeans but his keys are not there either.

"Have you checked the end table or the dresser?" I ask.

"I wouldn't have put them there," he mumbles, pulling on his jeans in the dark. "I must have left them in the truck."

Turning on the bedside lamp, I blink as my eyes adjust to the light. Reaching across the bed, I pick up the keys from beside Thomas' wallet on the nightstand. Without a word, I hand them to him and shut out the light. He is muttering under his breath as he opens the door and gives the keys to Jason.

Returning to bed, he is instantly asleep while I stare at the ceiling in the dark. The Cummings diesel in our Dodge Ram clatters to life and for a moment, its headlights cast deformed shadows on the far wall. I hear the crunch of gravel beneath the all terrain tires as Jason maneuvers the truck in the tight confines of our campsite. Finally, he returns to the trailer and once more all is quiet.

I snuggle deeper under the pile of blankets covering our bed but still sleep won't come. My troubled mind is going a hundred miles an hour. I'm worried about Jessica. Beneath her forced gaiety, I sense her quiet desperation. My friend Madison hasn't been herself either. Something's bothering her and it's more than a baby who won't sleep through the night, I can tell you that. But always my thoughts return to the two things that now seem to haunt my every waking moment—the strange things that are happening to my body and my mother's plans to remarry.

If Thomas had to go to work in the morning, I'd let him sleep but we're on vacation and I need him. Deliberately, I place my frigid feet against the back of his knees; giggling childishly when he barks a complaint.

"Keep those things away from me. They're like blocks of ice."

Now that he's awake, my self-control slips and a strangled sob escapes my throat.

Instantly, Thomas is apologetic, "I'm sorry, Honey" he whispers, acutely aware of the close quarters we share with the others. "I didn't mean to snap at you."

Still sobbing, I bury my face against his warm shoulder. Holding me close, he asks softly, "What is it, sweetheart? What's troubling you?"

"I miss my daddy and now I'm losing my mother too."

Ever a man of few words, Thomas says nothing, letting me sort through my feelings. In a voice I hope only he can hear, I continue, "I can't believe she's planning on marrying someone we've never even met. We know nothing about the man for heaven's sake. Is he a widower? Is he divorced? Does he have children? For all we know he could be a gold digger who's marrying Mom for the insurance money. And asking us to change our vacation plans, so we could meet them in Dallas to get acquainted was the last straw. She's being selfish, just plain selfish."

When it becomes apparent that my emotion has spent itself, Thomas takes a deep breath. "Your mother called while Jason and I were in town."

Instantly, I feel myself grow stiff with tension. *Breathe,* I tell myself. *Take two or three deep breaths.* Feeling calmer, I ask, "And...?"

"She was worried. She'd been trying to reach us all day and was on the verge of calling the highway patrol."

"Does she never listen? I specifically told her there would be days when we would be without cell phone service. Really, Thomas, I don't know why I even bother."

Sighing, he says rather wearily, "Becca, your mother is almost sixty years old. You're not going to change her."

Hoping to avoid an argument, I swallow my frustration. "Did she have anything else to say?"

"Actually, we had a rather interesting conversation. She's sorry for springing the wedding plans on you, but it's all happened so fast she says it just bowled her over."

"That's all the more reason for her to slow down and think things through."

"You'll get no argument from me in that regard, but I do think you'll have a hard time convincing your mother." Pausing to consider how best to proceed, he finally says, "She did tell me a little about Prince Charming. He serves as the pastor of a small congregation called the Church of the Comforter in Cleburne, Texas, not too far from Fort Worth. They met at a Singles Retreat and to quote your mother, 'It was love at first sight.'"

I nearly gag at the thought. What does that say about her relationship with my father? Did the thirty-nine years they spent together mean so little?

"Your mother claims that as a young teenager, she had her heart set on becoming a minister's wife. When she was sixteen your father came along and swept her off her feet. The rest, as they say, is history."

Thomas is trying to lessen my concerns, but everything he tells me only makes the situation worse for me. Is my mother saying that her marriage to my father was a mistake? Did she spend her entire married life regretting the fact that Daddy wasn't a minister? Was my entire childhood a façade, just an elaborate masquerade? Was she just pretending to be content, just pretending to love my father and me?

Turning over I face the wall, sick with grief. I can't talk about this anymore. It's too much for me to comprehend. Thomas rubs my back, trying to comfort me but I push his hand away, pleading exhaustion. Choking on what I see as Mom's final betrayal of Daddy's memory, I stuff the corner of my pillow in my mouth to stifle my sobs while searching for sleep.

THIRTEEN

For the third time this morning, Jason asks, "Does everyone have their topographical maps, the ones I had laminated for you?"

I can see the twins rolling their eyes at their adopted uncle as they step down from the trailer. A man on a mission, he's completely oblivious to their antics. He will allow nothing to distract him as he checks and rechecks the final preparations for the hike up the McIntyre Trail. Within the confines of our bedroom, Thomas and I refer to him as "Adrian Monk" after the quirky character on the USA network's popular television series. Living with his obsessiveness the past few days has given me a better understanding of why Jessica envies me. In comparison, Thomas' laid-back approach to life must seem like a godsend to her.

This morning, she is sitting in my favorite chair, near the fire, paying him no mind. Occasionally, she looks up from the book she is reading, takes a sip of her tea before reentering her own world. Unlike her I have children, meaning I have no life of my own. Right now, I'm rummaging around in one of the outer compartments of the "Runaway Bride" in search of insect spray and a bottle of 50 spf sunscreen.

At last I find them, at the bottom of the bin, under some fishing gear and, of all things, a golf club. When Thomas packed it, he said it was for defense, but I can't imagine what good it would do us buried back here. Returning to the fire, I take it with me and lay it on the picnic table so it will be close at hand. Squirting a generous portion of sunscreen onto the palm of my hand, I call for Brooklyn.

As she begrudgingly makes her way toward me, I can't help thinking how beautiful she is, her blonde hair streaked by the sun. Today, she has chosen pink and gray camouflage shorts, a silver ribbed tank with another pink striped one layered on top. Her lime green hooded sweatshirt is tied fashionably around her slight waist and her feet are clad in purple hiking boots, her hot pink socks folded perfectly over the top. A pink and green Estes Park baseball cap holds her golden hair off her neck. Large white sunglasses and glitter lip gloss complete the picture. Backwoods or not, my daughter isn't taking any chances—as she says you never know who you might run into on the trail.

Spotting the sunscreen, she whines, "I'm not putting on that goop. I'm allergic to it."

Pain and fatigue making me impatient, I snap at her. "Brooklyn, don't be childish. At this elevation, sunscreen is a must, especially for someone with your fair skin."

In an instant, her eyes cloud with tears and I'm reminded that while she may look sixteen, in many ways, she is still just a child and my sharp tone has hurt her feelings. Seeking to rectify the damage I have done, I continue in a more conciliatory tone. "Trust me, Darling, there is nothing worse than spending your vacation fighting the pain and agony of a second-degree sunburn."

For a moment, I'm tempted to show her the faint scars on my shoulders but then I think better of it. I remember, only too well, arguing with my mother over this very issue. She had insisted I cover myself with sunscreen and I flatly refused. Finally, my father intervened, allowing me to go swimming without protection. Mother just shook her head. All afternoon, Jessica and I splashed in the clear water of the South Platte River, oblivious to the sun's deadly rays. Covered in sunscreen, she suffered no ill effects, but by bedtime I was red as a lobster and whimpering in pain. Two or three days later, my shoulders were covered in tiny, pimple-like blisters, painful and pus-filled.

Reluctantly, Brooklyn extends her arms and I push the memory from my mind before covering them with sunscreen.

Next, we do her legs but she draws the line when I try to put sunscreen on her face. "Absolutely not," she says obstinately, "you'll ruin my makeup."

We are glaring at each other, neither of us willing to give an inch, when Jessica interjects, "Becca, give the girl a break. Her makeup will provide all the protection she needs."

Too stunned to respond, I watch as Jessica gets to her feet and walks determinedly toward the creek. Brooklyn is looking at me questioningly and I give her a tremulous smile. "Your Aunt Jessica is right. I don't know what I was thinking."

Dropping in a chair, I cover my face with my hands, fighting back my tears. It's not like this is the first time Jess has interposed herself between Brooklyn and me, but always before she did it with such good humor, using laughter to diffuse the situation. Today was different. She had an edge.

Brooklyn is still looking at me when Robert sneaks up behind and puts a grasshopper down the back of her ribbed tank. In an instant, she is shrieking and pulling at her top, trying to dislodge the foul insect. When at last, she succeeds, she smacks Robert soundly on his arm. "You're so juvenile!" she fumes, stomping toward the fifth wheel.

Not to be outdone, Robert calls after her, "I may be juvenile but at least I'm smart enough not to wear pink camo shorts."

"What's that supposed to mean?"

"For your information, sis, the entire purpose of camouflage clothing is to help you blend into your surroundings. Just think about it."

We all have a good chuckle at that one but before things can get out of hand I inject playfully, "Hey, Buddy, get over here and let me smear this awful goop all over you."

After taking a couple of steps in my direction, he stops and turns toward Jason. "Hey, Uncle, wasn't there something in those park regulations about pink making black bears aggressive?"

The look on my daughter's face is priceless. Glancing down, she stares at her pink shorts and then she lifts her eyes to study Jason's face. Furrowing his brow in concentration, he plays along. "Well, now that you mention it, Robert, I think I do recall something along those lines."

Removing the sheaf of papers he has stored in his daypack, he begins flipping through them. "Here it is!" he exclaims. "Hikers in the Rawah Wilderness area should avoid wearing bright colors, especially pink, as bright colors often incite black bears to attack."

"Let me see that," Thomas demands, getting into the act. Pretending to read, he lets out a low whistle, "Although the bears' behavior is baffling, scientists say it resembles the reaction bulls have to red objects."

Pausing briefly, he glances at Brooklyn who has edged considerably closer to the "Runaway Bride," all the while peering nervously into the woods. Taking pity on her,

Thomas announces in a booming voice, "Brooklyn Thornton, everything you have just heard is a bunch of Bull-logna."

In an instant, her apprehension turns into anger and she stamps her foot, glaring at Robert who is doubled over with laughter. The rest of us are laughing as well and without a word Brooklyn storms into the trailer, slamming the door.

Suddenly aware of how we have humiliated my daughter, I start after her. Touching me on the shoulder, Thomas says, "Let me handle this. I think I owe her an apology."

Jason busies himself with the daypacks on the picnic table, checking and rechecking the supplies—trail mix, water purification tablets, candles, matches in waterproof containers, and first-aid supplies. Jessica has not returned from the creek and Robert is poking at the dying fire with a long stick, pretending innocence. I'm ashamed of myself. I should have stepped in and put an end to the teasing before Brooklyn got hurt. No one meant any harm but that is no excuse.

Turning when I hear the trailer door open, I am pleased to see Brooklyn descending the steps, a mischievous grin spread across her face. Stepping through the door behind her, Thomas is wearing a bright pink pullover shirt. It's one I bought for him two or three years ago, but until today he has steadfastly refused to wear. More than once, he has told me that "real men don't wear pink!"

Proudly Brooklyn announces, "Daddy and I are a team."

Thomas gives me a wink before placing his arm gently around her shoulders. As they head up the trail together, I can't help thinking that I've never been more proud of him or of her for that matter.

As soon as the four of them disappear around the bend, I feel myself fading and I am thankful that I have most of the day to simply lie around and read. I can't help thinking that if I feel like this at thirty-seven what am I going to be like at fifty. Maybe it's the altitude? Not likely since I've been struggling with exhaustion for weeks. It seems I can never get rested. Laying the lounge chair back, I squirm until I have found a comfortable position, then I let myself relax. As I am nearing sleep, my thoughts drift toward Jessica. She's got a bee in her bonnet but I can't imagine why.

CHAPTER FOURTEEN

When I awaken, the sun is almost directly overhead eliminating whatever shade I once had. Putting a forearm over my eyes, I struggle to escape the grogginess of my mid-morning nap. Slowly, I become aware of a painful prickling in my scalp. It feels kind of like ant bites. I try to ignore it but the stinging is relentless and I sit up, brushing at my hair furiously. Getting no relief, I make my way into the trailer to examine myself in the mirror. My face is red and blotchy, the irritation extending into my hairline, but I can't see any ants or insects of any kind for that matter. Soaking a clean wash-cloth in cold water, I blot at my face, at last getting a small measure of relief.

After I have been out of the sun for a while, I begin to feel a little better. The prickling sensation is almost gone, replaced by a weariness that nearly drags me down. Trying to ignore it, I set about making a sandwich and a pitcher of lemonade. As I work, I glance out the window above the sink and see Jessica coming up the path from the creek. She is walking slowly, her head down, arms folded across her chest as if she is holding herself together.

Taking a second plate from the cupboard, I prepare a sandwich for her, being careful to make it just the way she likes. Whereas I am into condiments—lettuce, tomatoes, pickles, olives, relish—she wants nothing but a slice of bread with a smear of mayo and a cold cut. My pallet is more discriminating, requiring the subtle blending of both taste and textures. It's just another way in which we are so different and yet, she is my dearest friend.

Hearing the door open, I turn toward the small table, sandwich plates in each hand. Giving her my warmest smile, I set the plates on the table saying, "You're just in time, girl-friend." Turning back to the counter, I collect two glasses and the pitcher of lemonade. Although Jessica's silence lingers thick as a San Francisco fog, I plunge ahead determined to put this morning's misunderstanding behind us.

Chatting gaily, I tell her about the spoof the guys pulled on Brooklyn, and Thomas' pink pullover shirt. I laugh heartily but she refuses to crack a smile.

"Please, Becca," she says, deliberately drawing out her words.

The stress of the last few weeks has taken its toll and my patience suddenly runs out. "What's your problem?" I snap. "Did you have a fight with Jason or is this just that time of the month?"

For just an instant, I think she might slap me, then her anger is gone as quickly as it came, replaced by an unspeakable sadness. Reaching across the table, I place my hand on her arm. "I'm sorry, I shouldn't have said that."

When she doesn't respond, I ask, "What is it, Jessica? What is it?"

"Don't do this, Becca," she pleads, her sapphire eyes brimming with tears. "Don't insult me by pretending you don't know what this is about."

Desperately, I search my mind for something, anything, but I can think of nothing that I have done. I look at her but she won't meet my eyes. Instead, she toys with her half-eaten sandwich, pushing it around on her plate. Now, she reaches over and removes my hand from her arm, deliberately withdrawing from me.

Finally, she speaks, never looking up. "She's my mom too, at least that's the way I think of her, even if you don't."

Slowly, it dawns on me. Somehow, she has learned of my mother's plans to remarry. Maybe Mom called her or perhaps Jason overheard Thomas on the phone with my mother. It doesn't really matter. Now she thinks I've been deliberately keeping it from her. No wonder she's hurt. Realizing how betrayed she must feel, my heart goes out to her but once more she's withdrawn behind a wall of silence. I want to explain myself, but I hesitate, fearing that anything I say will simply sound self-serving.

She is crying now, soundlessly, silent tears streaking her ashen cheeks. Looking at her, I think my heart will break. How could I have been so blind, so caught up in my own stuff, that I didn't see what she has been going through? When Daddy died, she lost the only father she's ever known and now she must be as devastated as I am by mother's insanity.

Moving around the table, I kneel beside her chair and take her slight frame in my arms, praying she will not push me away. For a moment, she is as stiff and cold as an ice princess, then her self-control deserts her and she is sobbing into my shoulder, clinging to me for dear life.

"I'm sorry, Jessica," I whisper into her thick hair. "Please forgive me. I never meant to hurt you."

Lifting her wounded eyes to mine, she sobs, "I just want to belong, that's all. I just want to be part of the family like when we were kids. Mary's the only real mother I've ever had; Richard my only father. It hurts when I feel like I'm being left out."

"Oh, Jessie, you silly goose," I say, striving for a lighter tone. "I would never leave you out. We're the original 'Bonko Babes,' the dynamic duo, nothing can separate us."

She gives me a hint of a smile and I plunge ahead, "The Johnson family wasn't complete until you stepped into the picture, Jessica Montrose Goldstein. You're the piece that made our puzzle complete. You got that, girlfriend?"

Reaching for a tissue, she wipes her eyes, and then blows her nose. Giving me a brave smile she says, "Bet your beetles, Babe," reverting to the language of our childhood.

"Right as rain, alligator," I reply in kind, wishing we could truly shed our troubles as easy as that.

CHAPTER

FIFTEEN

Three weeks have passed since the hike up McIntyre Trail and we've been back in Tulsa for several days now. The mountain of laundry we brought home from Colorado seems to grow daily, and is beginning to resemble Mount Hood—making the trek between the garage and kitchen nearly as treacherous as climbing that dangerous peak. Just thinking about washing and folding all that laundry makes me weary and not for the first time, I wish for the luxury of a live-in maid.

The twins will be leaving for church camp in just a few days and Thomas is scheduled to fly to Clearwater, Florida, for his annual business meeting that same week. Trying to get all of their clothes ready is almost more than I can handle. If we could afford it, I would simply send the three of them to Kohl's to buy everything they need for the entire week.

Mom and her fiancé, Keith, have scheduled a get-acquainted trip to Tulsa for the first week in August adding additional stress to my life. I know I can't pretend she isn't getting married but I don't have to like it either. She just makes me so mad. Thankfully, Jess has promised to come around whenever possible to serve as a buffer between Mother and me.

How has it come to this, I wonder, when Mother and I once were so close, or so it seemed? Reexamining our relationship from an adult perspective, I can see that she and I have always been just slightly out of step; like we were dancing, but each to a different tune. As long as Daddy was alive, we seemed to get along because he heard both songs. With his attuned ear and leadership, the dance worked. Now that he is gone, and especially with the introduction of Keith into the mix, all that I can hear is the clanging; the final cymbal ringing harsh and strident.

On top of everything else, the symptoms I have been experiencing over the past three to four months have become progressively worse. The fatigue, brain fog, joint pain and swelling, dry eyes and mouth, blurred vision, numbness in my extremities, and migraine headaches, can no longer be ignored. My primary care physician has scheduled a series of tests, so here I am at my fourth appointment in as many days. Lucky me.

The heavy door closes with a sucking sound as the white-coated technician exits and I am left alone in the cold, dimly lit, vacuum-sealed room; just me and this multimillion dollar piece of equipment. I can't help thinking that the doctors must believe there is something seriously wrong with me, as I'm being subjected to the most sophisticated medical tests available. Already, I have had a CAT scan and a MRI. The procedure for which I am scheduled at the moment is called a PET scan. In preparation, I have been injected with radioactive intravenous fluids and strapped to a narrow slab of steel covered with a frighteningly thin pad. In moments, the steel slab will slide forward until my head is centered in a magnetic ring called a scanner.

Since the doctors have been uniformly tight-lipped, I have been forced to conduct my own research on the internet. What I've discovered has filled me with dread. The possibilities are ominous—a cancerous brain tumor, Parkinson's disease, Multiple Sclerosis, or even the early onset of Alzheimer's. I almost wish I could return to the bliss of ignorance but of course I can't. Having eaten of the tree of knowledge, I must now live with the consequences.

"You may feel free to sleep, Mrs. Thornton," says the voice in my ear before the machine revs up. *Fat chance,* I think, as the sound becomes increasingly deafening. For the next two hours, I grit my teeth against the noise, shifting uncomfortably on the cold slab, the pain in my tailbone getting harder and harder to ignore.

An eternity later a canned voice in my ear says, "We're all done here, Mrs. Thornton," and at last the deafening roar of the magnetic field slowly winds down.

"Now, that wasn't so bad, was it?" asks the technician as he comes through the sealed door to unstrap me from the monstrosity taking images of my brain.

I smile sweetly, thanking him for the five star accommodations. All the while I'm thinking, *that's easy for him to say. He wasn't the one who spent the last two hours strapped to a narrow slab of steel in the middle of an LAX runway.* Taking his proffered hand, I pull myself to a sitting position, hand him the headphones, and tug the bright orange earplugs out, dropping them into the trash can.

Waiting for him to lower the "bed," I use the time to put on my earrings and run my fingers through my hair. At last, I'm free to go. Following close on the heels of my "captor," I exit through the door and hurry to escape the gloomy confines of the Imaging Center. The wait for the elevator seems to take forever and I punch at the up button feverishly. The last three hours have exacerbated my claustrophobia and now it feels like the basement walls are closing in on me. Finally, the elevator dings and I step through the yawning doors, weak with relief.

Unfortunately, my brain seems to have locked up and I can't remember which floor I want. Staring at the control panel, I try desperately to remember where Thomas is waiting for me. Which button do I push? I must choose...make a decision. My eyes flit from one silver disc to another...SB...B...L...M...1...2...3...4.... I feel a panic attack coming on so I remind myself to breathe. *In, out, in, out,* calmer now, I even manage a small smile.

A medical technician hurries into the elevator, reaching around me to punch the button corresponding to the large "L." Silently the elevator begins its ascent and when the doors open unto the lobby, I spot Thomas. He must have heard the elevator ding because he has looked up and when he catches sight of me he smiles. Getting to his feet, he hurries across the lobby to meet me. Weak with relief, I step into his embrace and for a moment he holds me, kissing the top of my head.

Looping my arm through his, we walk slowly in the direction of the truck. "How does a relaxing lunch at Memories of Japan sound?" he asks, giving my hand a squeeze.

"Mmm," I manage, "you and sushi, my two favorite things."

Even though the doctor has made it clear that I must listen to my body and not overdo it, I push myself onward, determined to enjoy this too rare mid-day rendezvous with my husband. Never a man much given to words, Thomas has grown increasingly quiet in the face of my illness. I wish he would talk to me about what's happening to my body but I can't push. Fifteen years of marriage has taught me that I can't make Thomas talk until he is ready. In his defense, I must say that Thomas has become much more solicitous toward me. Now, he opens the door to the Dodge Ram and helps me get in.

The Oklahoma sun has turned the truck into an oven and I wait impatiently for the air conditioner to work its magic. I can feel my shirt sticking to my back and everywhere the sun has touched my skin it stings, like I'm being attacked by invisible bees. With an effort, I push these thoughts from my mind, determined to enjoy my time with Thomas. The truck has heavily tinted windows and as it begins to cool down I can feel my body relaxing. Thomas has turned on the stereo and now I lose myself in the soundtrack from *Somewhere In Time*.

Although the restaurant is located in Broken Arrow, the traffic is unusually light on 71st Street and we make good time. Thomas lets me out by the door before driving off in search of a parking place. While waiting for him to return, I find that I am struggling to repress the memories of the past four days. There's nothing to be gained by going there and yet my mind seems to have a will of its own. As morbid as it sounds I can't help wondering, *Who will take care of the twins? What about Thomas?*

He has returned and now we enter the restaurant, the bell above the door announcing our arrival. So Li comes to greet us, her ancient features breaking into a smile. "Mr. and Mrs. Thornton, it so good to see you. Come in. Come in."

I return the smile as best I can but it is obvious that I'm not my usual self.

Showing us to our favorite table, So Li gives me a look of concern, "You okay, Mrs. Thornton? You not look so good."

Knowing how even the effort at small talk can at times be overwhelming, Thomas answers for me. "She's been under the weather lately, especially since returning from our vacation."

"Aaah," So Li nods knowingly, "vacation wear anyone out. I know just what you need. I be right back."

She turns toward the kitchen, her back ramrod straight, her feet, deformed from binding, making it impossible for her to take anything but the tiniest of steps. She must be nearing eighty—a refugee from another time and place—and I can't help wondering about So Li, her life…the sorrows and the joys.

"Becca?" Thomas' deep voice is tender with concern. "Kisses for your thoughts?"

"I was just thinking about So Li," I reply, my heart warming at his use of our "special" phrase.

On feet of silence, So Li has appeared at my shoulder, bearing a steaming cup of her healing brew and a bowl of endamame, my favorite Japanese appetizer. Setting the platter down first, she carefully places the hot brew in front of me.

Thomas immediately reaches for one of the tasty soy beans. Catching him with his fingers in the dish, So Li gently smacks his hand, saying, "Those Mrs. Thornton's favorites. You keep hand away."

Turning back to me, she explains kindly, "This my mother's recipe. It fix you right up. Drink it."

I reach for the sugar but So Li stops me. "No, no, Becca, sugar take away healing power of tea. You must drink plain."

Giving her my kindest smile, I take a sip of the tea. It is awful and I nearly gag, causing me to decide right there that I would rather be sick for the rest of my life than drink that foul brew. So Li is waiting for my reaction so I nod and say, "That's strong stuff."

"Very good for you, very good." Reaching into her apron pocket, she pulls out her order pad. "I take order now, yes?"

After she has gone, I surreptitiously add sugar, being careful to place the empty sugar packages in my purse. There is no way I want to offend this wonderful woman but neither can I drink her healing brew without sweetening it. To my way of thinking, a little deception seems the best solution. I'm not hurting anyone, except maybe myself and only if sugar is truly bad for you, something which I strongly doubt.

Looking up, I realize that Thomas has been watching me. Giving him a sheepish grin, I shrug my shoulders. "What can I say? I'm a sugar addict."

He laughs softly and reaches across the table to feed me one of the tasty soybeans I love so much.

So Li delivers our entrées, departing only after we have tasted each one and given our approval. I have ordered a Lion King Roll, wrapped with soy paper instead of sea weed. It is a succulent combination of fried shrimp, cucumbers, cream cheese, and crispies; topped with fresh avocado, fish eggs, and paper thin shavings of raw salmon. Thomas has ordered two entrées—a Dynamite Roll and a Volcano Roll. Having never tried either one, I have no idea what he is eating but he seems to be enjoying himself, so they must be tasty.

Too soon, our meal is over and Thomas looks at his watch. "I suppose I better take you home and head for the office. With the annual meeting next week, there are still a lot of reports I have to go over."

I know he has to go back to work but I want him to stay with me. When I'm alone everything seems so much worse. I don't say anything but I grip his hand and give him a look he can't misinterpret. Knowing how much I need him, it nearly tears his heart out to leave me but what choice does he have?

"I know, I know," I say motioning for him to get the truck.

While waiting for him to return, my cell phone vibrates and I check the caller ID, hoping it's not my mother. It's an "out of area" number that I do not recognize so I let it go to voice mail. Through the tinted windows, I see the Dodge Ram Mega Cab approaching so I steel myself to leave the safety of Memories of Japan and return to the real world—a world of pain and sickness. At least, for me, that's what it has become and there is no end in sight.

CHAPTER

SIXTEEN

The exhaustion that now threatens to take over my life has returned with a vengeance and I am tempted to sleep the day away. For just a minute, I consider canceling lunch with Jessica and simply returning to my recently vacated king-size bed but then I think better of it. The twins are at camp and Thomas is out of town and I'm determined to take full advantage of this opportunity.

Shopping, eating, and a chick flick—what could be better? Combine that with the company of your dearest friend and you've pretty much described most women's

Mecca. I suppose we could toss in a manicure, pedicure, and a massage but who can actually afford all that?

Even though it feels like the entire Jenks High School Marching Band is doing practice drills in my head, I push through the pain and slowly make my way to the bathtub. I'm determined that nothing short of death is going to keep me from getting myself dressed and out the door.

With my strength waning a little more each day, getting dressed has become a challenge. As a result, I've had to make several adjustments in my daily routines, especially in regard to my makeup. For years, I prided myself on my artistic detail with makeup. Thinking back on it, I'm amazed to think how much time I used to invest in this ritual. Wearing three varying shades of eye shadow has now been trimmed down to just one and I usually forgo eyeliner altogether. I've discovered that by pressing the mascara wand a little closer to the eyelid it gives the illusion of liner and it's much less trouble. It's amazing how these few shortcuts conserve both my time and more importantly, my energy.

Cutting my nearly waist length hair to a short, choppy style, was a painful but necessary decision. My friends were aghast at first, but now, they love it. And it's so much simpler and, truthfully, much more fun. Now, with little effort, it looks adorable. Five minutes to dry, a glob of goo to run it through, flip it up and I'm ready to go. Yep—life's simpler this way.

It may be simpler but by the time I've finished getting ready, I still feel as if I've run the Boston Marathon and today is no different. Gritting my teeth against the ever-present joint pain, I push myself up and cross the bedroom to the full-length mirror. Taking one last look, I appraise my efforts. My stylish bi-level bob is tastefully mussed, with a London Blue crystal bobby pin placed precisely above one ear. My makeup has finally achieved that difficult balance between the "Pancake Look" and the "Natural Look," effectively covering the acne that has mysteriously attacked my complexion since the onset of my other symptoms. Struggling with exhaustion, I am determined to continue.

Next, I appraise my outfit; keeping in mind the "H.A.S. Rules of Shopping."

H is for hair. Remember, whatever goes on must come off. So I never wear a shirt or any item of clothing that goes over my head because taking it on and off will mess up my hair.

A is for accessories. Not only is taking jewelry on and off time-consuming but it can easily get lost or, worse yet, caught in the lace on that ugly chartreuse blouse you never should have tried on in the first place. I've found that by wearing only the simplest pieces of jewelry, I can forgo this kind of problem.

S is for shoes. You're going to be doing a lot of walking so comfortable shoes are a must. This is a hard one for me since I'm a firm believer that shoes make the outfit. I can't bear the thought of stepping out of the house unless my shoes and outfit are perfectly coordinated. On more than one occasion, I have been forced to choose between cutting my shopping trip short or buying a more comfortable pair of shoes because the ones matching my outfit were killing my feet. Of course, you know what I chose!

I thought I was on to something but I should have known it couldn't last. The first time I came home with a new pair of shoes I didn't need, Thomas let me get away with it. The next time I pulled that stunt, he gave me a knowing look, raising his eyebrows skeptically, letting me know that he was on to me. Giving him my most beautiful smile, I high-tailed it into the bedroom where I quickly placed that pair of red suede Kenneth Cole boots in the back of the closet. I was hoping that if they were out of sight, Thomas might forget about them and not insist that I return them.

Before my next shopping excursion, he left a sweet little post-it note on my Dillard's charge card. It said, "No new shoes, today, Honey," with a sweet little smiley face in place of his name.

These are the things that I keep in mind as I glance over my attire. Do I look nice? And do I obey all the rules. I think so. I've chosen a deep red gaucho pant, a red, white, and blue striped sleeveless button-up blouse and a cropped blue-jean jacket. Instead of my perfect but uncomfortable red rhinestone wedges, I have chosen my white-with-blue-beading satin ballerina slippers. My Akoya pearls provide the finishing touch.

Last night, I switched the larger bag I normally carry for a smaller, more compact one that's ideal for a long day at the mall. My lunchbox-style faux crocodile purse is made to be worn across my body making it easy to carry and it has just enough room for my ID, a credit card or two, a lipstick, my cell phone, and keys. What more does a woman need?

I'm checking my makeup one final time when I hear my cell phone ringing. Thinking it might be Thomas or one of the kids, I rush to dig it out of my purse, not even bothering to check the caller ID.

Out of breath, I manage a shaky, "Hello."

"May I speak with Rebecca Thornton, please?"

"Who's calling?" I ask, not recognizing the voice.

"Pastor Keith Thompson. I serve the Church of the Comforter in Cleburne, Texas."

Confused I reply, "I'm sorry. Do I know you?"

Laughing warmly, he says, "We've never met but we'll soon be family. I'm your mother's fiancé."

Off balance, I laugh nervously, before blurting out, "My mother put you up to this, didn't she?"

Taking no offense, he replies kindly, "Actually, your mother knows nothing about this call. It was a kind of spur of the moment thing. I do intend to tell her that I've talked with you, probably over dinner this evening."

Having no patience for this, I curtly demand, "How did you get this number?"

"Mary and I have exchanged personal family information, including our children's cell phone numbers, in case an emergency should arise. As you well know, a crisis is no time to be searching for contact information."

Trying hard to ignore the kindness that seems to flow so easily from him, I ask, more sharply than necessary, "Rev. Thompson, is there a purpose for your call?" Seemingly unfazed by my rudeness, he replies, "During my quiet time this morning, the Lord brought a passage of Scripture to mind and I felt impressed to share it with you."

He hesitates, waiting for my permission to continue. Finally, I acquiesce. Clearing his throat, he says, "The Scripture reference is Exodus 3:7 and 8."

Before he can say more the doorbell interrupts and Beethoven's Ninth's Symphony echoes down the hall. I glance at my watch. Twelve fifteen. Jessica's right on time, providing me with a perfect excuse for ending this unwelcomed telephone call.

"I'm sorry, Rev. Thompson, but my appointment is here." Snapping my cell phone closed without giving him a chance to respond, I fish in the bottom of my purse for a pen and a scrap sheet of paper. Hurriedly, I jot down the reference and drop the paper on my makeup table before heading for the door.

I grab my keys off the hook in the entry, turn off the alarm, and open the front door. "Hey, sweet friend," I say, forcing a smile, pushing back the guilt I feel at my uncharacteristically rude behavior.

Jessica looks dazzling, especially considering all she's been through these past few weeks. She's clad in a simple white and gold cotton tunic, over black stovepipe jeans that accent her lean legs. Checking out her shoes, I see she is wearing gold metallic tennis shoes—comfortable but stylish.

Turning to lock the door, I spot a dazzling baby blue Saab convertible sitting in my driveway causing my jaw to drop. Before I can say anything, Jessica says, "Jason bought it for me. I just picked it up this morning."

I walk around the stunning automobile nearly sick with envy, my hand running over its fenders and down its sides oh-so-lovingly. Cars, especially convertibles, are a secret passion of mine, Jessica and Thomas being the only two people in the world who know this about me. I've dreamed of owning a car like this forever.

Smiling teasingly, she dangles the keys in front of my face. "Would you like to drive?"

Like a teenager being given her first chance behind the wheel, I snatch the keys from her hand and head for the driver's side of the car.

Laughing at my excitement, Jess says, "I knew you would flip the moment you saw it. Whereas, for me, it's just a really pretty car that happens to match my eyes."

I swallow past the sudden tightness in my throat as I recall all the evenings, I spent hanging out in the garage with Dad as he lovingly restored one "classic" car after another. Jessica couldn't stand to get her hands dirty but as I got older I worked right alongside him. His continuous commentary regarding horsepower and torque ingrained in me a love for sports cars of any vintage. Restoring cars and cheering for our favorite football teams was "our" special thing.

Desperately, wanting to somehow share this feeling with Jessica, I reach across the car and squeeze her hand, before slipping the key in the ignition. With the engine idling restlessly, I examine the gauges, explaining excitedly, "Jess, this beauty has a 2.8 liter 6-cylinder turbocharged engine that generates 250-horsepower."

My detailed explanation continues as I carefully back out of the driveway but Jessica simply looks out the window disinterestedly. Instead of heading for Woodland Hills Mall, I turn south toward the Creek Turnpike. The traffic is light and when I enter the turnpike heading west I punch it, enjoying the scream of the turbocharger and the sudden surge of power that pushes us back into our seats. Risking a glance at Jessica, I see that she is gripping the arm rest so tight that her knuckles have turned white. Throwing my head back I laugh, the rush of adrenaline giving me more energy than I've had in weeks.

Easing off on the power, I move into the right lane and exit onto Highway 75 toward downtown. Turning east onto 71st Street, I weave in and out of the traffic, marveling at the Saab's responsiveness. Crossing the bridge over the Arkansas River, I can't resist punching it one last time, exalting in the power at my command. At the red light on Riverside Drive, I try the stereo and I'm pleased to note that I've finally caught Jessica's attention. Reaching in the glove box, she extracts the newest Nichole Nordeman CD and soon we are singing along to her hit single "Brave."

In a matter of minutes, we are turning into the parking lot at the Woodland Hills Mall and already I'm coming down, the excitement of the adrenalin rush wearing off, leaving me tired in a way I can't even describe. Now, the Oklahoma sun seems a thing alive, attacking my skin even as it sucks life out of me. I don't understand what's happening to me but for the first time I realize that the sun has become my enemy.

Ignoring the prickling just below the surface of my skin, I look for a parking spot near the entrance to the mall to conserve my energy. It's useless. Every parking lot is jammed and although I continue circling, there's not a parking spot to be found. "This is worse than the day after Thanksgiving," I mutter, growing more and more frustrated.

Glancing at the clock on the dash, Jessica says, "It's almost 11:30. Whatdya say we get a bite to eat at Mimi's and see if the parking lot thins out any?"

Relieved, I respond, "Sounds good to me. I could use some fortification before doing what we do best."

I pause, catching Jessica's eye, and we say in unison, "Shopping!"

Laughing, we give each other high fives as we head for Mimi's Café.

CHAPTER
SEVENTEEN

A s we wait for the hostess to seat us, I can't help thinking that Jessica's suggestion to grab a bite to eat before hitting the mall feels like a gift from God. Hopefully, a leisurely lunch will renew my energies. Following the hostess to a table in the center of the restaurant, I sink into a chair, unable to suppress a soft groan. Jessica gives me an anxious look causing me to instantly regret my momentary weakness. Waving off her concern, I say, "It's nothing." I feel a twinge of guilt at my white lie but I'm not yet prepared to burden her with my illness.

"Are you sure you're all right?" she asks, reaching across the table to touch my hand.

Giving her my best smile, I shrug off her concerns. "I'm fine. Just a little tired. You know I don't sleep well when Thomas is gone. Spoiled, I guess."

Hoping to end this discussion, I squeeze the lemon wedge into my glass of water before taking a sip. Lately, I can't seem to get enough to drink. No matter how much I consume, my mouth is always dry. Picking up the menu, I pretend to study it while wrestling with my thoughts. I desperately need someone to talk to but I can't bring myself to burden Jessica, not now. She's hurting and I need to be strong for her. Until I know exactly what's wrong with me, I'm not going to trouble her with my fears. I will protect her as long as I can. I've been doing it my whole life and I'm not going to stop now. Besides, nothing's real until I've told it to Jessica.

A quick glance at Jess and I know I'm not fooling her but she lets it slide for the moment, for which I'm grateful. Motioning to the waitress, I order an iced mocha cappuccino in hopes that a high dose of caffeine will give me the kick of energy I so desperately need. Jess orders her typical—Dr. Pepper, no ice, just a squeeze of lime.

Once the waitress leaves, I say, "So tell me about the car."

"What's to tell?"

When I don't respond, she studies the table, playing with her silverware, rearranging it time and again. Tick, tock, tick, tock, the seconds go by until I still her hands with my own.

Belatedly, she lifts her eyes, blinking rapidly to keep from crying. "The way I see it," she finally says, "Jason bought that car as some sort of consolation prize for me."

Her voice fills with bitter irony as she tries unsuccessfully to mimic Jason's rich baritone, "'Honey, you can't have babies but don't fret, here's a new car instead. Now give me one of your pretty smiles.'"

"He said that?" I gasp.

"No, but he might as well have."

My throat tightens as I fight back a rush of emotion. "Oh, Jess." Grabbing her hand in mine once more, I whisper, "You know he meant well, don't you?"

Swimming with tears, her blue eyes lift to meet my own, "Of course, I do and that's what makes my revulsion so much worse. He won't ever be a Daddy and it's all my fault, yet, he goes out and buys me a fifty-thousand-dollar car to cheer me up."

The self-loathing in her voice rips at my heart and I long to comfort her, but what can I say? Finally, I squeeze her hand and whisper, "I'm sorry, Jess. So sorry."

Giving me a forced smile, she says, "Life wasn't supposed to turn out like this, was it? You weren't supposed to get sick and I wasn't supposed to be infertile."

Startled, I stare at her. "What are you talking about?"

"Don't play dumb, Becca. We've been friends for most of our lives. Do you really think I don't know when something is going on with you?"

She's opened the door for me but I can't walk through it, I just can't. Casually, I wave off her concerns. "It's nothing, Jess, really."

For just an instant, I see the hurt in her eyes, the rejection, and then it is gone. Feigning nonchalance, she motions for the waitress to take our orders. "You can be that way if you want, but you're not fooling me."

The last thing in the world I want to do is hurt my friend and yet I can't bring myself to tell her how scared and sick I am. To confide in her, I would have to face the truth myself and I'm not yet prepared to do that. Nor do I have any words of comfort for her. Nothing I can say will give her a child or take away the pain of not having one.

Our food arrives and we pick at it, neither of us having much of an appetite. We make small talk without really saying anything, long periods of silence emphasizing the hurt we both feel. I sense the beginnings of a migraine headache but I try to ignore it, not willing to let Jessica know how bad I'm feeling. Closing my eyes, I will the blurred vision to cease, almost welcoming the pain to follow as just retribution for the way I have wounded my friend.

When I open my eyes, Jessica is staring at the foyer, a puzzled look on her face. Cutting my eyes in the same direction, I see Madison's husband, Michael, waiting to be seated and he's not alone. There's a good-looking brunette with him. She's dressed in a stylish business suit and carrying a portfolio. "It's probably just business, Jessica."

"Monkey business, maybe," she retorts.

As we continue to stare, Michael leans his head close to the woman's to hear what she is saying. They share a laugh and the woman puts her hand on his chest. It's an intimate gesture and belatedly, she seems to realize that they are in public and quickly makes a show of reaching up to straighten his tie. The hostess arrives to seat them and as they are shown to their table Michael's hand never leaves her waist.

I can't help thinking that their behavior is a little too familiar for mere business colleagues; too familiar for old friends, as far as that goes. Still, I don't want to jump to conclusions. Michael is a highly respected businessman and a leader in his church. As far as I know, he and Madison have a great marriage.

As if reading my mind, Jessica says, "I know—he's an elder at church and well thought of but that didn't look right."

"If Thomas treated another woman like that, I'd claw his eyes out but then 'manners' have never been his strong suit."

"Manners?" Jessica asks, raising an eyebrow skeptically. "Is that what you call that?"

"You know how Michael and Madison are." I reply, trying to convince myself as much as Jessica.

"In case you didn't notice, that wasn't Madison with Michael."

Opening her purse, Jessica extracts her compact and a lip pencil and begins touching up her lips. "What are you doing?" I ask.

"Preparing for war," she replies, a touch of steel creeping into her voice.

"You're not thinking of confronting Michael, are you?"

"As a matter of fact, the thought had crossed my mind."

"Jessica, don't make a fool of yourself."

"Don't worry, Becca, I know what I'm doing." She finger fluffs her hair, uses her tongue to clean her teeth, and looks to me for final approval. "If I don't do this, I won't be able to live with myself."

At my look of concern, she adds, "Don't worry. I'm not going to make a scene. I'm just going to cause Michael a wee bit of discomfort."

Snapping her compact shut, she replaces it in her purse and stands to her feet a determined look in her eye. I've seen that look a thousand times and I know what it means. Once her mind is made up nothing is going to stop her. Taking a deep breath, I reach for my purse and hurry after her.

Michael and the brunette are seated in a corner booth sharing an appetizer when we approach. Glancing up, he recognizes us and for just an instant, I see a flicker of emotion touch his eyes; consternation maybe, but more likely surprise. Ever the gentleman, he stands to greet us, reaching for our hands. "Jessica, Becca. What a pleasant surprise."

I can't help thinking that either this is a purely legitimate business lunch or Michael is a consummate actor. "Please join us," he says, motioning for Jessica and me to sit down. I'm ready to decline but Jessica is already sliding into the booth beside the brunette. Motioning to the waitress, he says, "Bring the ladies something to drink, please." Looking at Jess, he adds, "A Dr. Pepper, with a twist of lime and no ice if I remember correctly."

Turning to me, he says, "You'll have to help me out, Becca. You hardly ever drink the same thing. All I can remember is that it has to have lots of caffeine and even more sugar."

When the waitress leaves, Jessica immediately introduces herself to the brunette. "Becca and I are Madison's two closest friends—Madison being Michael's wife, of course. We go all the way back to elementary school. We've been looking out for each other since first grade. We may keep things from our husbands but there are no secrets among the three of us."

Trying to redirect the conversation, Michael interjects, "Allow me to introduce Lori Hays. She is our newest associate and we were going to use the lunch hour to go over some things. I suppose we could have done it at the office but it's hard to get anything done with the phone ringing all the time and people running in and out."

Before I can reply, Jessica responds, her tone slightly patronizing, "I'm sure working at the office must be terribly inconvenient, especially, when you don't want to be interrupted."

Lori glances Jessica's way, trying to decide if she is being nice or if she is implying something other than what she has just said. Jess gives her a sweet smile before turning to Michael, "Of course, I've told Jason that if he needs to meet with a good-looking colleague off site, he had better invite me or he'll find himself sleeping on the couch."

Michael laughs but it seems a little forced. "Thank God Madison's not so insecure or I'd never get anything done."

While they've been bantering, I've been studying Lori and I couldn't help noticing her portfolio. It's a rich chocolate brown leather with gold filigree lettering. Her name is prominently displayed along with a company name and it's not Monroe and Associates. Of course, that may not mean anything. If she's new at the company, she may not have had time to replace her portfolio, still the one she is carrying looks awfully new.

"So," I ask, "what made you decide to leave advertising?"

Before Lori can respond Michael jumps in. "Actually, Lori worked for one of the largest Public Relations firms in the city before she decided she wanted to do something different...more substantial. Commercial real estate gives her a chance to help develop Tulsa in a more concrete way."

If Michael's embarrassed to have his wife's two closest friends "catch" him at lunch with another woman, he hides it well. He doesn't seem the least bit disconcerted. Lori's discomfort, on the other hand, is obvious but that may be nothing more than feeling like the odd man out among three old friends. Still, I can't shake the feeling that something is amiss here. Something our pastor said last week keeps coming to mind: "There is no lie so odious as that which uses the truth to deceive."

The truth: Michael and Lori probably have a legitimate business relationship.

The lie: Under the guise of business, they are carrying on an inappropriate relationship of some sort.

As much as I want to believe otherwise, I'm convinced Michael is using the truth to deceive and now my heart hurts for Madison.

Glib is the word that comes to mind. Michael is so glib! Nothing seems to faze him. I'm sure he will call Madison as soon as we leave. I can almost hear him now. *"Hello, Honey. You'll never guess who I ran into at lunch today—Jessica and Becca. Yes, at Mimi's. Lori was with me. Lori Hays, the new girl, I was telling you about. What's going on with Becca anyway, she didn't look so good?"*

Taking a final sip of my Latte, I get to my feet, fumbling in my purse for my sunglasses. Although I now have a full blown migraine headache, I manage my good-byes and make my way toward the door as if nothing is amiss. Having been plagued with migraines since high school, I know what's in store for me. Shopping is now out of the question. All I want to do is retreat to a dark room, curl up and sleep.

Hurrying to catch up with me, Jessica asks, "Are you all right?"

"I'm having one of my migraine headaches. You'd better take me home."

Once we reach the Saab, I slump in the seat and close my eyes. Jessica quickly raises the convertible top, knowing how sensitive I am to light at times like this. Even though my eyes are tightly closed behind my sunglasses, I can still sense the light and it jabs like an ice pick. Gritting my teeth, I refuse to groan, willing Jessica to get me home as fast as she can.

Although it's less than three miles to my house, the drive seems to take forever. When Jessica finally turns into the circle drive and stops under the portico, I'm ready to collapse. She hurries to open my door. Taking my arm, she helps me out of the car and to the front door where I fumble in my purse for my keys. When I finally get the door open, I forget to disarm the alarm and the screaming of its siren causes me to cover my ears and moan with pain. Frantically, I punch in the code and almost immediately, the telephone rings. I'm tempted to ignore it but I don't dare. It's probably the security company and if I don't answer it, they will send the police out.

Jessica watches from the doorway but there's nothing she can do, so I wave good-bye and blow her a kiss while giving the security company my name and code word. Moving to the front door, I watch as she pulls out of the drive. She has lowered the convertible top and her hair is blowing in the wind, tendrils catching in her lip gloss. She brushes them away before putting the baby blue beast in drive and disappearing down the road.

Closing the door, I lean against it trying to gather my strength. With Jessica's departure, there's no need for me to pretend to be stronger than I am. Slowly, I slide down the heavy door to the cold floor, too tired to traverse the short distance to the master bedroom. As bad as the migraine is, it is not what has done me in. What I cannot bear is the possibility that there may be something seriously wrong with me—something medical science cannot cure.

Whatever has attacked my body did not come on suddenly but slowly, over a number of weeks, perhaps even months. At first, I tried to ignore it, tried to simply push through the pain and exhaustion but to no avail. With each succeeding week, it seemed I was confronted with a new symptom—forgetfulness, mood swings, extreme joint pain, parched mouth, and unbelievable exhaustion. Although I've undergone a number of tests, there still has not been a definitive diagnosis and without a diagnosis there can be no treatment.

The thing I find most disconcerting is the depression. Yes, depression. I don't want to admit it but that's what it is. Although I've always been an optimistic person, now I regularly battle feelings of hopelessness and I often find myself weeping for no reason. I'm sure Daddy's death is part of it, but this is more than grief. Never have I felt so alone, so abandoned by God. That's how it feels—like a door has been slammed in my face and bolted—locking me out. But I will not believe it is so; I cannot or I will die. God is my only hope and I will not let go of Him. More importantly, He will not let go of me! And as long as He is with me, I can bear anything—pain, sickness, grief, even death.

Having regained a little strength, I push myself to my feet and make my way down the hall and into the master bedroom. In the bathroom, I rummage in the cabinet until I find my migraine medicine and swallow the tablets dry. Glancing at my makeup table, I see the scrap of paper with Exodus 3:7 and 8 written on it. On an impulse, I pick it up and carry it with me to the four-poster bed. In too much pain to undress, I simply collapse on the bed, clutching that Scripture reference the way a drowning person clutches a life preserver.

CHAPTER

EIGHTEEN

It's midmorning and Starbucks is buzzing. While Jessica waits to get our coffees, I head for the two easy chairs in the corner by the window. Making myself comfortable, I inhale the rich aroma, thinking for the thousandth time that as much as I love the flavor of coffee, it never tastes as good as it smells. For two days, I have done almost nothing but sleep and for the first time in weeks I feel nearly human. It seems I'm gaining a little strength and today my joint pain is manageable. It's a good thing too because Thomas gets home tomorrow evening and the twins return from camp the day after that.

Jessica hands me my drink saying, "One iced caramel macchiato, shaken not stirred, with extra caramel." I laugh as she takes the chair beside me. She's having a plain cappuccino as usual and as she takes a sip I shake my head. "Boring…"

"So," she asks, "is this just a fun day at the mall or are you planning some serious shopping?"

"Pretty serious," I reply. "I need to update my wardrobe for fall. I'm looking for a pair of high-heeled ankle boots, at least one pair of black leggings, anything in gold, a tulip skirt, one great suit, a skinny pair of jeans—well at least as skinny as I can fit into—and one of the new outerwear coats."

Looking at me over her cappuccino she says, "Planning on breaking the bank, are we?"

"I won't be able to get it all today but that's what I'm looking for. Hopefully, I can pick up an item or two every couple of weeks and by mid-September I should be all set."

"That sounds like a plan. So what do you want to get today?"

"Anything on my list will do, but I would like to get the black leggings as soon as possible."

"Did you say leggings?"

"Sure did."

"You have got to be kidding."

Smiling widely, I say, "Nope, I'm not kidding."

"Leggings, as in the 1980s, Madonna, leg warmers, skinny jeans, shoulder pads, and the whole nine yards?"

"That's right, Jess. Everything but the shoulder pads. Where have you been? Don't you read *Vogue* or *InStyle* anymore?"

Looking down her nose at me, Jess says teasingly, "No, Miss Fashion Plate, unlike you and Madison, I have a job. I can't spend my days reading fashion magazines."

"What?" I cry, pretending to take offense. "Taking care of a husband and two teenagers isn't a job?"

A graphic artist, Jess is a sole proprietor of a business she runs out of her home. Most of her work is for clients located in New York City and other large metropolises, so I seldom see her work in print. As a result, I like to tease her about not having a real job. She, on the other hand, likes to kid Madison and me about being stay-at-home moms. It's all in good fun. In fact, Jessica's quick wit and good-natured sarcasm are two of the things I like best about her. We've been teasing each other since elementary school and I've always enjoyed our verbal sparring.

Finishing my iced caramel macchiato, I toss the empty cup in the trash bin and head for the door. Over my shoulder, I call, "Come on, Jess, it's time to hit the mall."

"Okay," she answers, hurrying after me, glancing down at the screen of her constantly ringing cell phone. Choosing to ignore this particular call, Jessica quiets her Blackberry Pearl before hollering, "This time I'm driving. I don't want you becoming too attached to my new car. You might start thinking it belongs to you and I've decided I'll keep it, consolation prize or not."

"That's my girl," I say, playfully tossing the keys her way before sashaying out the door and into the blinding sunshine of the Oklahoma summer.

⋯

As per our normal routine, we work our way through the racks of clothing collecting anything that looks interesting. Finally, we head for the dressing rooms, choosing the one that is set up for women with strollers. I suppose we're being tacky but we've always done it this way, at least as far back as I can remember. "The Bonko Babes" have always shared the largest dressing room; that's just the way we do things. But today, standing in front of the mirror next to Jessica's perfect size six pre-baby body, I'm questioning the wisdom of this tradition.

I don't consider myself unattractive, but I am starting to show some wear. No doubt about it, bearing twins did a number on my figure. Standing next to Jessica I look almost dowdy. Glancing at her slim figure and flat, stretch-mark-free stomach, I am suddenly overcome with that little green monster. I glare at my reflection, thinking my stomach looks like a bowl of cottage cheese with a few sprinkles of purple cabbage. Yuck!

But my self-critique doesn't stop there. Oh, no! There's so much more. Turning my back to the mirror, I begin studying my backside. Somehow over the years, it seems to have shifted. Now, instead of being narrow and round, it is wide and flat. Yep, I might as well wear a sign that says, "Wide Load."

And don't get me started on my bust. Before I breastfed the twins, I was a perfect size 32D. That's right. I had a "Barbie Doll" figure. Now, well, it's simply too deflating to talk about.

Noticing my sudden quietness, Jessica inquires, "Becca, what's wrong?"

Indicating the stacks of clothing, I've chosen to try on with a flick of her manicured hand, she adds, "You haven't tried a thing on. You've just been standing there glaring at your reflection. And what's with the strange looks you've been sending my way?"

Turning my critical gaze upon her, I snap, "Look at yourself, Jess. I mean really look."

Self-consciously, she examines herself in the mirror.

"Now, look at me."

We are both in our bras and underwear. If it wasn't so pathetic, the comparison would be hilarious. Me and my five-foot-four-inch-size-twelve-mother-of-two-thirty-seven-year-old body standing next to her five-foot-nine-inch-size-six-pre-baby-thirty-six-year-old body. There's no comparison. *Life definitely dealt her a better set of genes. Still, I wouldn't trade my twins for anything, not even a body like hers.*

"Well, Jess," I say in a self-mocking tone, "I guess I'm just feeling a little sorry for myself this morning. I've been mourning the passing of my youth. You know, saying good-bye to the good ol' days of summer."

"What are you talking about?" she asks confusion coloring her words.

"How can I explain it?" I nibble my lower lip. "Let's just say I'm missing the way things used to be before the cold winds took hold of my body and blew everything permanently south for the winter."

When she still doesn't get it, I make a show of pointing to my sagging breasts and then to my ever widening behind and finally, we are both laughing, my silliness having once again saved us from ourselves.

"Becca, you're a hoot!" she says, giving me a hug, the warmth of her friendship somehow lightening my load.

Suddenly my insecurity seems so petty and I start to giggle like a schoolgirl. Thomas loves me and my children love me so what's the big deal? Besides, with my sense of fashion, once I put on clothes I can still turn heads; not that that's important. Still, I would like to do something about my sagging boobs and why not? Given the advances in plastic surgery there's no reason I can't have a pert pair.

Quietly, in a conspiratorial whisper, I say, "Jessica, I'm going to get me some girls."

Confusion clouds her eyes again. "Becca, you already have Brooklyn."

I chuckle. "Not a daughter, Jess." Then indicating my sagging breasts, I say "You know…Girls!"

Her eyes widen in disbelief. Then in a voice loud enough for my grandma to hear, she shouts, "YOU'RE GETTING A BOOB JOB!"

"SHHH! JESSICA!" I say, my face flushed with embarrassment. "You don't have to announce it to the whole world."

From the dressing room two doors down, a woman calls to me. "You go, girl! I did it and it was the best thing I ever did!"

Mortified, I say just loud enough for the stranger to hear, "Thank you."

"You're welcome. Just remember, it's pretty painful. But like they say: no pain, no gain."

"Yeah, okay," I say, hoping against hope that she will just drop it.

Now, she's standing outside our dressing room door. Opening it just a crack, she hands me a card with her phone number. "Give me a call if you'd like to talk. I can recommend a great surgeon."

Once the door closes, Jessica grabs my arm. Intrigued, she asks, "Are you serious? Are you really going to get a boob job?"

I shrug. "I've been thinking about it for a while, but I didn't decide until just a minute ago."

"So have you discussed it with Thomas? What does he think?"

"Not recently. I brought it up once, months ago, and he just laughed. Pulling me into his arms, he kissed me on the end of my nose and said, 'Becca, I love you just the way you are.'"

"You're still going to do it, even though Thomas isn't enthused about it?" Jess presses.

"This isn't about Thomas, Jess. It's about me. I need to do this for me."

"Why?" she asks, genuinely puzzled.

Once more, I am reminded of how different the two of us are. Blessed with a nearly flawless body she hardly gives her appearance a second thought. With almost no effort, she looks stunning and at thirty-six she is as youthful looking as she was at twenty-five. She has her own insecurities, of course, but they have nothing to do with her body. In that regard, she is the least self-conscious person I have ever known. God knows I wish I were more like her.

In my mother's eyes, physical beauty was of utmost importance; consequently, I've always based my self-worth on my appearance. I know it's dumb but I can't help it. Now that my body is aging I'm plagued with self-doubt. Sometimes, I look in the mirror and I want to cry. Of course, I don't try to explain any of that to Jess. She would never understand.

Instead, I don my clown face once more. Hiking up my bra, I thrust out my chest in an exaggerated pose. "Never let it be said that the cruelties of aging can't be undone. With the help of modern medicine these girls will rise again."

Throwing her head back, Jessica roars with laughter and I can't help but join in. Life is beautiful and for the moment my pain is forgotten and Jessica's barrenness isn't all-consuming.

NINETEEN

In my rear-view mirror I see the police officer approaching. Tapping on my window he tells me to move along, so I shift my Navigator into drive and pull out. Thomas' flight from Orlando is late and the officer and I have been playing tag for the past forty-five minutes. Apparently, you can remain parked in the passenger pick-up zone no longer than five minutes at a time. It seems like an insane rule to me, like so many of the security rules they have put in place since 9-11. To my way of thinking, five minutes is more than enough time for a terrorist to detonate a car bomb, but what do I know. If the authorities are really serious about protecting our airports maybe they shouldn't allow us to park near the terminal at all.

Thomas tried to tell me it would be best if he drove himself to the airport and left his truck in long-term parking but I wouldn't listen; nor did I bother to check with the airline to make sure his flight was going to be on time. Being the optimistic person I am (Thomas calls it being naïve) I just assumed he would arrive on schedule and now I'm suffering the consequences. Apparently several flights have been delayed and traffic is beginning to back up, forcing me to circle the airport while I search in vain for a place to park at the curb. Finally, I give up and turn into short-term parking, selecting a spot near the edge of the lot, out of the sun.

When I left the house an hour and twenty minutes ago I was feeling reasonably good, having rested most of the afternoon so I would be able to enjoy the evening with Thomas. Unfortunately, the glare of the Oklahoma sun and the stress of the airport traffic have combined to physically and emotionally drain me. Reclining the seat, I lean my head back and close my eyes, hoping a quick nap will refresh me. Unfortunately, as is often the case when I am overly tired, I can't sleep.

I usually have a book with me for times like this, but I left the house in such a rush that I came without one and with nothing to read my mind wanders. I consider and discard a half a dozen topics before settling on my mother and her fiancé. Two weeks from tomorrow they will arrive for a get-acquainted visit. Knowing what a stickler my mother is for a spotless house, Jessica and Madison have offered to help me get ready for her visit but I have adamantly refused. I hate to admit it but it gives me a perverse pleasure to think of embarrassing her in front of her new love. Maybe, he'll decide we're "white trash" and change his mind about marrying her. Thomas thinks I'm being childish about the house and Jessica has suggested that I'm being passive aggressive but I don't care. My attitude is hardly Christian, I know, but if my mother thinks I'm going to make this easy for her; she's got another thing coming.

Finally, my cell phone plays "our song," letting me know that Thomas has landed. Digging it out of my purse, I mentally shift gears before saying, "Welcome home, Baby."

Fifteen minutes later, he has tossed his carry-on in the back of my Navigator, given me a hug and a kiss, and slid behind the wheel. As he turns toward the exit, I study his handsome profile, thanking God for my man. There's a cold sore on his bottom lip, just where I expected to find it. He hates to travel and if he has to be away from me for more than a couple of nights he always gets one. I know they're painful but I'd be disappointed if he returned from a business trip without a sore on his lip.

His dark hair is thinning on top and graying at the temples. He hates it but I think it makes him look distinguished. I wait until he has paid the attendant and exited the parking lot, and then I lean over and brush his cheek with my fingertips. "I've missed you," I whisper, blowing in his ear.

Although I'm not hungry, Thomas insists on taking me to our favorite Cajun restaurant—Jazmoz Bourbon Street Café on 15th Street. Once we're seated, he orders a dozen oysters on the half shell as an appetizer and like always he tries to get me to try one. Yuck! I love sushi but for the life of me I can't bring myself to eat a raw oyster. Silly, I know, but that's the way I am. Our entrées arrive and I toy with my coconut shrimp while Thomas wolfs down his crawfish etouffee.

There's a Cajun band and the noise and the crowd are nearly more than I can bear. Still, I'm determined not to let my weariness and irritability ruin the evening, knowing how much Thomas enjoys the atmosphere and the Cajun cuisine. Normally, I would be in the thick of things myself but tonight I simply don't have the strength. All I want to do is go home and spend a quiet evening, or at least what's left of it, with my husband. To my annoyance, Thomas orders a second espresso and sips it while enjoying the music.

When we finally arrive home, I'm nearly out on my feet but I'm determined that my illness will not ruin his first night back. Somehow I manage to make it through my bedtime ritual and I even put on one of my sexiest nightgowns. Thomas is not fooled. He knows me so well and tonight he can read the fear in my eyes. Without a word, he simply takes me in his arms. This is my undoing. The emotions I have kept so tightly suppressed come spilling out and I cry like a baby. When my tears have exhausted themselves, my knight in shining armor takes me by the hand and leads me to our bed. He has already turned it down and now he helps me into bed before stretching out beside me on the freshly laundered sheets. As I rest in his arms, I can't help thinking that it feels so good to place some of this load upon his strong shoulders.

"Becca," he murmurs, his voice thick with feeling, "you don't have to do this by yourself. Let me help you."

I try to protest but his finger on my lips hushes me.

"Don't shut me out, Sweetheart," he pleads. "I can't bear that."

Imperceptibly, I nod, tears welling up once more, thankful that he wants to share even this difficult time with me.

Brushing back my hair, he lifts my chin. Gazing deeply into his eyes, I'm overwhelmed at the love I see reflected there. "In sickness and in health," he says, reaffirming his wedding vows. "Don't you ever forget that."

We talk at length then, at least I do, and Thomas listens, never making light of my concerns with false assurances. I can tell that my fear makes him uncomfortable but to his credit he never turns away. When at last I have run down, I feel better somehow, more confident about the future. For several minutes we lay in comfortable quietness, content to simply hold each other. On the mantel in the living room my grandmother's antique clock chimes eleven times. Turning toward me, Thomas presses his mouth against my hair and prays, asking God for both strength and healing.

"Goodnight, Sweetheart," he says, after kissing me gently on the cheek.

As he turns over to sleep, I think my heart will break. Although I know he loves me, it is obvious that he no longer desires me. I can't help feeling that my sickness has made me unattractive to him. Biting my lip to keep from making a sound, I weep soundlessly into my pillow. *Is this the way it's going to be?* I wonder. *If my illness progresses, will I become less and less desirable to him?*

Although I have not uttered a peep, nor moved so much as a muscle, he senses my distress. Turning toward me, he asks, "What is it, Becca?"

His concern looses a fresh wave of grief and I turn my face to the wall, my sobs shaking the bed. Gently, he tries to turn me so I am facing him but I won't budge. I can't look at him, I just can't. The pain of his rejection is simply too much to bear. Finally, he gets out of bed, walks around to my side, and kneels on the floor so he can see my face. I try to turn away but laying his cheek next to mine, he begs, "What is it, Baby? Is there something you're not telling me?"

I hate myself for being weak. This isn't me. I'm Becca— super wife and mom, the life of the party, and tower of strength for my friends.

Instead of answering him I reach up, place my hands on both sides of his face and ignoring his cold sore kiss him squarely on the mouth. For an instant he hesitates, unsure how to respond, then I sense his desire. Now, his kiss is passionate and he draws me to himself, enfolding me in his strong arms.

After a moment he pulls away. "Are you sure you want to do this?" he asks, concerned about me. "Do you feel up to it?"

"Yes," I whisper.

Scooting over, I make room for him on the bed beside me. With a gentleness I did not know he was capable of, Thomas makes love to me. Each touch, each kiss is more intense, more sensitive than the one before. At last, we come together as God intended: one man, one woman, joined in holy matrimony, celebrating their love for each other.

Later, we are lying on the bed, my head nestled against his shoulder, the streetlight slanting through the blinds, casting bars of light across the comforter. Secure now that we have made love, I am able to share my earlier fears with him. "Oh, Baby," he says, "I'll always want you. I was just trying to be sensitive about your health issues."

"Well," I reply, punching his shoulder gently, "don't be quite so sensitive next time. If I don't feel up to making love, I'll let you know."

CHAPTER

TWENTY

Thomas and the twins have been home for almost a week now and it seems there are never enough hours in a day. The Women's Ministry leader from church called and asked me to be a discussion group leader for the Beth Moore Bible study. I accepted, of course, and when I told Thomas he just shook his head. To his way of thinking, I'm always trying to do too much. He's probably right but I love people and enjoy being involved in all kinds of activities.

Speaking of which, I'd better get going. Tonight's Bunko party is at Kathleen's and I can't wait. It feels like forever since I've seen The Babes. I wonder if Kathleen is starting to show yet? The theme is Mardi Gras and I've yet to decide on a dish. Normally, I'd head over to the Jazmoz Bourbon Street Cafe off of Cherry Street for Crawfish Etouffee, one of my favorite Cajun delicacies. But with so much on my plate right now, a quick swing through Popeye's Chicken for a large order of their seafood gumbo and red beans and rice will have to do.

Adam and Kathleen's starter home is located in what is charmingly referred to as "Midtown" Tulsa, an area steeped in middle-class American tradition. As I turn into their neighborhood, I can't help but marvel at the towering oak trees which spread their arms protectively over the neighborhood streets. It's like stepping back in time to a "Leave it to Beaver" episode, a place where I can easily imagine children riding their bikes—playing cards tucked in their front wheels making a comforting whap, whap, whap as they coast along.

Parking in the street, I survey their house noting its curb appeal. The yard looks manicured and Kathleen and Adam have stayed true to their home's history, never straying from its original 1920s vintage charm. Walking up the walk to their front porch, it's easy to imagine children playing hopscotch or roller skating somewhere down the block. And I can almost hear a mother calling her children to supper, reminding them to wipe their feet, and not to slam the door.

Ringing the bell, I wait patiently, noting that the evening air is thick with the threat of thunderstorms and heavy with mold spore. To the west, the summer sky is a kaleidoscope of angry purples and grays, pierced from time to time by a jagged flash of lightning. Glancing at the cars parked in the driveway, I realize that I'm one of the last to arrive. The first quarter-sized raindrops are pelting the sidewalks when Kathleen finally opens the door.

Pregnancy obviously agrees with her for she looks radiant, her abdomen curved and slightly protruding. She is clad in a floaty sundress of the creamiest buttercup, her auburn hair divided into pigtails and tied loosely with ribbon. "Becca," she begins, before holding up a finger and I watch from the other side of the screen door knowing instinctively what is coming next.

"Uh, uh, uh, Choo," she sneezes in her familiar way. "Excuse me," she manages, before beginning the process all over again.

I let myself in, catching the door with my foot to prevent it from slamming. "God bless you, Kitty Kat," I say, before heading for the kitchen.

"Thank yhoo," she replies, the last word slightly muffled from yet another sneeze.

I am about to cut through the dining room on my way to the kitchen when Jessica stops me. "Kathleen doesn't want anyone to go in the dining room until we're ready to eat."

Taking one of my Popeye's Chicken bags, she leads me down a short hallway and into the kitchen where Kathleen has set up a buffet table. Although much of the food is take-out, there's not a Styrofoam container in sight. Opening a cupboard door, Jessica gets two serving dishes and starts transferring the seafood gumbo into one bowl while I pour the red beans and rice into the other. I allow Jess to arrange my dishes on the buffet table noting the careful way she displays everything.

We return to the living room in time to hear Kitty Kat complain in a stuffy voice, "All this sneezing can't be good for the baby."

After eight babies, Autumn is our resident authority and from across the room, she pipes up, "Trust me. That kid's got more padding in there than ya think. Idn't that right, Karo?"

Karen, who works as a nurse on the Labor and Delivery floor at St. Francis Hospital, adds, "She's absolutely right, Kitty Kat. It's like being wrapped in layers, upon layers, of thick down comforters." Patting Kathleen's tummy, she continues, "I can't wait to see this little one brought into the world."

Straightening up, she asks, "Have you thought any more about working after the baby is born?"

Kathleen shrugs, "I don't want to but financially, there is no way I can stay at home with the baby. Adam doesn't make diddlysquat playing for the Tulsa Talons so for now, the modest income I make as an interior designer is what we live on."

Giving Kitty Kat an encouraging squeeze, Karen says, "It'll be hard at first especially leaving your baby at day care but you'll be fine and so will your baby."

When Kitty Kat still seems unconvinced, Karen continues, "I never had a stay-at-home Mom and neither did you. We didn't turn out too bad, did we?"

"That's debatable," I tease and then quickly add, "In reality, you both could be poster children for working Moms."

"Thank yhoo," Kitty Kat spews another sneeze and Michelle appears at her side, a box of Kleenex in her outstretched hand. "You're such a doll," Kitty Kat says gratefully, before being seized with yet another fit of sneezing.

Giving Kathleen a look of pity, Michelle pats her tummy saying, "Aah, the joys of pregnancy during allergy season in our great state. Just think—only six more months till the first freeze."

"Thanks a lot," Kathleen says from behind a wad of Kleenex, her voice sounding more and more like Elmer Fudd.

"Yeah, Michelle. That's the way to cheer her up," Karen injects, tongue in cheek.

Michelle takes a bow reveling in the attention and I'm so proud of her. Our little "mud-sucker" has blossomed since joining our group just a few months ago. She'll probably never be truly gregarious but at least she has developed the confidence to interact with the group.

Kitty Kat's sneezing fit finally seems to have passed and for the first time, I take note of all the work she has put into the preparations for tonight's Bunko party. Her living room has been completely transformed. Gone is the 1920s inspired Art Deco. In its place, the French Quarter has come to life, the heavy scent of magnolias filling the room. The windows are draped in gauzy fabrics of the richest emerald, amethyst, and gold creating a soft glow and a Billie Holiday CD is playing, her smoky voice adding the final touch.

"Wow," I say, smiling at Kathleen. "This is really amazing."

Stepping forward, Autumn interjects, "Well, I sure hope you ladies don't expect anything like this when you come to my house in a couple of weeks. You'll be lucky if I manage to dig out my sombrero, put up some streamers, and zap Cheez Whiz on some nachos for y'all on Mexican theme night."

Catching the spirit, Kathleen banters, "If I had eight kids, you wouldn't get anything like this either. Y'all would show up at my house for Mexican night and find a note on the door, 'Kid's are driving me crazy. Gone to Mexico!'"

We all laugh and I can't help thinking that she has no idea how right she is. In reality, she probably doesn't have a clue how radically her life is going to change after her baby arrives. Add a couple more and there will be days when she will feel like she's ready for the loony bin. As much as I love my twins, there were times when I was ready to give them away. Thank God, Mom lived nearby. She was a lifesaver.

Coming up beside her sister, Jess places her arm around her shoulders and says rather proudly, "You'll be a great mom, Kitty Kat. You're cut out for it."

"Thanks, Jess," Kitty Kat replies giving her a quick squeeze. "To tell you the truth, there are days when I wonder if I'm really ready for this. I mean, what do I know about taking care of a baby?" She wrinkles up her nose, while shrugging her shoulders in that universal gesture of complete and total helplessness.

"Boy, do I remember that feeling." I chuckle. "After the twins were born, I spent three days in the hospital. That's it. Then, the doctor came in all smiles and said, 'Everything looks great here, Mrs. Thornton. I'll get the discharge papers ready and you can take your babies home.' When he walked out, I looked at Thomas, my eyes the size of soup spoons. 'Do they come with an owner's manual?' I squeaked."

The laughter of The Bunko Babes fills the room and Karen says, "See, everyone has misgivings in the beginning. It's only natural."

"Hey, Kathleen," Michelle asks, growing weary of all this baby talk, "What's the banner say?"

Strung across the fireplace mantle is a beautiful banner in the traditional Mardi Gras colors of purple, green, and gold. It reads: "Laissez Les Bons Temps Rouler."

Giving us all a cocky little grin, Kathleen answers, "It's French for 'Let the Good Times Roll' which is exactly what we are going to be doing and very soon but to..." Again her nose crinkles and it looks like she is going to sneeze but at last this one passes and she continues, "...tonight, we're going to do things a little differently."

Turning to her sister, she adds with a wink, "Jessica, the bag, please."

With a great flourish, Jess presents a large gift bag. Reaching inside, Kitty Kat pulls out one amazing mask after another, along with a dazzling array of beaded necklaces. "Oohing" and "Aahing," we make our selections. I have chosen a mask resplendent with fans of dark iridescent emerald feathers. Violet sequins flash flirty winks of light in all directions, while brilliant baubles dangle down each side. Never having been a big fan of the "less is more" concept, I pile on the beads wrapping the strands around my wrists and ankles as well as draping them around my neck.

Pirouetting for my friends, Autumn teases, "Becca, what have you been up to?"

Confused, I give her a blank look.

Michelle steps in to clear things up. "She's referring to the beads."

"What?" I reply, still without a clue.

Several of The Bunko Babes are laughing at my naiveté and I'm starting to feel embarrassed and a strange feeling that is for me. Finally, Michelle explains the hedonistic Mardi Gras tradition in which women are given strands of beads for exposing their breasts.

Glancing down at my chest, I begin to giggle. "Given the sad shape of my cleavage, they'd probably make me give'um back!"

Once more, the girls erupt with laughter. When they finally settle down, Kathleen tells us that before the Bunko games can start we are going to enjoy a sit-down dinner.

Opening the doors to the dining room with a flourish, she presents us with the piece de' resistance of the evening. She has hand made place cards with our names written in perfect calligraphy. As I search for mine, I am overwhelmed at the amount of effort she has put into tonight's gathering. Each table setting includes a gold charger plate, formal flatware, a crystal goblet, and a cloth napkin with a tragedy mask napkin ring. She has thought of everything, down to the minutest detail.

I glance in Madison's direction to judge her reaction, knowing instinctively that out of all of us, she alone can fully appreciate how much work has gone into this evening's preparations. But tonight, Madison is in her own world and I think I know why—Michael. Remembering the way he flirted with that Lori woman, I would like to give him a swift kick in the pants followed by a right cross. I know that's not nice but maybe it would knock some sense into him.

As I look across the table at Madison, I can't imagine how Michael could ever be interested in another woman. Always attractive, Madison is stunningly beautiful tonight, her pure blonde hair pulled back in an elegant chignon, porcelain features flawless though obviously etched with worry or stress. Her posture is stiff and restrained, yet her elegance remains. My heart aches for her and I wonder if she knows about Lori. If she does, I know that there is nothing I or anybody else can do that will erase her hurt. And for me, that is the most difficult pill to swallow.

Listening to the music of laughter as The Babes banter back and forth, I can't help thinking how like life this is—joy and sorrow sitting at the same table. Without exception each of us has our challenges—marital difficulties, financial problems, health issues, infertility. You name it and we have it. And yet, God has given us joy in the midst of our struggles. The strength He gives us through family and friends sustains us even in the darkest hour and He will not fail Madison. Of that, I am sure.

CHAPTER

TWENTY-ONE

An hour later, we have finished dinner and Autumn and I are playing Bunko at the high table with Michelle and Mercedes. The M & M Babes—as we refer to them—are on a roll. They're kicking our booties, with Michelle doing most of the damage. That girl has a way with the dice. I've never seen anyone so lucky. If it only happened now and then it wouldn't be any big thing, but she does this week after week. I can't help thinking that she'd clean up if she ever went to Vegas.

Our Bunko group is talking about going to the regional Bunko Tournament in Nashville, Tennessee. If our plans actually come to fruition, Michelle should be a shoo-in with her luck and on her way to The National Bunko Tournament where she could make some serious money. It probably won't happen—with husbands and kids, school and jobs, but it's fun to think about. The truth is we're fortunate to get together for our weekly Bunko night.

Usually, I'm competitive to a fault but tonight I can't seem to get motivated. With Madison's sorrowful countenance etched in my mind, I keep flashing back to the scene at Mimi's Café. Although, Michael tried to pretend that woman was just a colleague, I know better. They were simply too familiar and now my friend is hurting. I wish there was something I could do but I can't bring it up until she does. The last thing I want to do is create a problem, especially if there isn't one.

"Hey, Pollywog," Autumn says, snapping her fingers in front of my face. "Keep your mind in the game. We're gettin' our rears beat here, just in case you haven't noticed."

I chuckle morosely. Holding up my score pad, I point to the empty spot next to our names. "That's quite obvious, partner," I reply in a teasing voice. "What do you suggest I do about it? Close my eyes and wish real hard? Or maybe, I should blow on the dice?"

"At this point, I'm ready for you to try almost anything."

Michelle, oblivious to our good-natured bantering, continues her ritual before each roll of the dice. Now, she releases them and they tumble across the table coming to rest with three 3's showing. "Bunko," she shouts, her eyes sparkling with pleasure.

Autumn and I slide our chairs back and prepare to head for the low table when Mercedes suddenly bursts into tears. Before any of us can react, she bolts for the bathroom and locks the door. Turning to Autumn, I ask, "Do you have any idea what that was about?"

Shrugging her shoulders, she replies, "Not a clue."

Ever the perfect hostess, Kathleen says, "Why don't y'all get some desert and I'll see if I can find out what's going on."

When she hasn't returned in fifteen minutes, I excuse myself and head down the short hallway toward the bathroom. Kathleen is sitting on the floor a helpless look on her face. Through the door, I can hear Mercedes weeping. Gingerly, I lower myself to sit on the floor beside Kitty Kat.

"How's it going?" I inquire, in a muted voice.

"She won't talk. She hasn't said a word."

"Why don't you rejoin your guests and I'll see what I can do?"

Gratefully, she gets to her feet and turns toward the dining room. When she has gone, I lean my forehead against the bathroom door, "Mercedes, it's me, Becca."

Nothing. Not even a peep.

From the other room, I can hear the murmur of conversation, punctuated from time to time with a burst of laughter, but from the bathroom only weeping.

"What is it Mercedes? Did you receive some bad news from Argentina?"

We carry on this one-sided conversation for several minutes more and when I am about to give up, she finally speaks. "Oh, Becca, they're taking my Douglas from me," she wails, her words garbled by her tears. "If something happens to him, I will die."

Slowly, it begins to dawn on me. Like so many others, Douglas joined the National Guard to finance his college education, never expecting to get called up. Of course, everything changed when the United States invaded Iraq. Now, tens of thousands of the United State's finest—many of them parents and spouses—are risking their lives to fight terrorism in Afghanistan and Iraq. For just a moment, I try to imagine what I would feel if Thomas were being sent to Iraq or worse yet one of the twins. I shudder, understanding a little better the fear that now grips Mercedes.

Douglas is a MK—a missionary kid. His parents are career missionaries serving in Buenos Aires. Four years older than Mercedes, they met during his parents' first term in Argentina. From day one, Mercedes had a crush on him, but for years, he was largely unaware of the little dark-haired Argentine girl who worshipped him from afar. She had eyes only for him and as far as she was concerned he was a *galán*, 'a handsome young man.'

I can't decide if love is blind or if beauty is simply in the eye of the beholder. Douglas is a dear, a really neat young man but I would never describe him as handsome; gangly maybe, or awkward but never handsome. He is six feet five inches tall, weighing one hundred and seventy pounds soaking wet, with flaming red hair—hardly the stuff of heart-throbs, except in Mercedes' eyes.

Mercedes, on the other hand, is an Argentine-born Italian beauty with thick dark hair and high cheekbones. A cross between Catherine Zeta Jones and Eva Longoria, she turns heads every time she walks into a room. I've told Thomas more than once that Douglas is one lucky man to be married to such a beautiful woman. Douglas seems to think the same thing and on more than one occasion, I've heard him say that he looks better when they're together.

They've been married just a little over a year, Mercedes having finally caught his eye when he spent Christmas vacation in Argentina with his parents. The wedding was in June, right after he graduated from college, following a five-month courtship by correspondence. Bidding her parents and siblings good-bye, Mercedes boarded a jet and flew with her new husband to the United States where they planned to build a life together. Thinking about it now, I can't help but admire her courage. She's hardly more than a child herself, closer to the twins' age than my own.

At last, her sobbing has stopped. I hear the water running and I imagine she is washing her face. With a flawless complexion, she wears almost no makeup so she doesn't have to worry about messing it up. Finally, I hear the door unlock and I push myself to my feet, gritting my teeth against the pain. When the bathroom door opens, I reach for her and she flings herself into my arms.

Embracing her, I realize that I'm nearly old enough to be her mother and I can't help thinking of her more as a daughter than a friend, especially now. Try as I might, I can't imagine what it must be like for her. She's in a foreign country, thousands of miles from home, and her husband is being sent to war. Without family, she must feel totally alone. My heart goes out to her, especially, when I imagine Brooklyn in a similar situation.

"Don't worry, Honey," I say, "we'll be here for you while Douglas is gone."

She gives me a grateful look, not trusting herself to speak.

"Are you ready to rejoin the others?"

When she nods, I take her by the hand and turn toward the living room. Jessica and Kitty Kat are chatting but the rest of The Bunko Babes have already gone.

"I'm sorry, Kitty Kat," Mercedes says, tearing up again. "It looks like I ruined your party."

"Don't give it a second thought," Kathleen says, motioning for Mercedes to join her on the couch.

As I settle into the easy chair, Jessica looks in my direction questioningly. "Douglas and Mercedes have received some bad news. His National Guard Unit has been called up and he leaves for Iraq in two weeks."

At the mention of Douglas' impending departure, Mercedes turns pale and her lip quivers but she does not cry. Kitty Kat reaches over and gives her hand a squeeze.

"May I share a passage of Scripture with you that has been a great comfort to me?" Jessica asks, surprising me. I know she loves the Lord but she's never been one to attend a Bible study or quote Scriptures. When Mercedes nods, she extracts a pocket Bible from her purse and reads:

> *"He will cover you with his feathers,*
> *and under his wings you will find refuge;*
> *his faithfulness will be your shield and rampart.*
> *You will not fear the terror of night,*
> *nor the arrow that flies by day,*
> *nor the pestilence that stalks in the darkness,*
> *nor the plague that destroys at midday.*
> *A thousand may fall at your side,*
> *ten thousand at your right hand,*
> *but it will not come near you."*

Mercedes eyes are shining and she silently mouths a thank you to Jessica.

Oblivious to everyone but Mercedes, Jessica continues, "Write those verses on 3 X 5 cards and put them all over your apartment—on your makeup mirror, on the nightstand beside your bed, on the kitchen counter, everywhere. Make several copies for Douglas. Pray those scriptures every time you're fearful."

Listening to Jessica, I can't help thinking that my lifelong friend is full of surprises tonight. I never would have thought she had it in her. Seeing the strength Mercedes has received from this Scripture, I'm reminded of the passage Pastor Thompson shared with me. Although it's been several days, I still haven't taken the time to look it up. In light of what's happened here tonight, I now regret the way I casually disregarded it.

I rack my brain but for the life of me I can't remember where I put the scrap of paper on which I wrote the reference. Surely, I didn't throw it away. If I can't find it, I suppose I could call him but I'd have to swallow my pride to do that. Maybe, that's what the Lord wants me to do—swallow my pride.

TWENTY-TWO

Driving home from Kathleen's, I reflect on the evening. While I was talking with Mercedes, the rest of The Bunko Babes decided to concede the evening's championship to Michelle. She graciously accepted the crown without making a big show of it. For the second time tonight, I am amazed at how far she's come in such a short time. She's become a more positive person and I can't help but think that The Bunko Babes have played a big part in her transformation. *Good job, God.*

The mere thought brings a tired smile to my face but it quickly fades as I'm reminded of Doug's impending deployment to Iraq and Mercedes concerns, not to mention Madison's troubles. Madison is such a private person and she tries hard to hide her feelings, still, I couldn't help but notice that her smile seemed forced this evening and her laughter slightly out of tune. Having been friends since childhood, I'm attuned to any shift in her moods, making me especially sensitive to her feelings. Hopefully, her melancholy wasn't so obvious to the others.

I'm so consumed with concern for my friend that I miss my turn. "Dadburnit!" I mutter, slapping the steering wheel with my open palms. Continuing down 71st Street, I turn left on Richmond and make the block. Two more lefts and I'm home. Hitting the garage door opener with my thumb, I pull into the center slot of our three-car garage and shut off the engine. Taking the key out of the ignition, I decide to give Jess a call and see if she's had a chance to talk with Madison since our chance encounter with Michael at Mimi's.

Impatient, I grab my cell and begin dialing before exiting my Navigator. Shutting the door with my hip, I remember to punch the alarm button on my key chain just before the siren alerts the entire neighborhood to my arrival. It wouldn't be the first time and I'm sure it won't be the last.

Where is she? I'm just about to hang up when Jessica answers the phone rather breathlessly. "It took you long enough," I snap. "Where were you?"

Accustomed to my "tudes" as she calls them, she snaps back. "None of your beeswax."

The use of the childish phrase is just the smack I need. "Sorry, Jess. That was uncalled for. Please forgive me."

I can hear the smile in her voice and I imagine she's wearing her "I'll have to think about it" look.

"Of course, silly girl," she says, a moment later. "What's up? Ya miss me already?" Her husky voice holds a teasing lilt and I chuckle in response. Few people can make me laugh like Jessica can.

"How'd ya guess?" I reply, playing along.

We banter back and forth a moment more and then I ask, "Have you had a chance to talk with Madison? She seemed really out of sorts this evening."

"That's hardly surprising." Jessica's voice is sharp and filled with disgust. "You'd be out of sorts too if your husband was fooling around."

For some reason I feel a need to defend Michael, not for his sake, but for Madison's. I don't want to think that my friend's husband is cheating on her. That would simply be too terrible, especially given Michael's high visibility in both the community and in his church.

"Let's not get ahead of ourselves, Jessica," I caution. "We don't know for certain that Michael is fooling around."

"For goodness sake, Becca, don't be so naïve. Michael is having an affair with that Lori woman. A blind person could see they have the hots for each other."

Surprised at the contempt in her voice, I return, "Mimi's is hardly the place for a romantic rendezvous."

Brutal in her honesty at times, Jess fumes, "This is one time when your 'silver-lining,' 'star-seeking,' 'half-full' theology is blinding you to the truth even though it's staring you right in the face. Wake up and smell the coffee, my dear sweet friend. Michael and Lori are having an affair!"

I'm afraid she's right but I can't bring myself to admit it. Instead, I repeat my earlier question, "So, have you talked to Madison?"

"No. Given my state of mind, I'm afraid I would say something I'd regret. Even if Michael is a two-timing jerk, I don't want to hurt Madison. If she doesn't know what he's up to, I don't want to be the one to tell her. Besides, you're the expert when it comes to matters of the heart."

No longer able to bear the oppressive heat of the garage, I let myself into the house and quickly rearm the security system. That done, I collapse into one of the kitchen chairs not bothering to flip on a light. Cell phone pressed to my ear, I drop my heavy head onto my hand before responding, "I'm the expert? Since when am I the expert?"

"Since always, you know that. When we get our hearts broken—we go to Becca to get it put back together. You and Jesus are the heart healers. All The Bunko Babes know that!"

When I don't say anything, she adds, "We all need you, Becca. You're the glue that holds us together. You always have been and you always will be."

Smiling softly, my heavy heart is somehow warmed by the simple thought that I am needed. My friends think of me as a healer of hearts. Wow! What an honor. Quietly, I reply, "Thank you. That may be the nicest thing anyone has ever said to me."

Never comfortable with compliments, Jess hastens to change the subject. "Okay, goofy girl, so what's the plan? What are we going to do about Madison?"

"I've thought about inviting her to lunch," I muse, "but this really isn't the kind of thing to discuss in public. Maybe, I'll swing by Starbucks and get a couple of cappuccinos and just drop in on her. Do you want to meet me at her house in the morning, say about 10:30?"

"Only if you make it three cappuccinos instead of just two."

Chuckling, I snap the phone shut after a quick good-bye.

"Lord Jesus, I'd better get some sleep. We've got some heart healing to do in the morning and I am nothing without You."

CHAPTER
TWENTY-THREE

Beethoven's Ninth Symphony echoes down the hallway intruding on my prescription induced stupor. Rolling over, I try to ignore it but whoever is at my front door is sadistically determined. Gritting my teeth against the pain, I push myself up and reach for my robe. I tug it on and shuffle down the hallway, mumbling threats of bodily harm as I make my way toward the front door.

Foggy with sleep, I'm having trouble focusing. Vaguely, I remember taking something for pain prescribed by my doctor but beyond that I have no recollection. I didn't hear Thomas leave and I've obviously slept through my alarm.

Beethoven's Ninth again—intrusive and irritating. For at least the hundredth time, I wish I had never let Thomas talk me into having that doorbell installed. What seemed like a good idea when he suggested it, now grates on my nerves. I would give almost anything for a doorbell that simply chimes.

From the brightness of the sun streaming through the kitchen windows, I know it is late morning, but the house is quiet and I try to remember what the twins had planned. Slowly, it comes to me. Brooklyn spent the night with a friend and Robert... Well, I know he had something scheduled for this morning but for the life of me I can't remember what it was. It'll come to me in a minute.

At the front door, I place my eye against the peephole and peer out. Jessica is reaching for the doorbell again when I finally shut off the security system and unlock the door. When she sees me, her worried scowl is immediately replaced by an irritated impatience. Pushing by me into the foyer, she demands, "What's going on? I've been trying to call you for the last hour."

I struggle to make some sense of Jessica's irritation but try as I might I can't seem to get fully awake. Not accustomed to taking medication, my mind is in a fog. Mumbling an apology, I turn toward the kitchen thinking coffee might help.

Jessica continues to question me as I put water in the espresso maker and a heaping scoop of Limited Edition Papua New Guinea coffee from Gevalia. Opening the cupboard, I get two heavy mugs. Jessica takes her coffee black or with just a splash of milk. I pour a mound of sugar in the bottom of my mug and add heavy whipping cream before putting it in the microwave for a few seconds. By now, the espresso maker is hissing, a cloud of steam rising and the rich aroma of freshly brewed coffee is teasing me awake.

Filling both mugs, I hand one to Jessica before taking a seat at the table in the breakfast nook. I'm still not fully awake but the coffee is helping. Vaguely, I remember that I was supposed to meet Jess at Madison's house this morning but the details are lost in the haze left by the pain meds. Next time, I'll take less, maybe only half of a pill, no matter that the pain makes it impossible for me to sleep.

With an effort, I focus on Jessica who is sipping her coffee. From beneath the table, I can hear the tapping of her foot on the floor and I know she's still irritated. I suppose she has a right to be upset but it's not my fault the pain pill knocked me out. I had no idea how strong it was. I don't remember turning my cell phone off but I could have; or maybe Thomas shut it off knowing how badly I needed my rest.

Having made two or three stabs at polite conversation, I now fall silent. As much as I love Jess, she can be a real pain sometimes and right now, I don't feel like babying her. It's obvious that she expects a full-blown apology, or at least an explanation, but I can't bring myself to offer one.

Usually, I'm the one to give in. Sometimes, I apologize but more often than not I simply tease her out of her moods. If I can get her laughing, she will usually get over whatever it is that's bothering her but today, I can't bring myself to make the effort. Friendship, I reason, is a two-way street and it's time she started pulling her weight.

Having finished my coffee, I collect our mugs, rinse them out, and put them in the dishwasher. Jess pushes her chair back from the table but she does not get up. Instead she looks at me and shakes her head. "Becca, why are you doing this? Why are you shutting me out of your life?"

"Shutting you out of my life?" I ask incredulously. "Is that what you think I'm doing? I take a pain pill and sleep through my alarm and now I'm shutting you out of my life!"

"You know that's not what I'm talking about."

"It's not? Then pray tell, what are you talking about?"

"I'm talking about us, Becca—The Bunko Babes. The sisterhood where there are no secrets."

She has risen from her chair and is now standing directly in front of me. The pleading in her eyes is nearly my undoing but instead of opening my heart to her, I turn away and walk to the window. When I do, a dark place opens inside of me. Although I've fought it all of my life, a part of me is insanely jealous of Jessica. If I were to be completely honest with myself, I would have to admit that I hated sharing Daddy's love with her. When she came to live with us, I could hardly stand it when Daddy tickled her and wrestled with her on the living room floor. I hid my feelings well, but on the inside a part of me hated her.

In many ways, she is everything I've always wanted to be—a classic beauty, tall and slim, talented, artistic and creative, fearless, and independent. Truthfully, I've only bested her in one area—motherhood. I have two beautiful children and she has none. Although a part of me grieves for her, another part of me wonders if she deserves them. After what she did, what can she expect?

I will never understand why she didn't simply tell Bobby she was pregnant. He loved her and I'm sure he would have done the right thing. Even if he had refused to marry her, she had other options. She didn't have to have an abortion. We would have stood by her. We would have helped her decide whether to keep the baby or give it up for adoption. That's what made her decision so baffling to me...so inexcusable. That's why I can't help thinking she doesn't deserve to be a mother.

Yet even as I condemn her, I am appalled at myself. Who am I to judge? Who am I to cast the first stone? God knows I'm not without sin, yet everything within me wants her to suffer for her mistakes.

I am panting with the intensity of my feelings and I know I should leave the room until I have my emotions under control but I seem rooted to the spot. Under no conditions, should I speak, lest the poisonous thoughts that are flooding my mind wound or possibly even destroy the lifelong friendship Jess and I have shared. But having entertained these unholy feelings, I now seem powerless to exorcise them and against my better judgment, I hear myself voicing the resentments I have so long repressed.

"Why does everything always have to be about you, Jess?"

When she doesn't respond, I continue, my words hammering at her. "You never consider how your actions are going to affect anyone but yourself. You never have and it doesn't look like you ever will."

"What are you talking about?" she asks, her voice sounding small before the enormity of my accusation.

Turning, I see my words have found their mark. Her face is ashen. Suddenly sickened by what I have done, I scramble to divert her attention. "In Colorado, when we were on vacation, you didn't stop to consider how I felt when you learned my mother was getting married. No! All you could think about was why I hadn't told you. And now that you think I'm sick, all you can talk about is how I'm shutting you out of my life. Just once! Just once, Jess, you really should think about someone other than yourself!"

Without a word, she picks up her purse, walks out of the kitchen and down the hall toward the front door. I know I should run after her and beg her forgiveness but my pride will not allow it. She disappears around the corner and I hear the front door open and then close. Staring at the empty hallway, tears slide unheeded down my pallid cheeks, pooling where they may. Despair overtakes me and I slide to the floor, desperately wondering how I will ever be able to undo the hurt that I've inflicted upon my dearest friend.

CHAPTER

TWENTY-FOUR

When Thomas comes home from the office for lunch an hour later, I'm still sitting on the tile floor in the kitchen. My prolonged weeping has left my eyes red and swollen. I'm in excruciating pain; a pain, I welcome as my just due for the evil thing I have done. Yet, as painful as my physical suffering is, it is nothing compared to the hurt in my heart. When I think of what I did to Jessica, I am filled with utter contempt, with a self-loathing so pervasive that I don't know if I will ever be able to forgive myself. I've looked at my actions from every angle and no matter how I turn it, no matter how I try to rationalize it, I can only come to one conclusion. I am a vile person—heartless and needlessly cruel. At the core of my being, I am despicable. Beneath the facade of friendship, there lurks a petty person intent on belittling others in order to make herself look better. I don't want to believe this but, given what I did to Jessica, what choice do I have?

Nearly as bewildering is the fact that I don't know who this other Becca is. Where did she come from? I must admit that I've always wanted attention and that I've battled with jealousy when anyone else had center stage.

Suddenly a page from my journal, written years ago before the twins were born, comes back to me as clearly as the day I penned it.

From day one, I've had my hand raised
Pick me, pick me, lavish me with praise.
I stand at the front of every line
Desperate for love of any kind.

In every crowd I have to stand out.
Look at me, look at me, my heart would shout.
Over here, here I am, don't walk by
I sing and dance, I'm not shy.

Pick me, pick me, I'm pretty enough.
I've got brains and talent, I can do all kinds of stuff.
Pick me, pick me, I want to go.
Use me, mold me, I just need to know.

That in this life You have a plan,
One that includes me, wherever I am.

Whether I'm hurt, broken, or bruised,
Pick me, pick me, I want to be used.

Through prayer and a lifetime of spiritual disciplines, I thought I had overcome my insatiable need to be noticed and the jealousy that it birthed, but apparently not. Given what I did today, I can only wonder if I will ever be different, if I will ever be the Christ-like person I desire to be. I hate what I've done—what I am—and yet I feel powerless to change. If, after all these years of being a Christian, I am still capable of something like this, then what hope is there for me?

"Becca," Thomas asks, squatting before me, "what are you doing on the floor? Honey, are you all right?"

His concern is my undoing and another fit of sobbing overtakes me. Burying my face in my hands, I turn away from him lest he see what I've become—a mean-spirited person and shameful. I try to scoot away from him but my back is against the cabinet and I have nowhere to go. Trapped, I turn inward, fleeing as much from myself as from him.

Standing to his feet, Thomas goes to the refrigerator and returns with a tall glass of orange juice. "Drink this," he says. "I think you're having a low blood sugar reaction."

Obstinately, I try to push it away but he refuses to be put off. Gently but firmly, he insists that I drink it. The first swallow or two nearly gags me but almost instantly, I can feel my body responding. Greedily, I reach for the glass and finish off the orange juice in one long drink.

Sitting the glass in the sink, Thomas takes my hands and helps me to my feet. I'm stiff from sitting on the floor and my joints scream in painful protest as he pulls me up. I lean against him grimacing, my breath coming in short gasps. When the first wave of pain has passed I allow him to help me to the bedroom.

Once I'm in bed, my pillows fluffed and positioned, Thomas sits down beside me and reaches for my hand. I don't deserve his tenderness or his love, and I'm tempted to pull away, but I don't. My bruised soul is desperate for love and I allow him to hold me, even though, I'm sure he would find it hard to love me if he knew what I had done.

Even in his arms, I cannot keep my self-loathing at bay. In my mind's eye, I see Jessica's stricken face, my spiteful words sucking the color out of her flawless complexion. Disbelief clouds her eyes—*surely this isn't happening, Becca wouldn't treat me this way*—quickly turning to hurt, then despair. I wish she had slapped me or at least, screamed at me but she just looked at me, her hurt clearly visible in her face before turning away.

As if from a great distance, I hear Thomas speaking to me. "What is it, Becca?"

He is staring at me intently and I can't bear to look him in the eye lest he see the shame discoloring my soul. Closing my eyes, I shake my head from side to side. "It's nothing," I mutter.

"Talk to me, Sweetheart," he pleads. "Tell me what's going on. Let me help you."

"You can't help me, Thomas. No one can. It's beyond that."

I'm crying again and he reaches up to wipe a tear from the corner of my eye, his touch as gentle as the brush of a butterfly's wing. "What is it, Honey? What happened to upset you so?"

"I can't talk about it," I sob, turning my back to him, burying my face against the pillows. He continues to plead with me but all I can hear are the accusing voices within. *"Hypocrite,"* they scream, *"phony, faithless friend."*

Desperate to escape, I ask Thomas to let me sleep. After he shuts off the light, I will myself to be still. For several minutes, I force myself to breathe deep and regularly, pretending to sleep. Finally, Thomas eases off the bed and tiptoes out of the room, closing the door softly. When I am sure he is gone, I allow myself to weep, sobbing into my pillow.

I weep for Jessica, for the bitter regret that is her daily bread, and for the pain of her childless future. I can't help thinking that it seems so unfair. As a teenager, she made a rash decision in a moment of weakness and now, she is forced to live with the consequences for the rest of her life. And I weep for the terrible thing I have done and for the pain I have caused her. *What was I thinking? How could I have thrown it in her face?* For just a moment, I consider calling her and begging her forgiveness but then I think better of it. Why would she want to talk to me after what I did? I want to apologize to her but given my emotional state, I can't risk her rejection. Maybe later.

Hours later, I awaken, my bedroom dark. From another part of the house, I hear voices and I realize that Thomas and the twins are having dinner. Probably takeout from that new Chinese place or maybe, hot wings. A fresh wave of guilt overtakes me and I wonder how long it has been since I cooked dinner. Once, it was an important family time and I tried to make every meal special. The twins seemed to enjoy sitting around the table talking long after we had finished eating. Now, I've become an emotional wreck, a recluse, huddling in the darkness of my bedroom and my family has been reduced to eating takeout or pizza. TV sitcoms or mind-numbing video games have replaced family conversations.

In the darkness, I review my life, realizing that the life I now live bears almost no resemblance to the life I had just a few months ago. I'm still married to the same man, we still attend the same church, and I'm still Mommy to my precious twins but that's where the similarity ends. Months ago, Daddy was still alive and we were making plans to celebrate the folk's fortieth anniversary. Now, he's buried in the cemetery located at 51st and Memorial, the victim of a massive heart attack. Before Daddy's death, I was a dynamo, involved at church, having lunch with my friends, playing Bunko with The Babes, doing stuff with the twins, redecorating the house... Most importantly, I was happy, fulfilled, a contented person. Now, I'm locked in a prison of pain, stalked by an undiagnosed illness that seems to be sucking the very life out of me. And worst of all, I've become an emotional see-saw capable of erupting in anger or dissolving in tears at a moment's notice.

CHAPTER
TWENTY-FIVE

It's Friday morning and last night's thunderstorm has left behind a blanket of humidity transforming a moderate 88° into a sweltering sauna. Thomas and I are on our way to meet with Dr. Steven Martin, my HMO appointed Rheumatologist. Hopefully, he will have a diagnosis and a treatment plan. The uncertainty is killing me, not to mention the illness itself. The sooner, we can get all of this behind us, the better.

Two weeks have passed since Jessica and I had our falling out and nothing has been resolved. I know I should go see her or at least call but I can't bring myself to do so. I want to blame my illness, and truthfully, it is all I can do to get dressed most days, but in my heart I know I'm being stubborn. *Why do I always have to be the one to apologize?* Just once, I would like for Jess to make the first move, never mind that I was the one who wounded her.

Usually, our spats don't last more than an hour or two and then we're back to being the best of friends but not this time. We haven't spoken in two weeks and in the thirty years, we've been friends that's never happened, not once. I'll admit that this was more than a spat but I didn't expect it to turn into a reenactment of the cold war. At first, I was inconsolable, blaming myself for everything but the more I've thought about it, the more I've come to believe that Jessica's not lily white either. She's at least partially to blame. What was she thinking snapping at me the minute she walked in? Couldn't she tell I was sick?

Thomas says I'm being foolish, that I'm choosing pride over friendship, but that's only part of it. Being sick has forced me to slow down and I've been doing a lot of thinking. It hurts me to say this, but it seems that many of my friendships are far more important to me than they are to the rest of The Babes. *Over the years, am I not the one who has kept us together? Am I not the one who initiates the contact, makes the plans, and goes out of my way? If it weren't for me, we would have drifted apart years ago.* If they don't feel the same, maybe these friendships aren't worth pursuing... including Jessica.

Years ago, Daddy told me that there are three kinds of friendship—teeter-totter friendships, clinging vine friendships, and hit-and-run friendships. Some people, he said, are only cut out for hit-and-run relationships. When they're with you, they're loads of fun and they make you feel like their best friend but when you're apart, it's like you don't exist. They blow in and out of your life and if you can't get comfortable with that, you probably aren't cut out to be their friend.

Clinging vine friends, on the other hand, wrap themselves around you. You are their only friend and they want to spend every moment with you. They expect you to meet all of their emotional needs. Initially, they make you feel indispensable but before long their neediness will smother you. If you cannot establish appropriate boundaries and maintain them, then you had better run for your life.

Finally, there are those special friendships that are built on mutual respect. Teeter-totter friendships is what he called them; friendships in which each person gives and receives nurture and encouragement. These are the healthiest relationships and the hardest to find. Fortunate is the woman who has a friend like that and she should do everything in her power to protect and preserve that friendship.

Thinking about Daddy, my throat gets tight and my heart hurts. I miss him so much. If he were here, I'd know what to do. I can't believe the twins are going to have to grow up without him. So much wisdom lost....

Sensing the shift in my mood, Thomas reaches over and gives my hand a squeeze, "It's going to be okay, Baby. Jesus is with us."

Turning into the parking lot, he heads for the portico where he lets me out. Although I have already seen the doctor a number of times, I'm still required to fill out a lengthy form. Before I can complete it, Thomas sits down beside me and starts leafing through an outdated copy of *Sport's Illustrated*.

Finally, a nurse calls my name and we are ushered into the doctor's office rather than an examining room. Dr. Martin has not yet arrived so I study his cramped office. The wall of windows behind his desk is covered floor to ceiling by heavy, deep brown, brocade drapes that reek of dust. The desk and file cabinets are piled high with files and medical textbooks. Oversized chairs and pieces of mismatched furniture overpower the limited space, leaving just enough room to squeeze between the desk and the chairs. Claustrophobic in the best of situations, I soon find myself searching frantically for some way of escape. My hands tug at the neckline of my blouse, my toe taps nervously, and I begin gnawing my nails.

Eventually, Dr. Martin enters and takes his place behind the desk, settling his ample frame into an ancient, executive chair of faded black leather. After greeting us, he picks up my thick medical chart, leans his chair back precariously far, and immediately becomes absorbed in studying the latest test results. From time to time, he puts on a pair of scratched spectacles for a closer look, letting out a little "humph," before resuming his reading.

Several times, he lowers his chair, turns to us, points and opens his mouth to speak. We sit up a little taller. Thomas leans forward. I squeeze his hand a little tighter. Dr. Martin simply closes his mouth and returns to his reading. After the third time, I am wrung out. Finally, after what seemed a lifetime, he clears his throat and turns to me. "Mrs. Thornton, you have an autoimmune disease known as Systemic Lupus. It is a chronic disease but once we get it under control, you should be able to live a fairly normal life."

He continues his explanation but I'm not listening. I finally have a name for this beast that has been ravaging my body. *Thank You, God!* I feel like jumping up and down. I want to celebrate. *Now that we have a diagnosis, we can finally get down to the business of getting me well. I just need to get on the right medications. I've heard of lupus. At least, I think I have and it's not that big of a deal.* It feels like this humungous load has been lifted off of my shoulders. My entire body feels light, airy, like if Thomas wasn't holding my hand I just might float away. I'm so relieved.

Why does Thomas look so concerned? I thought he'd be as relieved as I am. What's the doctor talking about now? Just get me my prescriptions and let me out of here. I'm in the mood to celebrate.

"It's imperative," Dr. Martin explains, his somber words finally penetrating my premature euphoria, "that you get plenty of rest. Not all patients who have Systemic Lupus suffer from photosensitivity but you obviously do, so you must wear 50 SPF sunscreen under your clothes anytime you go out-of-doors. You must never wear shorts, short sleeves, or be without a hat or umbrella when you are outside, even for just a few minutes."

Turning to Thomas, he says, "I strongly advise you to get limo tint on all your vehicles to minimize the effect of the sun on Mrs. Thornton."

I interrupt. "Doctor, are you saying that the sun is making me sick? I wasn't just imagining that?"

He nods his ascent.

"What about drugs? Surely there's something that will cure this, isn't there?"

"I'm afraid not, Rebecca. In fact, most of the medications you will be on will actually increase your sensitivity to sunlight. We will have to carefully manage your medications as each of them has potentially dangerous side effects."

Suddenly, this diagnosis doesn't sound nearly as promising as I first thought. "What kind of side effects are we talking about?"

He removes his spectacles and begins rubbing the bridge of his nose. "Prednisone is the most frequently used medication for the joint pain. It is a steroid and some of its side effects include: weight gain, acne, thinning of the bones, increased susceptibility to infection, a moon-shaped face, and development of what's commonly referred to as the "lupus hump." It's a hump that forms right at the base of your neck. Then there's…"

I hold up my hand. "Stop, please stop. I don't want to hear any more right now. Just tell me what I have to do to get back on my feet and I'll worry about the side effects later."

Giving me a look of sympathy, Dr. Martin adds, "If you'd like, Rebecca, I can fill Thomas in on the rest of the details, give him the brochures and the prescriptions, while you schedule your next appointment with the young ladies at the front desk. We'll only be a few minutes."

Grateful to flee the disturbing details of my treatment, I grab my purse and the exit paperwork before escaping out the office door. Leaning against the wall, I try to get my emotions under control. While fumbling in my purse for a tissue, a scrap of paper flutters to the floor. When I bend to pick it up, I see the Scripture reference from Pastor Thompson. Momentarily, I'm shamed to realize that I still haven't looked it up, but I determine in my heart that I will now.

When I finish with the paperwork, Thomas is still sequestered with Dr. Martin so I try to make myself comfortable in the waiting room. There is a Gideon Bible lying on the end table, so I pick it up and turn to Exodus 3:7 and 8.

The Lord said, "I have indeed seen the misery of my people in Egypt. I have heard them crying out because of their slave drivers, and I am concerned about their suffering. So I have come down to rescue them from the hand of the Egyptians and to bring them up out of that land into a good and spacious land...."

Tears flood my eyes, tears of gratitude and hope. Grateful for God's Word to me, I read it a second time, paraphrasing it so it addresses me personally: "The Lord said, 'Becca, I have **seen** your misery. I have **heard** you crying out because of your sickness, and **I am concerned** about your suffering. So **I am coming down to rescue you** and to bring you into a good and spacious place....'"

I am sitting with my eyes closed, the open Bible hugged to my chest, when Thomas touches my arm. "Becca?"

"Let me show you something," I say, tugging at his sleeve.

Reluctantly, he lowers himself into the chair beside me. Opening the Bible, I point to the appropriate verses. After reading them, he looks at me questioningly, "So?"

"Thomas," I say with more enthusiasm than I've felt in months, "this is like an email from God. He's telling me that He sees my situation. He hears my prayer, He cares about me, and He's coming down to rescue me!"

Slowly, it dawns on him. "Wow!" he says, "that's cool. What did you do, just open the Bible to that verse?"

"No. This is the passage Pastor Thomas gave me weeks ago. I just hadn't looked it up."

"Wow!" he says again, "an email from God."

TWENTY-SIX

I say a quick prayer for wisdom, while struggling to press the doorbell. The two iced caramel macchiatos are sweating profusely making them increasingly difficult to manage, especially with my Kate Spade clutch, precariously clinched under my left arm.

Beads of sweat gather under the rim of my scarlet hat, slowly trickling down the sides of my face. Following the doctor's orders, I'm clothed from head to toe, every inch of my skin sunscreened. Pressing the doorbell for the third time, I can't help thinking this wasn't a very good idea. The sun is merciless and all I can think of is how good it would feel to be back in my cool, darkened bedroom. Finally, the massive door opens and I am face-to-face with my friend or what appears to be a caricature of her.

The always perfect Madison is a mess. Her beautiful platinum blonde hair is bedraggled and piled on top of her head, held in place by a burnt-orange scrunchy. She hasn't put on makeup, not even gloss, and her lavender eyes are puffy. The Yale T-shirt she's wearing is faded, as are her tattered cutoffs.

I'm stunned. You might catch Autumn or me running around the house looking like that but not Madison. For years, she's gotten up an hour before Michael in order to do her hair and makeup. She never wanted him to see her unless she was looking her best. All I can do is stare slack jawed.

Trying to cover my surprise, I thrust one of the iced caramel macchiatos toward her as I step into the air-conditioned comfort of her ornate foyer, luxuriating in the artificial coolness. Madison breaks the silence. "Why on earth are you dressed like that?" Catching herself, she hastily adds, "I mean, you look absolutely adorable but you're going to have a heat stroke, goofy girl!"

I laugh, "I am a little warm."

"Let me put that in a real glass," she says, reaching for my drink, "while you get out of some of those clothes."

Removing my large, red straw hat, I ask, "So, where are the kids?"

"Meredith is down for her nap," she tosses over her shoulder, "and Mitchell is having his reading time in his room." Her voice trails off.

Quickly, I remove my blue jean bolero jacket and give a huge sigh of relief. To my way of thinking, few materials retain heat better than jean and my red and black T-shirt has a huge wet spot between my shoulder blades to prove it. doctor's orders or not, I'm not giving up my crop pants and today, I'm wearing a black pair with red espadrilles. To compensate, I wear extra sunscreen. Besides, the only time my ankles are exposed to the sun is when I'm walking from the car to the house.

Comfortable now, I take a moment to enjoy Madison's incredible house. Located in the historic district of Maple Ridge, her home is resplendent, not only in elegance, but in history as well. Every time, I turn west off of Peoria onto 16th Street, it's like stepping back in time. It is so easy to imagine ladies and gentlemen arriving for balls in horse-drawn carriages wearing fabulous gowns and formal attire. Built in the late 1890s, the home still has all of the original light fixtures including the massive chandeliers.

Before joining Madison in the kitchen, I make my way to the ballroom where I am transfixed by its splendor. The glossy floor is mahogany and one complete wall is floor to ceiling paned leaded glass windows, over which the wizened maples stretch their limbs in protection. This morning, the sun is streaming through the tall windows catching the crystals of the magnificent chandelier, casting a brilliant display of rainbows throughout the room. Overwhelmed by the sheer beauty, I revel in what my son has always referred to as "God's Promise."

"Here you are," Madison says, a smile in her voice. "I should have known."

"Oh, Maddy," I gush, "if I were you, I would just live in this room."

She shakes her head at my silliness and hands me my coffee in a new glass with fresh ice. "Drink up before it's nothing but water."

"Where do you want to sit?" I ask, feeling the sudden need to get off my feet.

"Back here. You haven't seen the kitchen and breakfast area since I redid it. I think you'll like it."

Madison speed walks, continuing to talk a mile a minute. Given her disheveled appearance and almost frenetic behavior, I'm sure something is troubling her but it's obvious she doesn't want to talk about it and until she does, all I can do is make myself available. I know her well enough to know that she's not going to talk until she's ready.

My mind can't keep up with her endless chatter about designer fabrics, paints, cabinet styles, and countertop choices. When I remodeled my kitchen, I stripped the cabinets, stained them a new color, chose a different color of paint, and bought new decorations from discount stores like Stein Mart and Tuesday Morning.

Stepping into Madison's kitchen is like walking onto a set for *Architectural Digest*. "Wow," I whisper in awe, momentarily forgetting the purpose of my visit. "This is fabulous."

Coming up to me, she gives me a hug. "Thanks, I knew you'd like it. Both Michael and I felt it was imperative that we return the home to its original beauty, including the kitchen."

There's the tiniest hitch in her voice when she says his name and my heart hurts for her. Maybe, she found out about Lori and this is Michael's way of trying to make it up to her. If so, she's going to be hard-pressed to ever forget his indiscretion. Every time she sets foot in this kitchen, she will be reminded of what he did.

Continuing her tour guide monologue, Madison says, "We had to purchase appliances modeled after the ones that were in use in the early 1900s. State of the art antiques, I think they call them. Don't they look authentic?"

"They do," I answer, as I take in the gorgeous red and silver cookstove. The amount of silver trim is mind-boggling and the detail work is amazing. Running my hand along the edge, I quietly say, "This is more like a piece of art than a stove. I'd be afraid to cook on it."

"I'd be afraid to have you cook on it," Madison teases. "I'm glad you like what we've done. You're the first of The Babes to see it."

"Well, I'm honored, even though, I had to show up uninvited." I pause, giving her a chance to explain her recent seclusion but she pretends not to notice.

"Enough about me," she says, sitting down at the table and toying with her now watery caramel macchiato. "How are you? I know you must be frantic trying to get things ready for the big weekend. Are you nervous about meeting your mom's fiancé?"

Taking a deep breath to calm my frustration at her evasiveness, I reply, "I'm not trying to impress anybody so I don't care whether my house is perfectly clean or whether or not we make a good impression."

"Of course you care, Becca," Madison interjects. "You're hurt right now but the time will come when the hurt will be gone and you will want a relationship with your mother's new husband."

"It's too soon," I say, tears threatening to cloud my vision. "Dad hasn't even been dead a year. It's just feels so wrong."

Before I can say more, Madison pops up, grabs our watered-down macchiatos and heads for the sink. Pouring them down the drain, she says, "What's with you and Jessica? Are you two having a tiff or something?"

I give a stiff smile before replying, "Don't be silly. Why would you think a thing like that?"

Glancing over her shoulder, she heads for the new "old-fashioned" refrigerator where she fills our glasses with ice water. Returning to the table, she hands me my glass. "I only mention it because you two seemed a little cool with each other at last week's Bunko game...."

She leaves the sentence unfinished, perhaps hoping I will pick it up and give her the inside scoop on Jessica and me. Of course I don't, having absolutely no desire to go there. A part of my mind can't help marveling at the choreography of our conversation. We're operating on different agendas but we're each probing, digging for the truth, while trying not to be overtly intrusive. I can't help wondering if my attempts are as transparent to her as hers are to me.

I take a long drink of ice water, reveling in the refreshing feel as it slides smoothly down my throat, yet dreading the moment I stop drinking and the dreadful dryness returns. Over the rim of the glass, I see the vague outline of a child entering the room.

Putting the glass down, I smile softly as Mitchell toddles toward his mother. With hair so blond it is almost white and eyes dark as pitch, he is a startling child. Today, he is clothed in a forest green Polo shirt and crisp navy blue shorts. In his pudgy right hand, he holds a brightly colored card. Having recently turned three, Mitchell thinks of himself as a big boy now and he tries hard to speak like one, as well.

Tugging on his mommy's cutoffs, he politely asks, "Mommy, I found a pretty. Please, look." He holds the object a little higher for Madison to inspect.

She sits him in her lap before taking the card from him. "Well, Mitchell, let's see what you have here." Glancing over the front of the card, she starts to read, then pauses uncertainly.

"Open, Mommy," Mitchell says, insistently tapping his finger on the card. When she still hesitates, he turns his megawatt smile upon her.

Mussing his hair, she whispers with a catch in her voice, "Yes, it is so very pretty." She kisses the top of his head before opening the card with trembling fingers.

Watching her from across the table, I find that I'm praying it's a card that Michael has bought as a surprise for Madison. Or it's a card that's fallen out of some box of memories from high school and Mitchell just happened upon it. Anything, anything but a card from Lori. *"Please, God, let Jess and I be wrong about this."*

Madison's face, already unnaturally pale, loses all color when she finally opens the card. I watch as her eyes dart over the words. For a moment, I think she's going to lose it but she doesn't and I have to admire her self-control. In her place, I don't think I could manage it. She begins tickling Mitchell and he squeals with delight. As she tickles him, she questions him. "Where did you find that pretty little card, you Munchkin? Huh, huh?"

More squeals. A pause from tickling, "On the floor, in Daddy's closet," Mitchell answers.

Tickling commences again. "And what were you doing in Daddy's closet?"

Squeals, pause, answer, "Hide-and-seek with Baby Bear."

After a few more minutes of play, Mitchell is off again and we are at last alone. Softly, I ask, "What's with the card?"

Without a word, she tosses it across the table. It's from Lori and she signed a lot more than just her name. Sickened, I lay it aside and reach for my friend's limp hand. "I'm so sorry."

She turns away, unable to look at me, embarrassed, as if the shame were hers. Stumbling to the sink, she vomits, gagging on her sobs. I move to comfort her but she waves me away. Now, I'm sorry that I have come. She doesn't want me to see her like this but I can't leave her; not now.

Mitchell has returned to the kitchen and now he runs to his mother, burying his face against her leg. He is sobbing, frightened by his mother's grief. I watch in amazement as Madison collects herself in order to comfort her son. "It's okay, Honey," she says hugging him. "It's okay. Mommy just got choked but I'm better now."

CHAPTER
TWENTY-SEVEN

Thomas is a bit miffed when I stubbornly refuse to make any special preparations for the upcoming weekend with my mother and her fiancé. Normally, my "good breeding" would kick in and I'd be rushing around stuffing things here, there, and everywhere—snapping at Thomas and the twins to do the same. But today, much to my husband's chagrin, I am comfortably ensconced in my favorite chair reading the latest offering from best-selling author Anita Shreve. He's running the vacuum cleaner and barking orders at the twins, while occasionally glaring in my direction. But I ignore him.

With my feet curled beneath me and our loveable cat "Catty" pretzeled around my ankles, I've no doubt I appear to be the picture of calm and contentment. If the truth be known, my insides are raging—closely resembling the turbulent waters of the Bering Sea. Right now, my light lunch is being tossed around on merciless waves of acid.

Brooklyn bounces into the room all sunshine and enthusiasm. "I sure do wish they'd get here." Plopping down on the couch, she grabs one of the throw pillows and hugs it close to her chest. Her beautiful blue eyes sparkle as she continues, her voice slightly muffled by the pillow. "Isn't it romantic, Mom? Mimi's in love and she's getting married."

Sighing dreamily, Brooklyn's head drops back against the sofa and a wistful look colors her features. Staring into space, my teenage daughter is completely lost in her make-believe world of romance. Watching her, I am suddenly overwhelmed by a deep yearning to be young again, to be thirteen one more time, to see Daddy, to touch him, to say good-bye. Time...it all boils down to time and Mom is simply moving too fast. She isn't thinking straight and even though, I probably won't be able to change her mind, I've got to try. The Lord knows I could use Jessica's support, but she's still not speaking to me. Her petulance seems childish to me and I can't help but think that fight or not, I would never allow her to face something like this without my unwavering support.

A dark green, four-door Honda Accord turns into our circle driveway, jolting me from my internal musings.

"They're here," I say, wishing I could retreat into my bedroom and close the door.

Letting out a piercing scream, Brooklyn springs from the couch. "Robbie, they're here." Flinging the door open, our little drama queen bursts onto the stoop and down the side-walk to their car where she waits impatiently for Mimi's exit, dancing excitedly all the while.

I groan at the tell-tale beeping of the alarm system and I hurry to get to the control pad before the deafening sirens go off yet again. It's happened so often that I'm on a first name basis with every employee at TNT Security. Before I make it into the foyer the sirens erupt and then abruptly fall silent only to be replaced by the ringing of the telephone.

Grabbing the cordless phone off the coffee table, I surmise that Thomas must have punched in the cancel code at one of the other keypads. With the phone to my ear, I auto-matically go through the routine using a touch of humor to cover my embarrassment. Mom is just rounding the corner as I am hanging up. Taking a deep breath, I paste a smile on my face before moving to greet her and the man she has chosen to replace my father. Of course, she doesn't view it that way, but I do.

"Becca," she gushes, as I lean in to accept her brief hug and a kiss on the cheek.

Her surprisingly soft and elegantly manicured hand pats my cheek as she continues, "Sweetheart, this is my Keith."

"It's a pleasure to meet you, Rebecca," Keith says extending his hand.

After the slightest hesitation, I offer him a limp hand. Pretending not to notice, he gives me a warm smile before turning to beam at my mother, who has returned to his side where she cuddles up to him. I stare in horror as she places her left hand lovingly upon his chest.

What is going on? Where's her wedding band? The one she has never removed since Daddy put it on her finger over forty years ago? And what is that monstrosity she's wearing in its stead?

My stare has turned into a glare and I am dangerously close to crossing that invisible line between expression and explosion. Taking a deep breath, I try to control my emotions. Not wanting to make a scene in front of Brooklyn, I give myself a good talking to.

"What's the big deal?" I ask myself. *"You knew they were engaged. Surely, you didn't expect her to wear the same ring with both husbands?"*

"Of course not," I reply. *"That's ridiculous. I just hadn't thought it through and therefore, I wasn't prepared for the shock of seeing them together—and her wearing his ring."*

The silence is deafening, roaring in my ears. At last, I find my voice and I reach for my mother's hand, saying, "Wow! What's this?"

It's all I can manage. There's no way, I can congratulate her or wish her well, although good manners demand it. Truthfully, I'm amazed that I was able to say what I did.

"Hello, everybody," Thomas says as he steps into the living room, breaking the uneasy tension. "I hope I didn't miss too much. I had a few last-minute things to take care of, but now I'm all yours for the rest of the weekend."

Giving Mom a squeeze and a quick hug, he immediately extends his hand to her fiancé. "Keith, I assume. I'm Thomas. Becca's better half...oops, I mean other half," he adds, after I elbow him playfully in the side.

"It's nice to meet you, Thomas," Keith replies, "Mary has told me all about you."

Glancing around the room, Mom asks, "Where's my handsome grandson?"

"Off saving the world, I'm afraid," Thomas quips, "the game world that is. I've told him he has five minutes to close out or he's grounded for the rest of the weekend. He should be coming in right about..." he is watching the second hand of his wristwatch very closely. "Now."

"Hey, Mimi," Rob says as he turns the corner in just the nick of time. "You're sure looking fine."

I watch in wonder as my fifty-eight-year-old mother blushes like a schoolgirl.

Swatting Robert playfully on the arm, she says, "You silver-tongued devil. Keep talking like that and you'll have all the girls banging down this door. Just you wait and see."

Brooklyn rolls her eyes exaggeratedly. "They'll have to get past his clown feet and sweaty palms first, Mimi. And that's a pretty hard sell."

We all laugh, including Robert, who is used to his twin sister's good-natured ribbing.

Normally, I'm a gracious hostess but today I can't bring myself to play the part. Accustomed to me taking the lead, Thomas looks at me questioningly and I quickly glance away. The weight of his stare is nearly more than I can bear but I refuse to budge.

Finally, Thomas slaps Keith chummily on the back, saying, "How about I get you and me a glass of ice tea and let's go out on the deck and leave these ladies to themselves."

The men share a hearty laugh as they begin walking toward the kitchen. I take a perverse pleasure in imagining Keith's distaste when he sees the dirty floor, the dishes stacked in the sink, the bills piled on the counter by the phone, and the layer of dust coating all of the appliances. Although, he's been careful to maintain a neutral expression I'm sure he hasn't missed the "lived-in" look of our house. Hopefully, it will give him pause as he contemplates his future with my mother.

After giving the guys time to get their ice tea and make their way to the deck, I head for the kitchen knowing my mother will follow me without hesitation. My assumption correct, it is but a moment before she is nipping at my heels like a chihuahua puppy.

To my dismay, I realize that the kitchen has been cleaned. Well, straightened might be more accurate but at least, there are no dirty dishes in the sink and the counters have been wiped clean. Normally, I would be grateful for Thomas' help but not today. All I can feel is frustration.

Doesn't Thomas understand that I want to embarrass my mother in front of her fiance'? Thankfully, he didn't have time to clean the floor, a fact I note with grim satisfaction. It only takes a moment for my mother to focus on it. Without a word, she heads for the broom closet. Quickly, she sweeps the floor, embarrassment fueling her efforts; that done, she fills a bucket with soapy water and proceeds to mop the kitchen. By the time she's through, the dishwasher has finished and she quickly unloads it, her disappointment in me evident in the way she sighs as she puts the dishes away.

From the deck, I can hear the murmur of conversation, punctuated by an occasional burst of laughter. Apparently, Thomas and Keith are getting along well which causes me no little distress. Doesn't Thomas realize this is our only chance to end this marriage madness? How dare he make Keith feel comfortable when I've determined to make this weekend as difficult as I possibly can.

Instead of joining me at the table in the breakfast nook, my mother has exited the kitchen. Thinking she may have gone to the bathroom, I wait a few minutes before going in search of her. I find her in the living room where she has retreated to nurse her disappointment in private. She is staring silently into space, her face a sorrowful mask. For a moment, I'm touched by her grief. Then, I remind myself of the sight of his ring on her finger.

Resolute, I enter the room, taking a seat across from her. "Where's Daddy's ring?" I ask, looking straight into her eyes without blinking.

Surprise and hurt causes her to blanch beneath her make-up and for just a moment, I'm shamed by my behavior. Then, I wrap my self-righteousness tighter around me, telling myself that it is she who is betraying my father's memory, not me. A tiny voice whispers that my behavior is a betrayal of his memory as well but I pay it no mind.

I watch as my mother struggles to control her emotions, refusing to cry no matter how deeply my words may have wounded her. Finally, in a voice tinged with hurt, she replies, "The ring your father gave me is in my purse, wrapped in tissue for safekeeping."

"May I have it, Mommy?" I implore, feeling suddenly like a lost child floating in a sea of strangers, my heart yearning for anything familiar to hold onto, anything to prevent me from drowning.

Her eyes shining with emotion, she whispers, "That's why I brought it, Baby. Just for you."

A crack appears in the armor around my heart and I touch my mother's leg before silently mouthing, "Thank you."

CHAPTER

TWENTY-EIGHT

Everyone is settled down for the night and I'm doing my lockdown ritual. Reflecting on the day, I'm emotionally and physically exhausted. Drained of every ounce of limited strength I had remaining, I cannot imagine how I am going to make it through the rest of the weekend. I knew this was going to be difficult but nothing I imagined could have prepared me for this emotional onslaught.

Even the most mundane details, like deciding where everyone was going to sleep, were fraught with emotional mines. Watching Keith close the door to the guest room, where Dad and Mom always stayed, was nearly more than I could bear. "No!" I wanted to scream. "No, it's not supposed to be this way. That's my daddy's room." Instead, I forced myself to walk down the hallway all the while thinking, *Daddy is gone forever and Mom is moving on with her life without him and there's nothing I can do to change things.*

I wanted to shake her or to have someone shake me and tell me this is all a horrible dream. But it's not a dream—a cruel joke maybe—but no dream. I feel like I'm being forced to betray my daddy for the sake of my mother's happiness. This can't be right. It just can't.

All these thoughts bounce around inside my head like so many pinballs, each one capable of breaching my defenses and wounding me in ways I can't even imagine. Turning the key in the final door, I hear the clunk as the deadbolt slides into place and I lean my head against the door overwhelmed by it all.

My eyes slide slowly shut and a shudder of grief moves through my body. Sorrow and sickness have combined to leave me so weary that I wonder if death would not be a relief. Yet, I know that joy comes in the morning and so I resist the depression that tempts me to give up. With God's help, I get hold of myself, grateful that my grief is once again firmly in my grasp—piercing but survivable.

Wiping my eyes, I shut off the final light and turn toward the master bedroom where Thomas awaits. As I do, I notice the light is still on in Brooklyn's room where Mother is staying. Desperately needing to speak with her alone, I decide to take a chance and see if she's still awake or if she simply fell asleep reading.

Opening the door a crack, I say, "I saw your light on and I thought maybe we could talk." I shrug giving her a small smile—hating the sudden insecurity I feel in my own mother's presence.

My offer hangs in the air between us and after a moment I turn to go, unable to bear the changes that my father's death has brought between my mother and me. Without Daddy, we are like an orchestra with no conductor...an opera singer with laryngitis. I don't know if we'll ever make beautiful music again.

"Rebecca, please don't go."

I pause, my heart pounding in my chest. Softly, I shut the door before turning slowly around to face my mother, my heart in my eyes.

She pats the bed beside her and without a word. I sit down allowing her to take me in her comforting arms. Incredibly, I'm a little girl again safe and protected in the circle of my mom's love.

Tenderly, she rocks me humming softly. When I was just a child she used to sing to me, songs of her own, making up the lyrics as she went. Much to my delight, she begins to sing one now.

Rebecca, I love you, Rebecca, I love you,
Rebecca, I love you, Rebecca, I love you.

I wilt in my mother's arms, finally able to release the stubborn hurt that has clouded my days since she informed me of her engagement. When my pent-up emotions have finally spent themselves, she hands me a tissue and I blow my nose. Pulling a chair close to the bed, I settle down for a long overdue heart-to-heart with my mom. When I do, I notice that instead of a nightgown, she is wearing an oversized man's shirt. "Is that one of Daddy's shirts?" I ask, hardly able to believe my eyes.

"Yes," she says, a tender expression giving her an almost youthful appearance. "I kept four or five of your father's shirts and I've slept in one of them every night since the funeral."

"But you're engaged to Keith," I stammer.

"Honey, what I feel for Keith will never change what I felt for your father. He was my first love and he will always have a place in my heart, just as Keith's first wife will always have a place in his heart."

Her eyes cloud with tears and one escapes, sliding silently down her age-softened cheek. Transfixed, I follow that single tear till it dangles precariously from the rounded edges of her jawline. Reaching, I rescue it with a gentle touch caressing the moisture between forefinger and thumb like a precious gift. I've never seen my mother cry, not even at Daddy's funeral. Her single tear both blesses and confuses me.

"Mom," I ask, posing a question that scares me, "were you truly happy with Daddy?"

Her answer is a long time coming and my question so softly spoken I'm beginning to wonder if she even heard me. At last she speaks, a sweet smile gracing her face. "My life with your father was all I ever hoped it would be—comfortable, full of love, and contentment. Like all marriages, we had seasons filled with a little more spice than I enjoyed but as you know that comes with the territory. Life with Richard was never dull and I don't regret a single minute of it. Marrying him and having you are the two best things that ever happened to me."

Exhaustion, stemming from the lupus, clouds my thoughts and I am finding it harder and harder to think clearly. I know I should head off to bed but I can't stop myself from asking one last question. "If you loved Daddy so much then how can you think of remarrying so soon? Daddy hasn't even been gone a year and you've already fallen in love with someone else. It makes no sense, Mom."

"Oh, Honey," she says, eager to make me understand, "don't you see that's exactly why I want to marry again? It's a testament to the relationship your father and I had. He spoiled me and because of him I don't think I could ever be content living alone. You can understand that, can't you?"

Mom looks at me imploringly and I glance down studying my tightly clasped hands.

Reaching out, she covers my hands with her own. "Please, Honey, I can't do this without your support. Give Keith a chance. I know he's not your dad. He doesn't want to take his place in your heart or mine. Don't forget, he's lost a spouse, too. His children don't think of me as their mother but simply as their father's new wife. Can't you do the same?"

I continue staring at our joined hands unable to meet the pleading look in Mom's grey eyes. The fact that Keith's wife died over three years ago, while Dad hasn't been gone a year, is a moot point as far as she's concerned and trying to discuss it with her is out of the question. *Well, it may not be a concern for her but it's a huge one for me. It's too soon. I simply cannot think of my mother with another man, not yet.*

Forcing myself to answer at last, I lift my eyes to hers and reply, "I'm doing the best I can, Mom. I'm trying. It's just a really difficult time for me right now."

"Is everything okay between you and Thomas?" she quickly inquires, marital problems being the worst thing imaginable as far as Mom's concerned.

"Yes," I respond, squeezing her hand reassuringly, "everything is fine in that regard."

When I pause, unable to say more, she asks, "Is it one of the twins?"

This time, I simply shake my head and concern clouds her features, then realization. Lightly touching my face, she inquires timorously, "What is it, Becca? What's wrong?"

Placing my hand upon hers, I press my cheek deeper into her palm savoring her touch. In a voice choked with emotion,

I tell her, "I have systemic lupus, Mom. It's a chronic, sometimes fatal immunological disease."

I could tell her more, lots more, but I don't want to frighten her. She doesn't need to know that if we can't get this disease under control, I may not live to see my twins graduate from high school. Or, if I do, that I may be a cripple confined to a wheelchair.

"I don't understand," she stammers, "you don't look sick."

Her words are meant to reassure herself as much as me and I belatedly realize that Daddy's death has wounded her in ways I can only imagine. Beneath her confident front, she is fragile, terribly afraid that death will suddenly snatch someone else she loves. I want to comfort her, to reassure her, but I can't. I simply do not have the strength.

Trying desperately to regain control of my emotions, I inhale deeply and say a small prayer before answering, "That's one of the most difficult things. Even on my worst days, I may not look sick but trust me, Mom, looks are deceiving. Right now, I barely have the strength to sit here."

As I continue to share what my life has been like over the past four months, my mother listens, nods in all the right places, and is appropriately sympathetic. Unfortunately, she doesn't pick up on my hints that I could really use her help and would appreciate it if she could stick around for a while. At this point, I am too hurt and afraid to come right out and ask for her help. After all, this way I can at least comfort myself with the thought that maybe, just maybe, she didn't understand what I was getting at. At least, that's what I tell myself as I struggle to fall asleep, the medication I took just a waste of time....

CHAPTER
TWENTY-NINE

The morning sun seeps around the curtains as I begin the daily stretching exercises prescribed by the doctor. He says it is the only way to maintain my mobility in the face of the onslaught brought about by the systemic lupus invading my body. Feet first, slowly, slowly pointing toes, rotating right then left. This process continues till I, at last, lie with arms tautly stretched above my head in that wonderful feline-like universal morning stretch, only mine has become more pain than pleasure.

I groan as I recall the barbeque planned for this afternoon. At Thomas' insistance, I have invited the original

Bunko Babes and their husbands to join the six of us for a backyard feast. Why did I let him talk me into it? What could have possessed me to think I could manage such an elaborate affair? Although I'm tempted to pull the covers over my head and burrow deeper into the darkened confines of my California King, I force myself toward the bathroom. Maybe a hot shower will help.

Twenty minutes later, I am blow-drying my hair when I hear a knock on my bedroom door. I hesitate thinking it is probably my mother. Although last night's conversation was mostly positive, we didn't resolve anything and I'm simply not ready for another go around. Reluctantly, I call, "Come in."

"Your breakfast, milady." Thomas announces from the doorway, a brunch tray in his hands.

"Do tell," I say, surprised by this unexpected kindness. "What possessed you to make me breakfast?"

Grinning sheepishly, he says, "Actually, your mom made it. I'm just the delivery boy."

I move the hair dryer so he can place the tray on the makeup table. Reaching up, I give his bicep a playful pinch, "Some delivery boy!"

Continuing the parody, he pulls a stiff white linen napkin from his back pocket and gives it a swift snap before laying it across my lap. I laugh in spite of myself and suddenly the day doesn't seem quite so impossible. Thomas has always been able to make me laugh and it is one of the things I love most about him.

"Will wonders never cease?" I tease, indicating the heavy-laden tray, which overflows with French toast, bacon, scrambled eggs, and my personal favorite, a chocolate-iced Krispy Kreme donut."

"That's not all yours," Thomas hastens to inform me. "Your mother insisted that I take breakfast with you." He delivers the last line with a snobbish British accent causing me to laugh yet again.

Ignoring all the nutritious foods, I reach for the donut. Picking it up, I take a bite. Inspired by Thomas' performance, I close my eyes and moan softly as if in ecstasy.

"I wish you'd make sounds like *that* when you kiss me!"

"I might, if you were smothered in sugar and then generously dipped in chocolate icing."

We both chuckle at the thought and I realize that Thomas has given me far more than sustenance. He's given me his love and the gift of laughter.

Softly, I say, "A dream home in Tulsa, Oklahoma—$350,000. A master suite fit for a queen—$25,000. A loving husband—priceless."

Two hours later, I'm sipping a glass of ice tea while comfortably ensconced in my favorite glider conveniently located in our air-conditioned, darkly tinted sunroom. I'm doing my best to conserve my strength for the onslaught of guests while trying to appear as if I'm still right in the middle of the preparations. That's no easy task. Especially considering, I don't want anyone to know how poorly I'm feeling.

Glancing up, I see Keith approaching, cold drink in hand. "Mind if I join you?"

Without waiting for my response, he makes himself comfortable on the love seat situated caddy corner to my glider. Propping his feet up on the footstool/coffee table, he leans back hands behind his head, "You've got the right idea here, Rebecca. Sit back, relax, and supervise."

When I don't respond, he sips his lemonade in silence, apparently content to wait me out. A gracious person by nature, rudeness is foreign to me, and I soon grow uncomfortable with my silence. Still, I cannot bring myself to speak and I wonder yet again, "Who is this person I have become?"

Finally, Keith leans forward, elbows on his knees, hands steepled thoughtfully. "I can only imagine how difficult this must be for you, Rebecca. Not only is your mother getting married, but to a man you don't even know. Not to mention the fact that it hasn't even been a year since your father died."

He pauses, giving me a chance to respond but I maintain my silence. "It's important for you to know that although I deeply love your mother, I don't want to take your father's place in her heart or in yours. You need to know that—understand that, if this is ever going to work."

Devoid of emotion, I inquire, "If what is going to work?"

"This," he reiterates, pointing his finger first at me then at himself. "If you and I are ever going to be friends, you have to know that I'm not trying to take your dad's place."

As if, I think, automatically reverting to Brooklyn's latest nonsensical response to anything she finds impossible to imagine. To my way of thinking, nothing could be more ridiculous than trying to imagine anyone taking my father's place.

Keith is unlike my father in almost every way, especially his physical appearance. Standing 6 feet 3 inches tall, my dad was at least 6 inches taller than Keith and well muscled from hard physical labor for most of his life. Keith is slim, almost slight, and soft-spoken, with the look of a scholar.

Daddy worked with his hands and they showed it. His hands were strong, rough, and weathered—hands that could fix anything. Hands that could catch you when you fell; hands that could make you feel safe, a man's hands. Keith's grip is firm enough but his hand feels soft and so much smaller. Of course, not many men have hands the size of hams like my father.

Undeterred by my stubborn silence, Keith continues, his deep voice resonate, "Based on the things your mother has said, your dad must have been an amazing man. I wish I could have known him."

Before I can stop myself, I say, "He was the best dad ever."

"You helped him restore classic cars, didn't you?"

I grunt a reply and he asks, "Did you have a favorite car, one that you really enjoyed working on with your dad?"

Instantly, I recall a 1957 Thunderbird and unbidden tears spring to my eyes. Turning away, lest Keith see my tears, I stare at the activity in the backyard with unseeing eyes, while indistinct images from those bygone days float on the periphery of my vision. I can't help thinking that I would give almost anything if I could have just one more summer evening in the garage with my daddy.

Finally, I manage a strangled whisper, "I can't talk about this now, please."

I turn my misty eyes to his in a sudden, unexplainable desire for his comprehension.

His face full of compassion, he responds, "I understand, Becca."

Getting to his feet, he reaches for my hand. Taking it between both of his, he squeezes gently. "Thank you for inviting me into your home and for giving this barbeque in my honor. I look forward to meeting your friends. If they are anything like you, it will be a joy."

I watch him as he goes to join the others in their frantic preparations and, although I hate to admit it, I think I could come to like him. That doesn't mean I want Mom to marry him, at least not so soon, but I'm beginning to understand why she's attracted to him. Unfortunately, the mere possibility of making a place in my heart for Keith makes me feel disloyal to my late father. "I'm sorry, Daddy," I whisper, "I'm sorry."

Amazingly, everything comes together just like Thomas promised it would. Of course, it helped that he called *The Rib Crib* and ordered enough food to feed an army and then swung by *Ehrle's Party Supply* off of Memorial and 41st to pick up the decorations. Mom and Brooklyn have transformed the backyard into a perfect rendition of a romantic Tiki destination. The hot tub has floating candles in a multitude of colors ready to be lit as the sun sets. A straw hut has been erected for the cold drink station and citronella candles, cleverly disguised as Tiki torches, are lining the deck prepared to be fired up at the first sign of mosquitoes. The only thing lacking is a seaside breeze, white sandy beaches, and the magical aromatic mixture of salt water, seaweed, and hibiscus.

I've retreated to a chaise lounge, situated in the shade of a towering oak tree. From my vantage point, I have a clear view of the proceedings and I can't help but marvel at my mother's joyous abandonment. How long has it been since I've seen Mom laugh like this? Maybe never. The years fall away under my watchful gaze and if I didn't know better, I would think she was only in her forties, so young and carefree does she appear.

"You've got to be kidding me," Jessica squeals in delight tossing her head back, her dark hair blowing in the wind. "Surely you didn't say that," she adds, placing her hand on Keith's arm for support. She's in her element and she is not to be outshined. Not tonight.

"I did, Jessica," Keith admits, somewhat sheepishly, "but please keep in mind that it was an inadvertent slip of the tongue. I meant to say 'lighthouses.'"

Still unable to believe it, Jessica continues, "You actually encouraged your congregation to be 'outhouses on a hill'? That's the funniest thing I've ever heard."

Keith has been regaling my friends with one ministry story after another, keeping them in stitches for the better part of an hour, and I can't help thinking that he's a gifted storyteller. He seems to especially enjoy poking fun at himself and Mom delights in his antidotes, her laugher ringing clearly above the others.

I'm glad for her but I can't help wondering how she can be so happy without Daddy? *How can Jessica be so blasé? How can she pretend that all is well when we haven't spoken in nearly three weeks? Michael has come with Madison and I can't imagine how she can act so normal after what he's done. I can only conclude that they must be cut from a different piece of cloth than I am.* Unlike them, I can't pretend everything is okay when it's not.

Everyone I love most in this entire world is standing right over there having a blast, laughing and carrying on. And here I am alone, observing life as it goes right on without me. It's my own fault. Not the sickness, but the way I'm handling it or maybe I should say not handling it. I've shut everyone out—isolated myself and in the process, I've hurt the very people I love most. But I'll fix it. I will, just not tonight...tomorrow. I'll fix everything tomorrow. Tonight, I simply can't do any more.

Silently, I slip into the house, taking refuge in my California King cocoon.

CHAPTER

THIRTY

It's Thursday evening and I'm on my way to the weekly Bunko party, hosted this week by Autumn. She lives with Rob and the kids on an acre and a half on the outskirts of Bixby, just south of Tulsa. When they bought the property seven or eight years ago, the house was a fixer-upper and it's still a work in progress. Rob is a gifted handyman but he has a tendency to get distracted before he finishes a project, hence, Autumn lives in the middle of a remodeling mess at all times. I can only shake my head in wonder. She just goes with the flow, ignoring things that would drive most wives absolutely batty.

Crossing the river, I turn west and head up the hill, squinting against the glare of the setting sun, the Navigator's A/C laboring against the sultry August heat. Slowing, I search for the driveway that leads to Autumn's house. Obscured by a wild tangle of weeds, I nearly miss it, chuckling as I think of the newer members of The Bunko Babes. This will be their first time at Autumn's and I can only imagine their reactions.

Although the driveway is narrow and sparsely covered with gravel, I find it picturesque as it winds through a grove of pecan trees, coming to a stop before a ranch style house of indiscriminate size. I'm careful to park with the Navigator facing the road, experience having taught me how difficult it is to get turned around out here in the dark. On more than one occasion, I've suggested getting one of the yard lights advertised by PSO but Rob always vetoes it saying it obscures the stars. Maybe it does but I'd still opt for the light. A couple of times I've nearly fallen trying to get to my car in the dark.

Appraising myself in the mirror on the visor, I fluff the necessary hair, put on a dab of cherry red lipstick, and cover it with gloss. Smacking my lips together, I blow a kiss at my reflection trying my best to ignore the deepening parentheses marring my cheeks and the sudden appearance of quotation marks between my brows. *What is it with women and punctuation marks?* Knowing it's a losing battle, I shrug it off and exit the Navigator.

Immediately, I begin to perspire, the humid heat wrapping itself around me like a wet towel. In the distance, I hear the clatter of the window units and I can only hope the house is bearable. The last time we were here, one of them wasn't working and I thought I'd die. Opening the rear door of the Navigator, I get a bowl of homemade guacamole, my contribution to the evening's Mexican food feast, and make my way up the walk, noting the construction debris littering one end of the porch that runs the length of the house.

Bunko nights at Autumn's are casual so I've traded my espadrilles for my recently acquired canvas Keds and my "perfect" white blouse for a sleeveless salmon tank with a collar to add a little flair. I wanted to wear shorts but heeding the doctor's instructions, I've settled for my most comfortable jeans, easily transforming them into crop pants. Unable to find anything cool to toss on over my tank, I settled for a brown fitted jacket. A low slung brown, leather belt and a pair of copper shoulder dusters complete the ensemble.

At the door Autumn greets me, raising an eyebrow as she surveys my outfit. "Isn't that a little much?" she teases me, knowing how I love the attention.

I grin. "You just wish you could carry it off, girlfriend. Besides, without accessories, how would one distinguish herself from the drab crowd?"

Giving me a saucy look, she replies, "A charming personality?"

Stepping back, I place a hand to my heart. "That hurts, really hurts."

Laughing, I hand her the bowl of guacamole. "By the way, where is the fam? Did you kick them out for the night?"

"Bet your Bunko Bank I did. They've invaded Tulsa's Incredible Pizza Place for the entire evening."

"Did you forewarn them?" I tease, a look of mock horror upon my face.

Smacking her head playfully with the palm of her hand, she laughs, "I knew I'd forgotten something."

Her joy is contagious and I find myself laughing with her as we make our way toward the kitchen. Inhaling deeply, I savor the moment, feeling better than I have all day. *Laughter,* I think, *God's medicine for the soul.*

Autumn is amazing. God has given her the incredible gift of acceptance. Around her, I feel free to be me. Whoever that may be, I know she will still love me. Agree with me? Support my stance? Maybe not, but she will always love me, tell me how it is, and be there to pick me up when I fall. In that way she's a lot like God. I wish I was more like her. In time....maybe in time.

Leaving me in the kitchen/dining room, she goes to answer the door. I take the opportunity to survey things and I can't help but note her lack of preparation. True to her word, she has hung her massive orange velvet sombrero from the dining room fixture but that's the extent of her decorations. There's a bowl of baked organic corn chips on the table with a jar of Cheez Whiz sitting beside it and some paper plates and napkins. I envy her carefree spirit and I can't help thinking that maybe more than any of us, she understands that Bunko night is about getting together with friends, not trying to outdo each other.

Hearing voices from down the hallway, I make my way toward what passes for the master bedroom. From the doorway, I spot Jessica and Kitty Kat appraising Rodney's unfinished handiwork. Unaware of the unresolved rift between Jessica and me, Kathleen waves me over.

Not willing to air our differences in public, Jess pretends nothing is amiss and I follow suit. "You gotta see this," she says, indicating the open wall that has been stuffed with straw salvaged from the barn.

"More like smell it," says Kitty Kat, a little green at the gills.

Giving her a sympathetic grin, I tease, "The morning sickness phase?"

"I don't know why it's called morning sickness," she snaps, without a hint of humor, "when it lasts all day."

Jess and I give each other a knowing look before saying simultaneously, "The mood swing phase."

Glaring at us, Kitty Kat says, "Excuse me."

We pretend to ignore her. Turning to Jessica, I say, "They're starting a little early, aren't they?"

She nods having lived vicariously through several of our friends. "Boy, I feel sorry for Adam. This is going to be a long nine months."

I nod in return. "Technically, it's about six-and-a-half months now."

"That's true, but who's counting?" Jess replies before looking straight at me.

"Adam!" we say, again reading each other like a recipe for boiling water.

"Will you two ever grow up?" Kitty Kat asks before turning on her heel and leaving the room.

Our eyes meet again and we burst into giggles just like we did when we were girls. As our laughter trails off, I venture a tentative peace offering. "It feels good to laugh and joke with you again, Jess. I've missed you."

The light leaves her eyes and I watch, deeply wounded, as she once again lowers the blinds to her soul, effectively shutting me out. "Jess?" I whisper, "Please...."

Before I can say anything else, Autumn calls us to the Bunko tables. Taking a seat at the low table, I hide my sorrow behind a smile and prepare to play. Mercedes gives me a shaky smile in return; reminding me that while I was wrapped up in the drama of meeting Mom's fiancé, she was enduring an emotional good-bye with her husband Douglas. That certainly puts things in perspective and I make a note to give her a call sometime this week as I hand her the dice. Sensing how fragile Mercedes is, and knowing how her emotional display at Kathleen's embarrassed her, Autumn interjects, "Let's get rollin', ladies. It's time to play some Bunko!"

Taking the dice, Mercedes tosses them high in the air. "Numero uno," she cheers. "Come on, Lady Luck!"

Although we are on opposite teams, I find myself pulling for my young friend, wanting everything to go her way. The purple die stops first on the number three. Mercedes brows draw close. The green one spins, tumbles twice before stopping on a five. Her full lips purse. The final die, red, teeters left, right, left…before coming at last to a stop. The transformation is amazing—from pensive to triumphant instantaneously. Glancing victoriously around the table, Mercedes proudly announces, "And that's the way it's done," before quickly swiping up the dice and repeating the process all over again.

Enjoying her enthusiasm, I retort, "Thanks for the reminder. Us old-timers have a tendency to forget things from time to time." That said, I take the opportunity to stuff a gooey chunk of monkey bread into my mouth, closing my eyes in sheer pleasure before licking every last sweet, sticky morsel off my fingertips.

Madison grimaces at my uncouth behavior. "There are forks on the table, Becca," she reminds me.

Unable to resist teasing her, I tear off an even larger, gooier piece. Opening my mouth as wide as I can, I shove the entire mess in, heedless of the caramel coating the corners of my mouth and running down my chin. "I know, Dawling," I reply, drawing it out like a true Southern Bell. "But it's so much more fun this way. Don't you agree?" I bat my eyes coquettishly hoping to complete the picture.

Chuckling, my sweet friend throws her hands in the air. "I don't know why I bother, Becca. You're hopeless."

I feel better just knowing I've made her smile, no matter that I had to play the fool to do it. Michael has moved out and taken a condo, leaving Madison and the children. At this point, he seems intent on destroying their marriage, refusing to consider marriage counseling even though his pastor has tried to reason with him. Although, she's the betrayed spouse, Madison can't help feeling shamed, as if she is somehow responsible for Michael's actions. She's going through a bad time and I want to be there for her.

The evening's Bunko game wraps up earlier than usual and for a change Michelle isn't the winner. Since no one seems ready to leave, we migrate toward Autumn's eclectic living room. Her decorating is a definite reflection of her lifestyle—easygoing, au natural. With eight rowdy kids, what furniture there is, is either broken down or frightfully stained. In addition, there are a number of bean bags scattered around the room and the younger ladies avail themselves of these, leaving the furniture for those of us who are less agile.

Watching Madison search for a place to sit, I don't know whether to laugh or cry. She's always fastidious but tonight she's downright compulsive; the thought of sitting on Autumn's soiled sofa nearly more than she can bear. After circling the couch a couple of times, she selects a spot and proceeds to brush it off, trying to be as inconspicuous as possible. Finally, she sits down on the very edge—back straight, knees together, and her feet flat on the floor. If I didn't know what was driving her, I would find her behavior hilarious but as it is, my heart goes out to her. When her life feels out of control, Madison fights the hardest to put her environment in perfect order and right now things are spinning out of control.

Stepping in from the kitchen, Autumn passes a platter of desert bars around the room but no one partakes. Frustrated, she says, "You're always talking about chocolate in whispered words of wonder, looks of pure pleasure upon your faces, and yet, you never touch the chocolate dishes I prepare. What gives?"

"It's carob, Autumn, not chocolate. Big difference, huge." Jessica shrugs her shoulders, smiling innocently before adding, "Enough said."

As if to prove us wrong, Autumn selects a "fudge bar" and takes a big bite. We watch as she makes a bitter face before placing the unfinished bar back on the tray. We grin knowingly as she concedes. Nothing can take the place of the sinful decadence of pure unadulterated chocolate. Our good-natured hoots and hollers follow her as she takes the tray back to the kitchen.

Returning from the bathroom, Kitty Kat carefully lowers her growing girth onto the couch, nearly squashing Madison in the process. Grimacing, she hastily apologizes, embarrassment coloring her face. "I'm so sorry, Madison. My brain has not yet recalculated my new size so everything's a little bit off."

Patting our young friend's leg, Madison says sympathetically, "Don't worry about it. Just be careful in parking lots and grocery stores. Those carts can be deadly."

"You can say that again," Karen pipes up.

We spend the better part of the next hour regaling Kathleen with humorous stories about our own pregnancies, laughing until there isn't a dry eye in the place. As good as our stories are, no one can top Autumn's, her "all natural" attempts at starting labor sound like a script for a slapstick comedy. She entertains us with hilarious tales, relating accounts of drinking Castor oil shakes, eating spicy foods, being intimate with her husband, getting specific types of massages, walking, doing jumping jacks, acupuncture—you name it, she did it. Most times with unsatisfactory results, the baby coming days later. Listening to all the talk, I can only say, "Thank God for epidurals, obstetricians, and formula. Not to mention the fact that my babies are now teenagers."

I risk a glance in Jessica's direction and find her eyes downcast, fingers picking relentlessly at the seam of her walking shorts. Her ebony hair falls across her shoulders shadowing her face from my concerned gaze. Regardless, I can imagine what she is thinking and what our conversation has done to her wounded heart. Anxious to rescue her, I decide to change the subject. Speaking up, I say, "There's something I need to tell y'all. Something, I should have talked about weeks ago."

Expecting another funny story, Michelle pops off, "If this is about getting a boob job, the gig is up. Jess has already told us."

Momentarily taken aback, I hesitate before continuing. "No, it's not about that." Another longer pause. "I'm sick, Babes, really sick."

Around me the laughter dies and the room grows quiet. Struggling to speak, I say, "I've been diagnosed with systemic lupus, a chronic and often life-threatening disease."

When I finish, I am weeping soundlessly, silent tears streaming down my cheeks. Almost as one, The Babes close around me, surrounding me with their love and support. There are many questions, embraces, compassion, shared tears, and prayers. When things settle down just a bit, I allow my eyes to scan the room, searching frantically for the one person who matters most, but she is nowhere to be found. Belatedly, I realize that by going public with The Babes before confiding in her, I have likely wounded my dearest friend yet again. This time there was neither forethought nor malice but that is of no consequence now. Jessica is gone.

THIRTY-ONE

Rushing through my good-byes, I give The Bunko Babes quick hugs and a muffled apology for my early departure. Although it is not quite ten o'clock on this Thursday night, I am the first to leave and that's a rarity. Okay, it's more than rare. If the truth be told, it's never happened before but there's a first time for everything, right?

"Ouch!" I complain, as I stumble in the dark, twisting my ankle. Pausing briefly, I rub my throbbing joint, while willing my eyes to adjust to the inky blackness around me. "This is why I don't live in the country," I mutter, as I continue toward my SUV.

Mentally, I berate myself for wearing my new canvas Keds instead of the leather ones. The dust from the gravel driveway is likely to stain them and it's my own fault. I wouldn't be so upset but I've been waiting forever for these overpriced tennis shoes to go on sale and tonight was the first chance I've had to wear them.

At last, I reach my Navigator and I let out a groan of relief at the chirp, chirp it makes as the doors unlock and the interior lights come on. Momentarily, I lean against the tailgate in exhaustion, amazed at how much the evening's activities have taken out of me. Eventually, I manage to push myself up and stumble to the driver's door. Gritting my teeth against the fire in my joints, I pull myself into the driver's seat.

Once inside, all pretenses crumble and my body begins to tremble from the pain I've kept in check by the sheer force of my will. Almost as disconcerting is the memory of the fawning of my friends. Although they meant well, I quickly tired of being coddled and continually forced to answer questions regarding my diagnosis. I just want things to be the way they used to be.

Frustration getting the best of me, I slam my hands on the steering wheel, fighting back my tears. I'm ashamed of myself. Everyone was wonderful to me, so why am I struggling with resentment? Truthfully, I don't know what I'd do without my family and friends—my husband Thomas, The Bunko Babes, my kids, my pastor, the people at church, they've all helped out immensely. The past few months would have been impossible without them. Still, I have become a stranger to myself and, with increasing frequency, I find myself alternating between bouts of depression and fits of nearly uncontrollable anger.

Behind me the porch light comes on, startling me into action. Jabbing the key into the ignition, I start the car and jerk it into reverse. Glancing at the digital clock on the dash, I am surprised to realize that nearly fifteen minutes have passed since I bid my good-byes. I have to get out of here. I can't bear the thought of having to explain why I'm still sitting here in the dark.

The disease that has attacked my body has affected my night vision as well, and now I squint into the darkness, backing haphazardly. Slamming on the brakes, I stop just in time, nearly colliding with Jessica's new Saab.

"What is wrong with me," I mutter, fighting back a rising panic. Hurriedly, I shift into drive and press hard on the accelerator, leaving a spew of gravel in my wake.

Exhaustion clouds my thoughts and I pay no mind to which direction I turn. I just need to get away...away from it all. I have never dealt with anything like this. I have lost control of my life. The person I used to be has ceased to exist. I am trapped—trapped in a failing body, suffocated by fear of the future.

Swiping at the tears blurring my vision, I try desperately to focus on the road. The usually familiar route suddenly seems foreign to me. I know I've been this way a hundred times before but at this moment, I haven't got a clue where I am. My mind seems to have deserted me and my heart hammers in my throat. Gripping the wheel tightly, I squint into the darkness, gasping at the sharp bite of pain traveling up my arms. Try as I might, I cannot stem the unbidden flow of tears.

It's not just the physical pain that has undone me, but the loss of control and the fear that are my constant companions. For weeks, I have been subjected to a host of humiliating and painful procedures. I have been poked, prodded, scanned, and scoped until I am convinced that these strangers know my body better than I do. All of this has been done in the name of medicine…in the hope of healing, but seemingly to no avail.

My foot is heavy on the accelerator but I am oblivious to the blur of trees and mailboxes flying past my window. Too late, I realize that there is a sharp bend in the road ahead. As if in slow motion, my mind registers this fact as my Navigator careens out of control. The last thing I remember is the screech of branches on shiny metal and then I am falling into a black hole.

CHAPTER

THIRTY-TWO

Pain awakens me, pulling me from the womb of sleep. Groggily, I try to roll over seeking some relief, but instantly freeze when a stabbing pain takes my breath away. Something is wrong, terribly wrong! Lying back, I realize my head is throbbing and for the life of me, I can't figure out where I am or how I got here. The last thing I remember is leaving home to go to the Bunko party at Autumn's house.

Gamely, I try to reconstruct the evening but to no avail. I can't concentrate. I keep losing my train of thought. It feels as if someone has dipped my brain in thick molasses. Opening my eyes, I squint into the darkness trying to acclimate myself to the unfamiliar surroundings. Moonlight is streaming through the partially opened blinds, casting shadowy bars across the foot of my bed and in the far corner, a dim lamp draws a soft circle of light around a chair in which a woman sleeps, a Bible lying open in her lap.

A door opens, spilling a splash of light into the room causing me to flinch in pain. On nearly soundless feet, a nurse in a white uniform comes to stand beside my bed. She wipes an instrument across my forehead, noting my temperature on a chart. After checking my blood pressure, she injects something into the IV line connected to the back of my hand. I want to ask her what I'm doing here but my words come out in an inarticulate mumble. Patting my hand, she exists the room leaving me to my confusion. Once more, a drug-induced sleep woos me and against my will I succumb to its soft embrace.

The next time I awake, day has come and from the hallway I hear the bustle of activity. Surveying the room without lifting my head, I see that the chair in the corner is empty but there's a purse and a Bible sitting on the window ledge. Whoever is sitting with me obviously hasn't gone far. After a moment, I hear a toilet flush and then the sound of water running. Directly, the bathroom door opens and my mother emerges, her makeup freshly done and her hair brushed. Seeing I am awake, she hurries to my side.

"Good morning, Becca," she says, concern evident in the tone of her voice.

"What am I doing here?" I ask, desperate to make some sense of my situation.

My question obviously pains her and she hesitates before answering. "Honey, how many times do I have to tell you? You were in an automobile accident."

My first thought is of Thomas and the twins and I cut her off before she can say more. "The twins?" I manage, fear strangling my words. "Thomas?"

Patting my arm, she says, "They're fine. You were alone when the accident occurred...."

Relief washes over me and I miss the rest of her explanation, "What did you say?"

Repeating herself, she tells me. "Apparently, you ran off the side of the road and lost control. You must have been driving pretty fast. The car rolled several times."

My back is killing me but when I try to change positions a spasm of pain seizes me, taking my breath away. Mom leans over me, brushing my hair back. "Take it easy, Honey. You have a broken collarbone, as well as a couple of broken ribs, one of which punctured your lung. In addition, you suffered a pretty severe brain concussion."

"Where's Thomas?"

"I sent him home last night. He hadn't left your side since the accident and he was nearly out on his feet."

"How long have I been here?"

"About thirty-six hours now, but you've been disoriented most of the time."

Thirty-six hours and I don't remember a thing; not a single detail. Nor do I remember the Bunko party or leaving Autumn's or the accident. All of that is gone and no matter how hard I try I cannot retrieve a single memory. The last thing I remember is flirting with Thomas in the closet while getting dressed. In spite of myself I smile, replaying the memory.

Coming up behind me, he wraps his strong arms around my not so girlish waist. Sighing, I lean into him, relishing his scent, his strength, his voice. "Hmmm," I purr. "You could make a girl want to blow off Bunko and stay home with her husband."

"Promises, promises," he replies, nibbling the lobe of my ear.

His breath is warm and heavy in my ear and I blush like a young bride on her wedding night as he whispers things only a wife is meant to hear. Reaching for the belt of my robe, he tugs gently on one end and I feel the satin bow give way. My eyes slide closed and I pull his arms a little tighter around me, tallying the time in my head to see if I can fit this wonderful little tryst in and still make it to Autumn's on time.

My reminiscing is cut short when a young doctor enters the room coming directly to my bed. Taking the metal file containing my chart from the nurse, he hurriedly scans it. Satisfied, he gives it back to her before addressing me. "So how are you feeling this morning, Ms. Thornton?"

Without giving me a chance to reply, he takes a light out of his breast pocket and shines it in first one eye and then the other. "Follow my finger with your eyes without moving your head," he commands and I do my best to comply.

Putting his light away, he asks, "What do you remember about the night of the accident?"

"Not much. Nothing really after I left my home."

"That's not unusual given the severity of your concussion; short-term memory loss being a common side effect. The good news is you should regain the full use of your memory over the next several days. Probably not all at once but you should begin to recall bits and pieces of what happened that evening."

As he turns to go, I blurt out, "When can I go home?"

"That's hard to say," he replies. "Given your concussion and the punctured lung, I think we had better keep you here for another three or four days just to make sure nothing develops."

I'm not happy with his answer, this hospital room being the last place I want to be but there's not much I can do about it. After he leaves, I ring for the nurse to help me to the bathroom. She tries to encourage me to use the bed pan but I won't hear of it. Reluctantly, she raises the back of my bed before helping me sit up. Although my ribs are tightly wrapped, the pain nearly causes me to pass out. Once more, she tries to get me to use the bed pan but I stubbornly refuse. I can do this. I can.

CHAPTER

THIRTY-THREE

The nurse has just gotten me back into bed when Jessica and my mom's fiancé arrive. Keith has come to take my mother to breakfast and then deliver her to my house for some much needed rest. Jessica, it appears, has come to sit with me even though, we still haven't resolved our differences. It's good to see her but her presence creates an undeniable tension in me, not to mention a lingering guilt.

Pushing those thoughts aside, I focus on my mother and Keith. I can't help noticing how she lights up in his presence, even though she must be exhausted after spending the night here with me. I'm trying to be happy for her but no matter how hard I try, I can't help feeling that she's betraying Daddy's memory. It's simply too soon for her to be in love with another man.

Although I can't remember a single detail of the Bunko party at Autumn's or the ensuing accident, the memory of my father's death is indelibly imprinted upon my mind and it only takes the smallest thing to trigger it. Watching my mother leave, Keith's arm comfortably around her waist, generates a sense of loss in me, followed by a spasm of grief. Almost without realizing it, I find myself reliving that tragic night and the grief filled days that followed.

Daddy had gone to the garage to work on one of his beloved classic cars as he did almost every night after dinner. Mom watched television all evening, then cleaned her face and got ready for bed. When Daddy hadn't come in by 11:30, she went to the garage to see what was keeping him. She found him lying face down on the garage floor, felled, as the autopsy would reveal, by a massive heart attack.

She had the presence of mind to call 9-1-1 and then telephoned us. We arrived just after the paramedics and I can remember watching in stunned disbelief as they wheeled him toward the ambulance. They took him to St. Francis Hospital but there was nothing anyone could do. He was declared dead on arrival and my world changed forever.

Standing alone before the open casket three days later, my mind refused to believe that the man laid out before me was the same man who fathered me, taught me to fish, swim, ride a bike, and most importantly, showed me how to live my life for Jesus. Although I stared long and hard, I couldn't find a trace of my daddy in that casket and I felt gypped. The man, lying so still and frozen in death, was just a ghostly reflection of my vibrant daddy, nothing more.

Others said he looked peaceful in death, as if he were sleeping. They were wrong. In life, even sleeping, Daddy didn't look like this man. He hardly ever wore a suit and tie and he certainly didn't sleep in one; nor did he sleep on his back with his hands folded across his stomach. No, if what they said were true, then I would have spotted just a hint of the smile that Daddy wore even in sleep. I would have noticed the flutter of his mustache as he exhaled, exhausted after a hard day's work at the coal plant in Oolagah.

Stepping closer to the casket, I finally reached out and caressed his cheek. When I did the tears I had been holding in came spilling out and I thought my heart would break. I had Thomas and the twins and that should have been enough but it wasn't. Daddy had always been my rock, my true north, and without him, my whole life felt out of kilter.

Mother saw me weeping and came to stand beside me, slipping her arm around my waist she pulled me close. I remember pulling away and telling her I wanted to be alone with Daddy. I didn't mean to hurt her but in that moment her presence was intrusive. Thankfully, she seemed to understand, giving me the privacy I so desperately needed.

In the background, I could hear the murmur of conversation as family and friends offered their condolences but in my mind, it was just my daddy and me. My eyes caressed his features trying hard to memorize every line and curve of his face; the sharp angle of his jaw, that slight bump on the bridge of his nose, the tic-tac-toe scar on his forehead that was no longer hidden behind waves of dark hair.

Softly, I kissed my fingertips trying to infuse all the words yet to be spoken and all the love yet to be shared into this one final touch.

I don't know how long I stood there with fingers pressed to my lips, tears blurring my vision but at last, I felt I was ready to say good-bye. Pressing my fingertips tenderly upon Daddy's lips, I whispered hoarsely, "Pick us out a great cloud, Daddy, soft, fluffy, and with a view of the universe. I'll be there before you know it."

Before I turned to go, I straightened his tie, even though it didn't need straightening and gave his hands one final squeeze. Lifting my eyes heavenward, I gave a quick two thumbs up and whispered, "I'll always love you, Daddy, big as God."

Later that evening, I shared a solitary meal with Thomas and the twins, mother having already gone to bed, exhausted by her grief. We ate in the kitchen at the bar, a single lamp our only light, leaving dark shadows in the far corners. Grief rendered the food tasteless; still I tried to force myself to eat out of some misbegotten sense of obligation to all the friends who had brought food in. To this day, I cannot remember a sadder meal.

For a minute or two more I lay with my eyes closed, teetering on the brink between the past and the present. Finally, I force myself to focus on Jessica who is studying me from across the room. It's the first time we have been alone together since our falling out and both of us are obviously uncomfortable. As far as I'm concerned, the fact that she has come to the hospital, at all, is an undeserved gift but when I try to say as much she brushes my sentiments aside saying, "What are friends for?"

For the better part of an hour we make small talk, being careful not to say anything that might offend. While I'm grateful for the conversation, in some ways the, studied way in which we tiptoe around each other is more painful than an open confrontation, especially when compared with the easy camaraderie we've shared for years. *Why*, I wonder, *can't we just make up and put all of this behind us?*

"Jess," I venture, "could I trouble you for a glass of water?"

"Of course," she says, bringing the water pitcher and a glass to the bed tray.

Before she can turn away, I reach for her hand, ignoring the painful protest from my broken ribs. "Please," I plead, "can we talk?"

"What is there to say?" she asks, hurt coloring her words. "I believe you've made your feelings perfectly clear."

"I never meant to hurt you. Please believe me."

"Do you really expect me to believe that after what you've done?"

"What exactly have I done, Jessica?"

"Please, Becca, let's not go there. It will only make things worse."

My head is throbbing and I know I'm in no condition to have this conversation but if not now, when? I can't go on like this. The stress is killing me—literally. It's a prime factor in systemic lupus, aggravating every symptom. If I didn't love Jessica like a sister, maybe I could just ignore things but I do love her and I can't just let our friendship die; not if there's any way to restore it.

Humbling myself, I say, "I'm sorry, Jess. Truly I am."

Her back is to me and for a minute I don't think she's going to respond, then she turns to face me, her countenance full of conflict. "What is it that you are truly sorry for?"

I pretend I don't know what she means, but of course, I do. She's talking about her abortion and the resulting infertility. She wants to know if I'm sorry for blaming her for what she did so many years ago and for thinking that she doesn't deserve to have a child. I hate myself for feeling this way but I can't help it. I will never understand how anyone could kill an innocent child before birth no matter the circumstances. I've fought my feelings for years but Jessica's decision will always be indefensible to me and I can't pretend otherwise.

Finally, I manage to say, "I'm sorry for hurting you."

Without a word, she turns her back to me and walks to the window. Her shoulders begin to quiver, then she is sobbing softly, a sound so sad I think my heart will break. "What was I supposed to do?" she asks, her voice muted. "He was my stepfather and a United States Senator to boot."

Stunned, I try to comprehend what she just said. All these years, I thought Bobby Henthorn was the baby's father.

From across the room, she continues her tearful confession while staring out the window. "When he came to my room the first time, I tried to tell my mother. She slapped me and called me a liar; accused me of trying to break up her marriage."

My head is spinning. Nothing is as it seemed. Jessica was not promiscuous...

"He gave me the money and told me to get rid of the baby or he would have me put into the juvenile detention center. Of course, he was bluffing but at sixteen I had no way of knowing that."

What have I done? All these years, I have misjudged my dear sweet friend, blaming her for things over which she had little or no control. Against her will, she was abused and manipulated and then forced to have an abortion to cover up the transgressions of another and I never gave her the benefit of a doubt. Not once.

Gritting my teeth against the stabbing pain in my injured ribs, I manage to push myself into a sitting position. After a moment, I scoot off the side of the bed and stand to my feet, swaying dizzily. It's only a few steps to the window where Jess is standing but it requires all of my strength to traverse that short distance. Using my one good arm, I pull her head against my shoulder, doing my best to absorb her pain.

Mingling my tears with hers, I beg her forgiveness. "Please forgive me, Jess, I didn't know. I didn't know."

After a moment, she says, "Let's get you back in bed before you pass out."

Once I'm situated, Jessica goes to the bathroom to try and repair her makeup, leaving me alone with my thoughts and what a hodgepodge they are. Her confession has turned my world upside down, dismantling my carefully constructed understanding of things. Lying on the uncomfortable hospital bed waiting for my pain to recede, I allow my mind to drift. Like slides projected on the screen of my mind, I recall one poignant incident after another. From these, I patch together a history of our relationship and more importantly an updated version of Jessica's childhood.

An illegitimate child, Jessica never knew her father. To this day, her mother refuses to disclose his identity. Jess thinks he must have come from a moneyed family because when she and her mother moved from California to Tulsa, Oklahoma, they suddenly had money to begin a new life. Being both beautiful and ambitious, her mother soon worked her way into the political machinery of the Democratic party. She proved to be a tireless worker, a charming hostess, and an incredible fund-raiser; traits that soon endeared her to the powers that be. Unfortunately, she had little or no time for her precocious daughter and as a result, Jessica became an unofficial member of our family and the sister I never had.

When Jessica was fourteen years old, her mother married the United States Senator from Oklahoma. Recently divorced, with rumors circulating about past indiscretions, he was anxious to create a new image as a family man. Within a week after the wedding, he demanded that Jessica move back home and limit her contact with me and my family. At his insistence, Jess was enrolled at Holland Hall, an elite private school and we saw very little of each other, although, we did continue to talk by telephone, especially when the Senator was in Washington, D.C.

Even though we hardly ever saw each other, I can remember thinking how different Jessica seemed. Normally vivacious, she became moody, withdrawn. Given what I've just learned I can understand why. And following her abortion, she went wild for a while—partying and doing drugs. It all makes sense now. Remembering how quick I was to judge her, a fresh wave of guilt rolls over me.

Jess returns from the bathroom cutting short my painful reminiscing. She has redone her makeup and her game face is firmly in place. It's obvious she doesn't want to revisit her confession, so I honor her feelings being careful not to say anything that might reopen old wounds. Although our relationship is still strained, we have taken a huge step toward restoring it. What I thought was a recent wound has really been festering in Jessica's soul since high school and it will take some time for us to work through twenty years of repressed pain. The fact that she has remained my friend all these years is a testimony to the kind of person she is and it portends good things for the future.

CHAPTER

THIRTY-FOUR

It took almost three days for my head to clear and longer than that for the pain of a broken collarbone and two broken ribs to become manageable but once it did, I began to wish fervently for the comfort of my own bed and a single night of uninterrupted sleep. Yet as much as I want to go home, I know I'm not in any condition to take care of myself. Thomas has suggested hiring a nurse to care for me during the day while he's at the office, but the thought of having a stranger in my home is nearly more than I can bear. I've tried hinting to Mother about coming and helping out for a few weeks but right now, she has a one-track mind. She can't seem to think of anything but Keith and the upcoming wedding. She seems unable to comprehend the seriousness of my illness or the fact that lupus, Prednisone, and broken bones make for a grim prognosis. Instead of it taking six weeks for my bones to heal, I'm looking at ninety days or even longer.

Glancing around the sterile room, I can't help but smile ruefully. After the twins were born, I used to pray for some excuse to spend a few days in the hospital. In my mind, it seemed kind of like a free vacation with 24-hour room service and around-the-clock care. Definitely a dream come true for a frazzled, sleep deprived, young mother of twin infants.

Now my dream has come true and it's not anything like I imagined. There's nothing glamorous about cotton gowns that reveal all your assets, having your fluid input and output measured daily, temperature taken, blood pressure monitored, and never forget your ever-present friend—the IV dispenser. No, this isn't a vacation. It's more like Chinese torture.

It's seven o'clock in the evening, one week after the accident and I've just selected my second novel of the day when I hear a ruckus in the hallway. Although my door is shut, I hear the patter of scurrying feet, followed by excited giggling and hoots of laughter. I'm still wondering what to make of it when my door is suddenly thrust open and a bevy of pajama clad women invade my room. I do my best not to laugh, knowing the pain it will cause me, but I cannot control myself. The thought of The Bunko Babes parading through the halls of St. Francis Hospital in their nighties is nearly more than I can bear, especially, when I catch sight of Autumn.

I'm aghast at my dear friend's attire but she seems completely unfazed. Shamelessly, she sashays around the room in a gorgeous black corseted number with a sheer, flowing skirt over matching, shimmering hosiery. Black satin mules and a feather boa complete the ensemble.

"Where in the world did you get that?" I ask, embarrassed at the thought of her being seen in public in that get up.

Striking a pose, she replies with a straight face, "HotMamas.com."

Jessica has brought a Boom Box and now she hits play and a sultry number fills the room. The Babes begin to clap to the beat and Autumn says, "Out of my way, ladies, a *real* woman is comin' through."

Laughing, The Babes move aside to give the Caucasian "Queen Latifah" plenty of room. Getting caught up in the mood, I say in my best downtown cool, "Lookit chu girl gettin' all down wit yo fine self."

My inept attempt causes Autumn to lose it and she doubles over with laughter, her ample body jiggling. Struggling to keep my own laughter in check, I squeak out, "I can't believe you actually wore that over here, parading through the entire hospital."

Stepping forward, Madison says, "Don't let her fool you, Becca. She ditched her trench coat just outside your door."

"Thank goodness for small mercies."

For a moment, I'm left alone on my bed as they scurry about the room in preparation for tonight's Bunko party.

Watching them set up card tables and unload picnic hampers of food, I'm so filled with gratitude at their kindness I think my heart will burst. The trouble they've gone to on my behalf causes me to tear up and I smile as I survey the room noting their nighties. Of course no one can top Autumn but Michelle, our little mud-sucker turned Bunko Queen, comes close. She's wearing a pair of Big Bird, bright yellow, footed pajamas complete with a bottom-flap for nature calls; her tiny feet wrapped in gigantic Oscar the Grouch slippers.

Unlike Autumn, Michelle did not hide her pajamas beneath an overcoat, thus exposing herself to the curious glances and snide remarks of all who saw her. Her willingness to risk embarrassment on my behalf touches me deeply and I make a mental note to do something special for her as soon as I'm back on my feet. Nothing comes easy for her, except Bunko, and therefore, I especially treasure her efforts.

While we're eating finger foods off of paper plates, I discover that tonight's pajama party was Madison's brainchild and I look at her with admiration. "You're amazing," I say, "especially considering everything."

Flicking me gently on the top of my head, the lace from her elegant dressing gown tickling my nose, she replies, "Oh, pooh! Don't look so surprised. I still know how to have a good time. Besides, 'Bunko in Bed' seemed the only way we were ever going to get back on schedule with you being in the hospital and all."

Feeling suddenly weepy, I give my sweet friend a grateful smile before quickly wiping away the single tear that has slipped down my cheek. "You know us high maintenance gals," I toss in trying to recapture our lighthearted mood. "We're not happy unless we're the center of attention."

"I hear that," Jessica says and The Babes all laugh—the mood restored.

Although it was exhausting, the evening was just what I needed; helping me to get my mind off of myself. If I have too much time alone, I begin to fret about the future, imagining all kinds of dire possibilities. To top things off, I won tonight's competition—a rare occurrence indeed—and The Bunko Babes championship tiara sets on my head at a jaunty angle. Needless to say, I'm feeling pretty good as The Babes repack their things and prepare to go.

One by one, the girls come by to give me a hug and bid me good-bye. Finally, only Mercedes remains and she pulls up a chair beside my bed. "Becca, I'd like to talk with you for a minute; that is, if you're not too tired."

"Of course," I say, willing myself to be attentive even though exhaustion is now laying claim to every fiber of my being. That's one of the most frustrating things about lupus. One minute, you can be absolutely fine and the very next you feel as if you couldn't put one foot in front of the other, not even if your life depended upon it. On my best days, I feel like a sleep-deprived mother of a colicky baby. On my worst days, I'm absolutely helpless. If the house was on fire, I couldn't get up, not even to save my life.

"I don't know how to say this," Mercedes continues, "so I'm just going to blurt it out. You're in no condition to take care of yourself or your family and I would like to help."

Before I can stop myself, I say, "Oh, Mercedes, that's an answer to prayer."

"For me, too," she replies. "With Douglas gone, I have a lot of time on my hands and it's been awfully lonely."

Now that I've had a moment to process her offer, I realize there are a number of logistical things we need to discuss. Before I can say anything, she hurries to assure me of her capabilities. "Being the oldest daughter, I've been working in the home since I was just a child. I'm a very responsible person and I work hard. I know how to cook and clean as well as do laundry. I can do the grocery shopping, run errands, and help with the twins."

When she pauses, I say, "I will need to discuss this with Thomas before making a final decision, but I cannot imagine why he would be opposed." Giving her my best smile, I conclude, "If he is I'll kill him!"

Jumping up, she bends over the bed and gives me a hug, being careful of both my ribs and my collarbone. Giving me a kiss on the cheek, she says, "I'm so happy. I can't wait to tell Douglas."

Her energy and enthusiasm are a little overwhelming, but I can't help thinking she's just what the doctor ordered. Freed from the responsibility of cooking, cleaning, and laundry, I will be able to concentrate on getting well. I'm sure I'll be back to my old self in no time.

When the nurse arrives to give me my bedtime medications, she grins at me and says, "Somebody had fun tonight."

I nod sleepily.

"Friends," she adds, before turning to go, "are a blessing from God and I can see that you are a blessed woman."

So I am, I think, *so I am.*

CHAPTER THIRTY-FIVE

Thomas and the twins are helping Mercedes move her things into the guest suite and I can hear snatches of conversation as they banter back and forth. Brooklyn wanted Mercedes to share her bedroom but I vetoed that, much to Mercedes' relief. Maintaining our normal routines is critical if this is going to work. Besides, as loveable as she is, Brooklyn can get on your nerves. She is quite the talker and has a penchant for being overly dramatic. Even a saint would be hard-pressed to share a room with her for any length of time.

The guest suite, located at the far end of the house, is far more practical. It has its own outside entrance as well as an oversized bedroom with a sitting area and a private bath. This will allow Mercedes a measure of independence while affording us the privacy we also need to function as a family. Mercedes has decided to keep her and Doug's apartment for the time being. If it appears we are going to need her for an extended period of time, she can always sublet it until he returns from Iraq. Besides, her parents are planning on coming for Christmas and they will need a place to stay.

Secretly, I'm hoping that our relationship will prove to be mutually beneficial, providing companionship and comfort for her while Douglas is gone and giving us the assistance we need during my recovery. As always when I think of Doug, I breathe a prayer for his protection. Only God knows how Mercedes would survive if something happened to him.

As soon as they've finished carrying Mercedes' things into the guest suite, Thomas and Robert excuse themselves, leaving the unpacking and settling in to the girls. The thought of it worries me some knowing how volatile Brooklyn can be if she doesn't get her way. She has definite ideas about how things should be done and I can only hope that Mercedes is strong enough to handle her. *Oh well,* I think, *if Mercedes can't handle her, the sooner we realize that the better.*

Brooklyn isn't malicious but she is strong-willed and highly opinionated. I love her without question, but there are definitely times when I could pinch her head off. When it comes to decorating her room or buying clothes, I've had to learn to back off. She has definite opinions and will defend her tastes to the death. As far as I'm concerned, the key to parenting a strong-willed child like her is knowing what's negotiable and what's nonnegotiable. If it's just about taste, I give in, but if it involves values, I stand firm. That one key has improved our relationship enormously.

At first, I try to pass the time watching television and then I attempt to read a book but I can't concentrate. No matter what I'm doing my mind is with the girls in the guest suite at the other end of the house but I don't have the energy to go there. Upon leaving the hospital, Thomas suggested renting a wheelchair until I recovered from my injuries but I nixed that idea. Now, I wish I had listened to him. Given another chance, I would choose mobility over vanity anytime! Instead of being confined to my bedroom, I could be in the guest suite with Mercedes and Brooklyn.

As it is, I strain my ears listening for the anticipated eruption. To my amazement nearly three hours pass and I haven't heard a peep out of Brooklyn—no melodramatic wailing or the slamming of doors. Nothing. Either Mercedes has allowed Brooklyn to make every decision or she has the guile of a snake charmer. Either way, I'm relieved. Who knows, the two of them may become best of friends.

Finally, I hear them coming down the hall and Brooklyn is talking a mile a minute, as my daddy used to say. "This is Robert's room," she announces. "You don't want to go in there. Trust me."

I smile at her melodramatics but I have to admit she's right. Robert's room is a scary place when it hasn't been cleaned and, as far as I know, no one has touched it since the week-end of the barbeque, more than four weeks ago. I can only hope that Mercedes doesn't change her mind about helping out when she sees what she's up against. I had planned to warn her but it seems little Miss Brooklyn has other ideas.

They must be nearing Robert's door because she says, "Mom and I have labeled this the 'Dead Zone.'" I hear her knock soundly once before throwing the door open.

"What's going on?" Brooklyn squeals.

Nonchalantly, Robert replies, "I don't know what you're talking about, sweet lil' sis."

"You cleaned your room," our little drama queen accuses.

"Of course, I cleaned my room. What do you think I am, a slob?"

Without another word, she storms out of his room and down the hall toward her own. I hear her door slam and I can't help thinking that she's far too competitive. Having planned on humiliating Robert in front of Mercedes, she's had the tables turned on her and she doesn't like it one bit. I can only imagine what Mercedes must be thinking and then I remember that she grew up in a family with several children and I relax. Sibling rivalry isn't anything new to her.

A minute later, she knocks on my bedroom door and I bid her come in. Although she's dressed casually in a pair of cutoffs and a T-shirt, her youthfulness and natural beauty make her look radiant. Next to her I feel like an old shoe, especially since my broken collarbone makes it nearly impossible for me to do my hair or put on makeup. Thankfully, the drapes are closed, casting the room in soft light making the contrasts in our appearances less obvious. That this should matter to me is silly I know but it does.

Pulling up a chair next to the chaise lounge where I am reclining, she gives me a warm smile. "Thank you, Becca," she says. "I feel better already. That empty apartment was just about to do me in."

Studying her profile in the dim light, I can't help thinking that she's grown a lot since learning that Douglas was being called into active duty. For two weeks, they were required to attend orientation classes here in Tulsa and then Douglas was sent to (Ft. Leonard Wood) where he underwent four weeks of intense training. Ten days ago, he returned to Tulsa for one week before being deployed to Iraq. Through all of that Mercedes has matured, becoming a remarkable young woman of faith and a passionate prayer warrior, her Argentine heritage standing her in good stead.

"I'm glad you're here," I banter back, trying to be light-hearted, "I don't think I could survive another week of Thomas' cooking."

We both laugh.

"You better watch what you're saying," Thomas teases, having overheard the last remark from the doorway.

"What have you heard from Douglas?" I ask as Thomas takes a seat on the foot of the bed.

"Not much," Mercedes replies, a tremor in her voice. "He sent an email to let me know that he had arrived safely but that's all."

She's trying to be brave but I can hear the fear in her voice. With good reason too, given what's happening in Baghdad. Squeezing her hand, I say, "The Lord will protect him. We have to believe that."

Uncomfortable with the direction of our conversation, Thomas claps his hands saying, "Let's get down to business." Reaching into his shirt pocket, he removes two sheets of lined paper and unfolds them. Addressing Mercedes, he continues, "There's almost no food in the house so I've prepared a grocery list. Here's my debit card. Why don't you take Brooklyn and head over to Reasor's at 71st and Sheridan?"

Once she has gone, I turn to Thomas. "Why did you do that?"

"What are you talking about? What did I do?"

"You interrupted our conversation and you sent her away."

"I don't want her upsetting you with all that talk about the war in Iraq. That's the last thing you need. Given everything that's happened this year, it's all I can do to keep your spirits up."

Irritated, I demand, "What makes you think you know what I need?"

Holding up his hands, he says, "Wait a minute. Where did that come from?"

Taking a deep breath to calm my rising anger, I reply, "Thomas, you mean well, I know that, but it's not working. You can't make me better by pretending my illness isn't life-threatening. You and I both know that my immune system thinks that my internal organs are infected and it is attacking itself. If the doctors can't get this disease under control, I'm going to die. Laughing and joking isn't going to change that."

Reaching for the bag of Hershey's kisses that is nestled on the mahogany side table among my Bible, the latest John Grisham book, my meds, and a chilled bottle of Fiji water, Thomas extracts a single silver wrapped kiss. Holding it in the palm of his hand, he says, "For you, my Queen, a kiss to calm your fears, to quiet your heart, and a kiss to ease your pain. Above all, a kiss to assure you, Milady, of my undying love."

"Stop it, Thomas!" I scream.

Caught off guard by the intensity of my emotions, he reaches for me but I push him away with my one good arm. "Don't!," I hiss. "Don't you touch me."

For the first time ever, I see my own fear mirrored in his eyes and it gives me hope. Maybe, just maybe, I can make him understand. "Thomas, this isn't going away. We have to deal with it."

"I can't," he wails, a heart-wrenching sob nearly choking him. "I can't deal with the thought of you dying."

With that he lunges to his feet and flees the bedroom leaving me alone with the reality of my disease and the possibility of my death.

Thomas is not a bad man, nor even an insensitive one, but like many of our generation, he has always used humor to keep reality at bay. I've been a willing accomplice; I'll admit that but no more. The things I've faced this past year have convinced me that laughter can only take us so far. At some point, we have to come to grips with reality. To do that we need faith and at least one person who will walk through the valley of the shadow of death with us. I had hoped Thomas could be that person for me but....

Reaching for my Bible, I hug it to my chest, drawing strength from the promises it contains. With God's help, I can do this. Picking up my pen, I make a list of the things I must do. 1) Write letters to each of the children. 2) Make a will. 3) Purchase a burial plot and pick out a casket. On second thought, I cross out casket. That can wait. I'm not trying to be morbid but if Daddy's death taught me anything at all, it taught me to be prepared. It's the least I can do for those I love.

CHAPTER

THIRTY-SIX

I awake in pain, feeling as if I haven't rested at all. That's the way it's been every morning since the accident. I'm regaining a little strength but my broken ribs still make it impossible for me to sleep in my California King. Instead, I spend my nights on the chaise lounge, a castle of pillows around me. I've tried the recliner in the living room but it doesn't work as well; besides I like sleeping in the same room with Thomas.

From the kitchen, I smell the rich aroma of freshly brewed coffee and I can hear Thomas moving about in the bathroom as he completes his morning shower and shave. Although

Mercedes has only been with us a few days, she's already proven invaluable. Not only are we eating healthier but the house is cleaner than it has been in years. I'm not just talking about straight but deep down clean. Best of all, she and Brooklyn are inseparable.

The only fly in the ointment is my old adversary—jealousy. Seeing how well the family functions without me makes me feel more than a little insecure, like they don't need me. I know I'm being silly but I can't deny what I feel. Still, I refuse to give into those feelings. Instead, I am determined to take every thought captive, bringing them into submission to Jesus Christ.

Although I've been a Christian for as long as I can remember, this is really the first time I've ever had to rely on my faith. Medically speaking, systemic lupus is incurable. The best medical science can offer is the management of the disease through medication and lifestyle. In the face of such a grim prognosis, I've turned more and more to my faith, looking to God for my healing. *And if I'm not healed, I am determined to praise Him for the promise of His presence in my life; for the promise that He will be with me in sickness as He was with me in health. If worse comes to worse, and I am faced with imminent death, I am determined to praise Him for the promise of eternal life. I will praise Him in all things and at all times. I will for He is worthy to be praised no matter what is happening in my life!*

Speaking of which, I have to admit that Thomas and I are hardly speaking at the moment. Without humor and silliness, it seems we don't know how to talk to each other. Given my situation, I've had time to do a lot of thinking and I can only conclude that for years we have used laughter to avoid dealing with the tough issues. If something was too painful, we would use humor to distract ourselves. It was an effective way of avoiding our problems but it never solved anything. I still like to laugh but I can't afford to pretend I'm not seriously ill just to protect Thomas' feelings.

My musings are cut short as Thomas exits the bathroom followed by a haze of steam and the fragrance of Grey Flannel cologne. Silently, I watch him get dressed, longing for the comfortable banter of a few days ago but not willing to return to our make-believe world in order to recapture it. Picking up his keys, he grabs his wallet on the way out the bedroom door.

"Hey," I call after him, "what about a good-bye kiss?"

He doesn't even bother to answer and it only takes an instant for my astonishment to turn into anger, my earlier spiritual thoughts notwithstanding. Even though I know Thomas is hurting, I can't find much sympathy in my heart for him at the moment. His continued refusal to acknowledge the seriousness of my illness or to allow me to talk about it has isolated me when I need him most. I have tried to be patient but this is getting old.

Without consciously intending to, I find myself remembering what Autumn did when her husband was, in her words, acting like a donkey. Who knows, maybe there's a way I can use something like that to bring Thomas to his senses.

As I recall, Autumn was six months pregnant and miserable. One evening, she was late getting dinner on the table and Rodney asked her what she had *done* all day. Big mistake, huge! Without a word she walked out, leaving him with seven kids to care for and a goat to milk. Getting into her dilapidated VW van, she drove around until she cooled down enough to formulate a plan. That's when she showed up at my house.

Knowing Rod's penchant for beginning his day with the classified section of the *Tulsa World,* she decided to place an ad. It appeared the following day:

> *Husband seeks assistance with pregnant wife, seven children, and small farm. Chores include cooking, cleaning, laundry, weeding the garden, milking the goat, wet nursing, homeschooling, and yard chores. Candidate must be willing to work for room and board only with no hope of advancement. If interested, please contact Rod Levitt at: Iamindeeptrouble@hotmail.com.*

Although the ad generated no applicants, it did produce a number of interesting emails, several of them from irate women. Apparently, Rob learned his lesson. To my knowledge, he's never again questioned how Autumn spends her time. And just in case he's ever tempted, there's a framed copy of the ad prominently displayed on the living room wall above the couch, surrounded by the children's birth certificates.

Of course, I would never do anything like that, especially since Thomas has been so supportive, at least for the most part. Still, recalling the incident has diffused my anger and I'm chuckling softly when Mercedes knocks on the bedroom door. "What are you grinning about?" she asks, coming to my side. I tell her and we both have a good laugh, imagining Rob milking the goat while trying to corral seven rowdy kids.

Taking my good arm, she helps me to my feet, being careful of my broken collarbone. Slowly, we make our way to the kitchen where she has prepared a breakfast of whole wheat toast, fresh fruit, and cheese. She nearly gags when I ask her to bring me the bag of powered sugar for my strawberries. Laughing, I tell her, "You can take away my pop tarts, but don't you dare touch my sugar!"

Two hours later, I am back in my chaise lounge trying to find a position where my ribs don't hurt. Mercedes has taken Brooklyn to the mall to shop for school clothes and Robert is at football practice, leaving me alone in the house. Try as I might, I cannot get over the fact that Thomas went to the office without kissing me good-bye. He's never done that in all the years we've been married. I cannot help worrying about the toll this disease is taking on our marriage. I've read the divorce statistics for couples who are dealing with lupus and they're not good.

I know I'm overreacting but I can't seem to help myself. In desperation, I reach for the phone and punch in Autumn's number. Today, I don't need answers or advice. I just want someone who will listen to me and love me, even in my misery. In the whole world, there's no one better at that than my oldest friend. Although we are as different as fire and ice, she understands me like no one else and more importantly, she accepts me.

The telephone rings several times and I'm just about to hang up when she finally answers, her voice comforting to my ear.

"Hey, you," I say, not trusting myself to say more.

Instantly attuned, Autumn responds, "Tough day?"

Closing my eyes, I sigh, grateful for her sensitivity. "That obvious, huh?"

"Only to me."

There's a scuffle in the background and she says, "Hold on a sec, 'kay?"

There's a loud "thunk" as she sets the receiver down. I can't help thinking, she's probably one of the few people in America who still owns a rotary dial telephone. It's big, black, and heavy like those you see on reruns of "The Andy Griffith Show" and other television classics.

"Chaos contained," Autumn reports rather breathlessly. "I'm all yours, at least for the next few minutes."

"I don't know how you do it," I say for the umpteenth time.

"Yeah, I know," she replies. "So what gives?"

"I'm just having a really hard day."

"Problems with Mercedes?"

"Heavens no, she's incredible! I don't know what we would do without her."

"That's good. Now are we going to play twenty questions or are you going to tell me what's troubling you?"

In a halting voice, I tell her about Thomas and me and the terrible stress this disease is putting on our marriage. I tell her I've gained twelve pounds since I got on the Prednisone and that I'm outgrowing all my clothes. I tell her that I feel worthless, washed up, weak as a kitten, fat as a cow, and dumb as a mule. I can't cook, I can't clean, and to top it all off…I can't even shop anymore! This last line is delivered through a mixture of laughter and tears.

"Oh, Becca," Autumn says, laughing with me, "you can be so melodramatic."

There's no judgment in her voice, just compassion and understanding and I feel better already. No matter what I do, or how ugly I feel, or how miserably I fail, she sees only the promise of who I'm becoming. She's one of those rare people who can know the worst and still, believe the best.

"You have our Father's eyes," I whisper.

"What?" Autumn asks.

"You have our Father's eyes," I say again, this time louder, with more conviction. "Like the Amy Grant song, remember?"

"Oh, yeah." Autumn hums a few bars and then begins to sing in a husky, slightly off-key voice. I join in trying to help her locate a key, any key.

We sing along humming when we can't recall the words. Gradually, our singing fades replaced by the ever-present crackling of the telephone line.

After a moment, she says, "You have His eyes as well, you know."

Choking up, I treasure her compliment. Still, I can't help wondering if it's deserved. *Do I have eyes full of compassion? Eyes that see good when no one else can?* At one time, I thought I did but lately it's been so hard. Still, I am determined, with God's help, to see others through His eyes, to try and see them as He does.

A loud clang can be heard in the background and I know my time is officially up. The walls have been breached. Fighting back my disappointment, I remind myself that I, too, once had small children, two of them at the same time, the same exact age, and everything was in complete disarray.

Sympathetically, I quip, "Houston, we have a problem," before saying a quick good-bye and touching the "End" button on my cell phone.

Setting with the now silent cell phone in my lap, I reflect on our conversation, marveling again at how Autumn can always make me feel better. Sure, maybe, I'd like it better if she would tell me that I'm irreplaceable, brilliant, beautiful, and the best shopper west of the Mississippi. You know, things that "really" matter in life. But truthfully, being told that I have my Father's eyes is the highest compliment I could ever hope to receive.

THIRTY-SEVEN

The past few days have been difficult but Thomas and I are finally getting things worked out, or maybe I should say we have come to an understanding. I've had to accept the fact that he will not discuss the possibility of my death; he simply isn't emotionally able to deal with it at this time. I'm bothered by this, but I'm not willing to let it destroy our relationship. For his part, Thomas has agreed to let me make whatever preparations I feel are necessary. He's even gone so far as to set up an appointment for me with the attorney who handles the wills and estates for the executives of the Williams Company where he's worked for the past twelve years. Hopefully, with God's help, we will beat this disease and all of these preparations will prove unnecessary; still, I will feel better knowing I've taken care of them.

It's been five weeks since my accident and I am about to go stir crazy being confined to this house. Having Mercedes here has helped but if I don't get out, I think I will lose my mind. I'm a people person and all of this solitude is driving me crazy. For my first venture back into the real world, I've decided to attend Bunko night at Karen's. I still can't drive but Jessica is coming by for me since Mercedes headed over early to help set things up. Now that it's almost time to go, I'm starting to feel guilty.

Turning to Thomas, I ask, "Are you sure you don't mind? We could take the kids and catch a movie or get some dinner if you like."

Shaking his head in amusement, he says, "Go on, we'll be fine."

When I still hesitate, he steps across the room and puts his finger under my chin. Lifting my head, he looks deep into my eyes, "Becca, I want you to go. You need it. Don't worry about us. We'll be fine."

Giving me a gentle nudge, he starts me out the bedroom door and down the hall before hollering, "Kids, say good-bye to your mom."

Brooklyn pokes her head out of her bedroom door just long enough to say, "Bye, Mom. Love you." Robert simply calls a good-bye over his shoulder, never looking up from his video game.

Hurt by their nonchalance, I glare at Thomas. Shrugging, he gives me one of his famous "What can I say?" looks.

Placing his hand on the small of my back, he propels me down the hall to the front door. "They're growing up, Honey," he says, "you knew it was going to happen."

Wistfully, I reply, "I just didn't think it would happen so fast."

Knowing Jessica is waiting, I give him a quick peck on the cheek before pasting a brave smile on my face but I can't fool my friend. Once I have gotten settled in the Saab, she asks teasingly, "Why so glum, Doodlebum?" Without waiting for me to respond, she shifts into reverse and backs out of the driveway.

Staring straight ahead, I have eyes only for what I see on the screen of my mind. Brooklyn with a cell phone glued to one ear and an ear bud from her ever-present iPod in the other. Robert, leaning forward, dark hair falling over his forehead as he concentrates on his latest video game. Finally, I reply morosely, "My babies are growing up."

"How dare they!" she says, feigning outrage. "The least they could have done was to ask first."

Her irreverent humor is just what I need, jerking me from my melancholy mood. Laughing, I say, "I don't know what I'm complaining about. I've been praying for them to grow up for years so I can get my life back!"

Soon we are bantering back and forth as we zip down the Creek Nation Turnpike. It's like old times—before I got sick, before Jessica and I had our falling out—and I'm grateful for every smile, for every kind word and touch that she shares with me. I don't deserve her friendship or her forgiveness, yet she has given me both for years.

"Thank you for being my friend," I say, reaching for Jessica's hand and giving it a squeeze. "You're an amazing woman and the closest thing to a sister I'll ever have." Suddenly, I am seized with a certainty, a knowing I can't explain or deny, and before I can stop myself I blurt out, "Someday you're going to make a wonderful mother, Jess. I just know it."

Taking her eyes off the road for just a moment, she gives me a skeptical look.

"I don't know how," I stammer, "but I just know you're going to have a child. Adoption, maybe? It only takes a little faith."

"A little faith," she replies in a shaky voice.

Gripping her hand tightly, I raise our fists in triumph, reaching as high as I can given my injuries. Together, we repeat in rhythm, "Just a little bit of faith."

I toss in a sassy, "Oh, yeah," and before we know it we've got ourselves a white girls rap goin'. "Just a little bit of faith….oh, yeah," I continue, at half my normal voice, while Jessica pounds out a mean beat on the steering wheel of her Saab.

"That's all it takes…oh, yeah,…just a little bit of faith…."

Every few seconds, my fantabulous friend tosses in a little boom-chicka-boom thang to keep it real.

I know we're acting like a couple of teenagers, but it feels good to just let our hair down and be silly. Besides, we've been doing this sort of thing since we were kids. By the time we arrive at Karen's house, I'm feeling better than I have in weeks, months really and it seems Jessica is too, although, I can never be sure given her penchant for disguising her deepest feelings. Still, she seems different and I have to believe that sharing her most shameful secret has somehow set her free. Learning the truth about what really happened has certainly changed me; teaching me that things are not always as they appear and that it is dangerous to rush to judgment. *Thank God for His mercy and for Jessica's.*

After parking in Karen's driveway, Jessica leaves the Saab running, allowing us to check our makeup in air-conditioned comfort. Reverting to a ritual we perfected as teenagers, we open the visor mirrors in synchronized rhythm. Like mirrored images, we quickly pass a finger gently under each eye, run our tongue over the top row of teeth, then the bottom, smile cheesily, place our forefinger in our mouth pulling it carefully through our lips to remove excess lipstick and ensure it won't get back on our teeth. Finally, we pucker-up and give ourselves a wink. In perfect synchronization, we shut the mirrors, flip up the visors, nod, and open our respective doors, all the while giggling like schoolgirls.

Coming around the car, Jessica says, "We haven't lost our touch, Sweetheart." And I can't help thinking how good it feels to shed our responsibilities for a few hours and just be silly.

Linking arms, we make our way up the walk to Karen's perfectly maintained Tudor style home. As always, the lawn is lush, the walks perfectly edged, and her flower beds are festooned with a rainbow of blooming plants, all perfectly spaced. I know they have a lawn service but Karen insists on doing her own flower beds. *How,* I wonder, *does a working mother of three girls, all under the age of five, keep a flower bed so meticulously? I can only conclude that she's a better woman than I am.*

"Wow," Jess mouths at me, apparently thinking the same thing.

The front door stands open invitingly, the storm door cutting out most of the suffocating September heat. Jess gives the obligatory knock, then opens the glass door. Heading for the kitchen, she calls, "Hello, is anybody home?" Feigning exhaustion, she tosses her store-bought cookies on the countertop before collapsing on one of the barstools. "I hope you ladies appreciate those cookies," she says. "I've slaved over a hot stove all day to make them especially for you."

Karen steps into the kitchen just in time to hear her last remark and hastens to enlighten Jessica to the fact that most cookies are baked in an oven and not on top of the stove. "Of course," she continues while setting the plates and flatware on the counter, "there are the infamous 'No-Bake Cookies' that are made on top of the stove. And let us not forget, Rice Krispy Treats—my children's favorites."

Tapping her on the shoulder, Jessica hands her the package of Keebler Grasshopper cookies. "What about these," she asks, "stove top or oven?"

Realizing she's been had, Karen's face flushes slightly but she just smiles and says with great poise, "I should have known. Jessica bake? We'd have a better chance of getting Becca to pass up a shoe sale."

We all laugh, except Madison, who is busy at the stove where she is warming up her yummy homemade sweet and sour sauce for the Chinese meat balls she's prepared. I would have zapped it in the microwave but not Madison. She claims it compromises the flavor. Be that as it may, I make a beeline for her.

I know these past weeks haven't been easy and with the accident I haven't been able to be there for her like I normally would. Coming up behind her, I rest my chin on her shoulder and quietly inquire, "How's ya doin', girlfriend?"

Lifting her ever elegant hand to my face, she pats my cheek before pulling my head closer to hers for a little squeeze. "I have good days and bad days," she says, giving me a sad smile. "I wish I could tell you the good days outweigh the bad but I can't."

Turning back to the stove, she continues stirring for a minute more, and then she adds, with an attempt at gallows humor, "They say divorce is like a death only you never get to bury the body."

I manage the obligatory chuckle, but I can see she's hurting in ways I can't even imagine. "That bad, huh?"

"Worse," she says, her words coming out in a rush. "Michael is making things so difficult. Now, he wants joint custody of the children. Why, I don't know. He hardly spent anytime with them when he was living at home. If he gets joint custody, they'll be spending half their time in daycare. I don't want to believe it but sometimes, I think he's doing it just to hurt me."

She's stirring furiously, blinking back her tears. I don't know what to say so I just put my arm around her waist and hold her. Finally, she speaks in a voice raw with emotion, "I hate what this is doing to me. I'm becoming such a negative person."

"You're not being negative, Maddy, you're just being real. Michael has jerked the rug out from under you, so to speak, and you're just trying to find your way."

Before I can say more, Karen calls from the dining room, "Is that sauce just about ready?"

"Coming," Madison says, lifting the pot off the stove and heading for the dining room. I shut off the burner and follow, reciting a portion of Scripture under my breath. (Yes, I do know a few scriptures by heart.) I quote it for myself and for Madison; reminding myself that God knows about our situations and that He has promised to rescue us.

Pausing at the door to the dining room, I breathe a quick prayer. *"Hurry, Lord Jesus,"* I pray, *"hurry and rescue us."*

CHAPTER

THIRTY-EIGHT

Mercedes has just finished telling us how Douglas proposed to her and how God miraculously provided Douglas with an engagement ring for her and my head is still spinning. I thought things like that only happened in the Bible. While I'm still trying to fit it into my twenty-first century, high-tech worldview, Karen calls for our attention as she prepares to present the tiara to Jessica who is tonight's winner.

The saucy mother of three is standing on a small wooden step stool, tiara firmly in hand. Assuming a pseudo-official posture, she announces, "It is with great pleasure that I bestow upon Jessica Goldstein this most coveted crown. It is to be worn with pride and dignity until next week, when once again, we will compete for the weekly Bunko championship and the right to wear The Bunko Babes' crown." Bending her knees slightly, Jessica lowers herself to Karen's petite height, allowing her to place the dollar-store tiara snugly upon her head. Stepping down from her pedestal, Karen lifts high her glass of sparkling apple cider and salutes.

"To the Queen!"

"To the Queen!" we repeat, lifting our glasses high in return.

Jessica is enjoying every minute of it, her eyes sparkling like London Blue topaz set off to perfection by the high gloss of her pitch-black tresses. Watching my friend, the tiara catching the light and casting flashes of rainbows across the floor, I smile thinking how incredibly beautiful she is and how blessed I am that she is a part of my life.

Feeling the weight of my stare, she turns and gives me a sassy grin, "Sorry, Becca. Better luck next time."

"Enjoy it while you can," I respond playfully.

Not wanting to be left out, Autumn pantomimes the irrefutably annoying paparazzi, making a whirring sound just like the motor drive on a fine camera. Striking a pose, Jessica is instantaneously in character, waving and blowing kisses to her adoring public before dashing through a doorway and out of the prying eyes of her fans. We all laugh uproariously, thoroughly enjoying the spontaneous performance.

They both curtsy, charmed by the applause.

"Encore, encore," we shout.

Autumn replies laughingly, "Sorry, dear friends, but true genius cannot be repeated."

"Aah," I say, "a one-hit wonder."

Surprised at my quick wit, Jessica says, "Very good. I'm impressed."

That's a high compliment coming from Jess, who happens to be the reigning champion of comebacks. "Thank you," I return smugly, "I learned from the best."

"Bet your beetles, Babe," she adds with a wink.

"Right as rain, alligator," I conclude, more content with my life than I have been in longer than I care to remember. I'm so glad I didn't stay home tonight, no matter how tired I'm feeling right now.

Seeing the party is about to break up, Madison says, "There's one other thing I'd like for us to discuss before we go. As most of you know, Michelle won the regional Bunko championship in Nashville which qualifies her for the Nationals in Las Vegas."

"No!" I scream, delighted for my young friend.

Breaking into a gigantic grin, she says, "Can you believe it? Your little mud-sucker is going to Vegas."

"Woohoo!" I shout, wishing desperately that I could jump up and down in celebration. Since I can't, I order the others to do it for me.

Instantly, they erupt into cheers, dancing around giving each other high fives and hip-smacks; just being crazy in an attempt to show support for our Mighty Mouse. She's only slightly embarrassed by all the attention and glowing with pleasure, as I am for her.

"Order," Madison calls above the din, laughing with genuine pleasure for the first time this evening.

After The Babes have settled down, she continues, "Since Michelle will be representing The Bunko Babes in Vegas I think we should raise the money to send her."

We erupt in another round of cheers and Madison waits for us to settle down before continuing. "I would like to volunteer to host a garage sale at my house. We can all contribute things and the proceeds will all go toward covering Michelle expenses. So, what do you think?"

We spend another fifteen or twenty minutes discussing the details—setting a date, assigning tasks, etc. By now, the evening's activities are starting to take their toll on me and I'm grateful when Jessica excuses herself to drive me home while the other Babes pitch in to help put Karen's house back in order.

Once in the Saab, I lean my seat back and close my eyes. Knowing how exhausted I am, Jessica drives in silence, the haunting music from the soundtrack *Somewhere in Time* covering the road noise. My mind drifts, replaying the events of the evening, finally settling on the story Mercedes told. I still don't know quite what to make of it so I venture a question. "Hey, Jess? What's your take on that whole engagement ring thing?"

"You mean the Doug and Mercedes fairy tale? With the engagement ring, UPS, no return address, God-provided thing?"

"That's the one."

"I believe it but only because it came from Mercedes. I mean, who ever heard of a diamond engagement ring just showing up in the mail?"

"Actually, it was UPS who delivered it."

"Whatever. Anyway, like I was saying it just sounds too good to be true, but I can't imagine Mercedes making something like that up."

"It just doesn't seem possible," I muse. "Since 9-11 UPS requires a return address on every package they ship."

"Are you suggesting Mercedes is lying?"

"No, but maybe she got her facts mixed up."

"What do you mean?"

"The package came to Douglas rather than to her, didn't it?

"That's what she said."

"Okay, then maybe there was a return address and Douglas just failed to mention it."

"I suppose that's a possibility. Still, I think we're missing the point here. However it was sent, God supplied Mercedes with a ring!"

We drive in silence for a moment, each of us lost in our own thoughts. Sighing deeply, I say, "It's so romantic."

"Isn't it," Jess responds, before adding, "who knew God was romantic?"

"Not me," I say, "definitely not me."

Turning pensive, Jessica says, "You know what our problem is, we're too self-reliant. Instead of trusting God, we just whip out the 'ole credit card. It's like, who needs God if you have Visa?"

"It's the fasting thing that would do Thomas in," I reply, only half in jest. "He would rather work a month of overtime than miss a meal. Besides with overtime, you know what you're going to get. With fasting and prayer, you never know what's going to happen."

"I guess, I've just always thought that God had more important things to concern Himself with than what size rock I have on my finger. But, hey, what do I know?"

Exiting the Creek Nation Turnpike onto Yale Ave., Jessica heads north toward 71st Street. After a moment, I say, "I'll tell you what...If UPS delivered a ring to Thomas with no return address and no way to track who sent it, I'd be calling them every single day and telling them exactly what Brown could do for me."

Picking up my cell phone, I pretend to make a call, "Hello, UPS?" I ask in my best snooty voice. "Yes, Brown can bring me the newest collection from Harry Winston Jewels, please. Overnight delivery. Name? Thornton, the soon-to-be Mrs. Thomas Thornton. You know the address. Yesterday, you delivered a flawless one-and-a-half carat diamond platinum engagement ring. Yes, yes, that's the place. Thank you so very much. And, oh, could you possibly toss in a couple pairs of the newest of Jimmy Choo shoes? You know, the ones fresh off the runway. I've just got to have them. I'm sure you've got my size on record somewhere."

We both laugh, before turning serious again. "Becca," Jessica says, her tone earnest, "I want to know God the way Mercedes knows Him. I want to know that He really cares about the things that concern me."

The traffic light turns red and Jessica brakes the Saab, pulling into the left turn lane before coming to a stop. Putting on the turn signal she looks at me, waiting for my response. Finally, I say, "I keep thinking that if God cares that much about a measly ring, then He must care about my sickness and about your infertility."

The light turns green and Jess makes a left onto 71st Street and we drive the rest of the way to my house in silence, each of us contemplating what it would mean to really trust God; to trust not only His sufficiency but His wisdom. Much of what I'm feeling is too deep for words, I couldn't explain it to Jess if I tried, so I just squeeze her hand and whisper good-bye. I watch until the Saab's taillights disappear around the corner and then close the door, sensing that something of eternal significance has happened tonight.

CHAPTER

THIRTY-NINE

The kids are back in school and life has settled into a comfortable routine at the Thornton household, thanks in no small part to Mercedes. It's amazing how effortlessly she has melded into our family—like she's always been a part. Weekday mornings, always frenzied heretofore, now run like clockwork. The same kids, who refused to get out of bed for me, now hop up without any prompting. They're at the table by seven A.M. ready to devour the well-balanced breakfast Mercedes has prepared. All I can do is sit back, shake my head, and thank the Lord for small blessings.

I shared breakfast with the fam for the first week but after that I decided to take advantage of this wonderful gift while I still could. Now, 'Cedes and I have our breakfast between nine and ten and then we have a devotional time together and prayer. Although I'm nearly old enough to be her mother, she has a spiritual maturity I can only wish I had. Having been part of the great Argentine revival, she's experienced things I've only read about in the Bible. When she first came to live with us, I envisioned myself becoming a spiritual mentor to her. Now, I think it's the other way around.

Glancing at the clock, I realize it's that time again and I carefully roll over and ease myself into a sitting position on the edge of the bed. My injuries are healing but it will be some time yet before I'm fully recovered. Still, I'm thankful for the progress I'm making. I can't tell you how wonderful it feels to finally be able to sleep in my own bed again. After six weeks of trying to sleep sitting up in my beautiful chaise lounge, I was ready to throw the thing out!

After pulling on my robe, I grab my pill case off the bathroom counter and head for the kitchen where 'Cedes will have a steaming cup of *coffee con leche* waiting for me. We now drink only the best coffees from Argentina, supplied by her family, and after drinking it, I don't think I'll ever think of Starbucks in the same way again.

Entering the kitchen, I'm surprised to find Mercedes seated at the table in the breakfast nook reading what appears to be a lengthy email. When I greet her, she hastily gets to her feet and hurriedly prepares my coffee, adding just the right amount of hot milk. The sugar, she leaves to me and I add several heaping spoonfuls much to her dismay.

She's apologetic as she bustles around the kitchen preparing breakfast. "I'm so sorry," she says, "I guess I lost track of the time."

"No problem," I say, taking a sip of my sinfully sweet coffee. Holding the mug snuggly between my two palms, I savor the entire experience—sight, sound, aroma, and taste. For me, coffee is about so much more than just something to drink. It's about relationships and revelations—a chance to share your heart with those closest to you.

While she cooks, I take inventory of my body. I'm still gaining weight and my face is badly broken out but I don't feel any worse than I did before the accident, except for my injuries, of course. I may not be getting any better yet but it does appear I have stopped my downward plunge or at least significantly slowed it down. *"Let it be so, Lord,"* I pray, *"let it be so."*

Turning my attention back to Mercedes, I watch as she places three slices of bacon on a paper towel and carefully blots the grease. On an impulse, I go to the counter and butter four slices of bread before sprinkling them with a generous amount of sugar and cinnamon. Placing them on a cookie sheet, I slide them into the oven and set it on broil. By the time she has our eggs ready they'll be done and we can enjoy one of my childhood favorites—oven-broiled cinnamon toast.

One thing I can say for the Prednisone, it makes me ravenous and I attack my food with a purpose. Across from me, Mercedes picks at hers, moving it around on her plate but not really eating. Finally I can contain my curiosity no longer so I inquire, "Was that an email from Douglas or did you get some news from home?"

Smiling wistfully, she says, "It was from Douglas."

"And?"

Extracting the folded pages from the pocket of her jeans, she slides them across the table toward me. "Maybe you should read it for yourself."

My heart lurches in my chest and I reach for the email, wondering what it contains that she couldn't bring herself to tell me. Maybe Douglas has gotten into some kind of trouble or worse yet been injured. Before picking up the folded pages, I risk a look at her. She is staring out the window, a pensive look on her face. With trembling hands, I unfold the pages and start to read. In an instant, I realize what she has done and I let out a screech. "You little twit. I'll get you for this."

Grinning, she reaches across the table to retrieve Douglas' email. "So sorry. I didn't realize that you couldn't read Spanish."

Her emotions are mercurial this morning and now her coffee-colored eyes blur with tears. "I miss him so much." Shrugging shyly, she asks, "You understand?"

"Of course, you miss him, Baby Girl. Of course, you do." I reach across the table and touch her hand, offering her what little comfort I can.

"Gracias, Becca, mi amigo. You are truly a blessing in my life."

"De nada," I reply, "Baby Girl, the blessing has been returned tenfold."

Unfolding the email, she gives me a shy smile. "There are some things that are meant only for me."

"Of course."

Clearing her throat she begins to read, her Argentine lilt like music to my ears.

"The flight from DFW to Buenos Aires is a piece of cake compared to what we had to go through to get to Iraq. First, we flew to Dover AFB in Delaware. From there, we flew to Spain where we stayed overnight and finally, into Baghdad. If you think coach class on a 757 is uncomfortable, you should try a C-5 military transport. One good thing was I had my sleeping bag and I could spread it out on the floor and sleep—well sort of.

"I liked Spain a lot and I think you would too. The air base was located in a valley with mountains on both sides. We were there less than twenty-four hours and it rained the whole time so we really couldn't see much but what I could see was beautiful. I struck up a conversation with one young man who

worked in the chow hall and I ended up giving him 'Witness the Passion' by Richard Exley. The Spanish version of course. God's hand at work from day one, amazing, huh?"

Mercedes lifts her dark eyes to mine and I see they are swimming with tears. Giving her an encouraging smile, I say softly, "Douglas' deployment came as no surprise to God. He has His hand on Douglas. He knows just where he is and every step he is taking."

She nods her head and resumes reading:

"We were really tense leaving Spain. No one said anything but we were all thinking about our next stop—Baghdad. For most of us, it would be the first time we had ever been in a war zone. As we neared touch down my tension seemed to increase tenfold. Although we control most of the military installations and airports in Iraq, no plane bearing the American flag is completely safe.

"Iraq is hot! Hotter than anything, I've ever experienced. It hurts to breathe. The air is so hot it burns my nose and throat. The countryside is stark and there's sand everywhere. You can't get away from it no matter where you go! The poverty is the worst I've ever seen and no one is safe from the insurgents, not even the children.

"Yet, as miserable as all of this is, I know this is where I'm supposed to be. The Iraqi people are

desperate for hope. Not just political hope but the eternal hope that only Jesus Christ can give. I don't speak their language and there are regulations against trying to convert anyone but I don't think that will be a problem. The best witness is a life lived loving and serving others and I can do that. "

She stops reading and looks at me, her eyes shining with pride. "There's more but it's personal."

"Thank you for sharing Douglas' email," I say, my voice choked with emotion. "Your Douglas sounds like a real man of God. I can see why you love him so."

"Si," Mercedes manages, dabbing at her damp eyes with a napkin, "he's handsome to and so sexy in his uniform."

CHAPTER

FORTY

The early morning air has a bit of a bite to it, as I clumsily climb into my new Chrysler 300M—my jumbo travel mug of coffee con leche, oversized Kate Spade bag, cell phone, jacket, hat, and key chain making it extremely challenging for me. Having no difficulty herself, Mercedes waits patiently in the passenger seat trying unsuccessfully to control her facetious grin. Finally, she takes mercy on me and helps me get my things into the car.

"Thanks for the help," I say, unable to disguise my irritation.

'Cedes shrugs. "You're the one who keeps complaining about being treated like an invalid..."

She just let's the sentence hang, unfinished. *Dang! She's gotten good at this over the past six weeks.* In spite of myself, I chuckle. "You've been hanging around Brooklyn too much."

"Oh, yeah," Mercedes asks, eyebrows raised, "How can ya tell?"

Giving her a wink, I quip, "You're gettin' sassy."

Heading for 71st Street, we settle into a comfortable silence, each of us lost in our own thoughts. It is early October and we drive with the windows down, enjoying the first hint of fall. Later in the day, the heat will return but not with the vengeance of August. Turning west toward Riverside Drive, I note the absence of traffic at this early hour.

Glancing at Mercedes, I remark, "It looks kinda like a ghost town, doesn't it?"

"Si," she agrees perusing the empty streets. "But then who gets up before six o'clock on a Saturday morning?"

"My point exactly."

Grinning she adds, "As Jessica likes to say, 'Life before lunch is highly overrated.'"

We both laugh.

The normally bustling intersection of 71st and Riverside is ghostly in the gray dawn and once more I'm assailed with second thoughts. *I hope we haven't scheduled this too early.* We merge onto Riverside heading north, then immediately onto Peoria without slowing down. As we drive, I point out historical landmarks and tell Mercedes about taking family portraits in Woodward Park when the fall colors were in full regalia. As we're crossing 21st Street the traffic begins to pick up but I'm so engrossed in my childhood stories that I pay it no mind and nearly rear end a Toyota Prius carrying what looks to be two eco friendly young moms.

Shakily, I say, "Shuy, that was close." Casting my eyes toward the heavens, I thank God for saving me from my carelessness. I mouth an apology to the young women in front of us hoping they can read my lips. Finally, I turn to Mercedes, "I wonder what the holdup is. I hope there hasn't been an accident."

Nearing the corner of 16th and Peoria, I'm amazed to discover that many of the cars are turning into Madison's neighborhood apparently heading for our yard sale. Glancing down at the dash, I check the time. 5:45 A.M. The garage sale doesn't start for another fifteen minutes and already people are lining up. I haven't seen anything like this since I was a kid living in Wolf Creek Estates. Every year, the entire subdivision would have a yard sale and the traffic would be backed up for blocks, as hordes of people descended on our neighborhood. Personally, I could never see the attraction but then I don't like antiques either. As far as I'm concerned, old is old

Pulling into the right lane, I zip around a line of vehicles trying to make a left-hand turn onto 16th and continue a few more blocks before taking a left and meandering through the picturesque neighborhood of Maple Ridge. Nearing

Madison's house cars are lined up on both sides of the street and there's not a parking space in sight. I had hoped to park in Madison's driveway at the back of the house but cars are blocking the entrance so I stop briefly in front of the house and turn the wheel over to Mercedes who drops me off and goes in search of a parking place.

As she drives away I turn toward the house and discover that Madison has erected a ten foot by six foot professionally printed banner in her front yard. It reads, "Yard Sale: Betrayed Wife Sells Sleazebag's Stuff." I nearly choke on my coffee spewing it everywhere, overcome with laughter. "You go, girl!" I shout as I punch the air with my fist several times.

Looking around I see that The Bunko Babes have been hard at work, probably since before daylight for the yard and driveway are covered with merchandise. Noting Michael's custom-made touring bike, his bow-flex total gym machine, and his golf clubs, I can't suppress a smile. Given the quality of the things we're selling, we shouldn't have any trouble raising the money to send Michelle to the National Bunko Championship in Las Vegas.

Making my way to the back door, I knock before letting myself in. I head straight for the kitchen where I see Madison hurriedly putting the finishing touches on an elegant tray of cold cuts, bread, cheese, and fruit. Following her into the garage, I see that she has prepared a refreshment table for her customers. Setting the tray on the table beside a coffee urn and a plate of pastries, she turns to me and asks, "So what do you think?"

Looking at my friend with pride, I stop her busy hands with my own. "I'm proud of you."

"You are?" she inquires, lifting luminous lavender eyes to mine.

I nod.

Impulsively, she hugs me. "Thanks. What do you think he'll do when he discovers what I've done?"

"What can he do?" I ask nonchalantly.

Laughing nervously, she says, "I guess not much."

"Oh, he'll blow and go, get red in the face, threaten another lawsuit, but honestly Madison, what can he really do? Demand half the profits?"

Her eyes downcast, Madison continues to fiddle with the preparations repeatedly rearranging the strawberries.

Again, I still her movements with a gentle touch. "Maddy, look at me."

She does.

"Don't empower him. Remember, he only has as much power as you give him."

She swallows hard against the lump in her throat and I watch helplessly as she battles her own inner demons. At last, she firmly grips my hand and looks me confidently in the eye, before pushing the garage door opener. "Let's do this," she says.

For the next four hours The Bunko Babes work without a break while I sit at the table and collect the money. I'm amazed at the number of people who will pay good money for someone else's discards, although, I do have to admit that the things Madison has donated are first rate, especially Michael's toys. A time or two I thought some of the guys were going to come to blows arguing over his things, the bow-flex machine in particular. I settled that one by selling it to the highest bidder.

By noon, the last of the stragglers have departed and we are gathered in the kitchen to total our receipts. Although I haven't worked nearly as hard as the rest of The Babes, I'm exhausted and in considerable pain. My injuries are nearly healed and the onslaught of the lupus seems to have slowed down, still, I'm a long way from being well and it only takes an excursion like this to remind me of how far I have to go. Kathleen finishes counting the cash and then uses a calculator to total the checks. Looking up, she says, "$3,127.35. That should be more than enough to send Michelle to Vegas."

The Babes are too tired to dance around the room but we do let out a rowdy cheer. When we finally quiet down Michelle thanks us profusely, giving Madison a big hug. Noticing how spent I am, Mercedes goes after the car and helps me get my things. She offers to drive and I gladly accept laying my seat back and closing my eyes.

As I review the morning, two events stand out in my mind. About ten o'clock an earnest young man arrived with a folded newspaper clutched in his hand. He hastily surveyed the remaining merchandise without finding what he was looking for. Approaching the table where I was seated, he placed the newspaper before me and pointed to a classified ad circled with a red marker. "Am I at the right place?"

Glancing at the ad, I scanned it quickly. *Must sell men's professional wardrobe, size 42 regular. Mint condition. 4 Valentino suits, 4 Oscar de la Renta suits, 12 pair of Ralph Lauren slacks, sweaters, oxfords, overcoats, ties, and dress shirts. Make an offer.*

Madison had listed her address and belatedly, I realized that she intended to sell Michael's entire winter wardrobe. Returning my attention to the young man who appeared to be in his late twenties, I noted that he was about Michael's size; a little trimmer perhaps. He was clean shaven, light brown hair slicked back, with a pleasant smile. His clothes were pressed, clean but worn and I couldn't help surmising that he was probably a recent graduate, undoubtedly having finished his degree at night. He likely needed the clothes for an important job interview. Immediately, my heart went out to him and I called Madison over. "This gentleman would like to see the men's clothing you mentioned in your ad."

"Certainly," Madison replied before turning her attention to the young man. "Come with me. The clothes are hanging in the utility room just inside the door."

Clearing his throat, he said, "Perhaps we should discuss the price. I've limited funds and I wouldn't want to waste your time."

"Nonsense. If you don't like the clothes, the price doesn't matter."

With that Madison turned toward the door and after a moment he followed her inside. They were gone about ten minutes and when Madison returned she was smiling, a sheaf of bills in her hand. Handing it to me, she said, "$87.50."

Stunned, I said, "You sold Michael's entire winter wardrobe for $87.50?"

Laughing, she bantered back, "I need the closet space."

Before I could say anything more she called to Michelle and Jessica, "Give me a hand here, ladies. Let's help this gentleman get these clothes in his car."

Michelle was carrying one final armload of clothes to the gentleman's car when Michael's silver Porsche 911 came roaring around the corner and skidded to a stop at the curb, directly in front of the banner. Paying it no mind, he stormed up the driveway to confront Madison, a rolled-up newspaper clinched in his fist.

Just then a black Ford F250 4X4 began backing into the driveway, stopping just short of the bow-flex machine. Two muscle-bound guys in tank tops and cutoffs climbed out of the truck and began loading the bow-flex. Instantly, Michael veered in their direction, "Leave that right where it is or I'll call the police and have you arrested."

Ignoring him, the two guys simply continued to load the machine into the back of their truck. "He must be the

Sleazebag," one of them muttered, loud enough for all of us to hear.

The other one glanced at the Porsche where Lori was sitting, "And she must be the trollop."

Michael continued to make threatening noises until the driver of the F250 reached inside the truck for a bill of sale. Glaring at Michael, he said, "Little man, you can go ahead and call the police if you want, but it won't do you no good. This piece of paper says I bought that bow-flex for $300.00." With that he climbed in his truck and drove off, leaving Michael fuming in the driveway.

As the truck turned the corner, Michael stormed into the garage to confront Madison. "You sold my bow-flex machine for a measly $300?" he screamed, slamming his hand on the table in front of her. "You must be an idiot. I paid over two thousand dollars for that machine."

I could see a flicker of fear in Madison's eyes but she conquered it and stood to her feet, meeting Michael's angry glare with a resolute stare of her own. As if on cue, The Bunko Babes moved to form a semicircle of support behind her like Mama Bears protecting a cub. Our message was clear, "Mess with one Bunko Babe and you will answer to all of us."

Struggling to control his temper, Michael fumed, "Could you give us a little privacy here? I'm trying to talk to my wife."

In response, we simply closed our semicircle a little tighter behind Madison. Incensed, he stormed around the garage, enraged but impotent in the face of our solidarity. Suddenly, he noticed the empty ceiling hooks where his custom-made bicycle normally hung and the empty wall peg where his golf bag and clubs should have been.

Turning back to Madison, he raged, "You didn't! Tell me you didn't sell my bicycle or my golf clubs."

Calmly, Madison replied, "You left them here so I assumed you didn't want them."

"You imbecile! Just because I left them here doesn't mean I don't want them."

"Sorry. I had no idea. You left Meredith, Mitchell, and me here and you don't want us."

"They weren't yours to sell," Michael whined. "You had no right to sell my things."

"You're hardly in a position to talk to me about rights," Madison said, in a voice cold with contempt. "But if you want to talk about rights I'll talk about rights. You had no right to betray our marriage vows and take up with that woman. You had no right to lie to me or to try to take the children from me. You had no right to throw away fifteen years of marriage. You had no right to divorce me...."

Infuriated, Michael interrupted her, "You'll be hearing from my attorney." Waving the newspaper with the classified ad, he continued, "You can't humiliate me like this. I'll be a laughingstock in the business community." With that he turned and stalked out of the garage, his back stiff with anger.

Thinking about it now, I can't help but admire Madison. She remained in control at all times and refused to be intimidated. After Michael drove off she told me, "I won't allow him to make me into something I'm not. I've never been a bitter or vindictive person and I will not allow Michael to turn me into one."

CHAPTER

FORTY-ONE

Just when I thought I was getting better, I'm blindsided by what my doctor calls a "lupus flare." Nobody knows for sure what sets them off—stress, exposure to the sun, over-exertion, or most likely some combination thereof. Be that as it may, for the past four days I've done almost nothing but sleep. I don't know what would have happened if Mercedes hadn't been here to keep the household going. She's truly a godsend.

Only now am I starting to regain a minimal amount of strength. I still can't do much, but for the first time in days I've managed to stay awake through an entire television show. Big accomplishment, right? Now I'm watching *What Not to Wear* on the learning channel. Stacey London has just given her trademark "Shut up!" when I catch sight of Brooklyn as she passes my bedroom door.

Hungry for companionship, I call, "Hey, Tiddlywinks, got a sec?"

Poking her head into my room, she says, "Hey, yourself."

"Would you like to watch a movie with me? We could pop some kettle corn and have some girl time."

"Sorry, Mom, no can do. Mercedes and I are just about to leave for the mall to look for my purity dress. Maybe tomorrow evening?"

I smile to hide my disappointment and call after her, "Have fun."

I maintain my composure until I hear the garage door open and then close, but once I know they have gone I give in to my despair. When my lupus flares, my feelings are all over the place. At the moment, I'm a basket case. I couldn't love Mercedes more if she were my own daughter, but right now I resent her terribly. What right did she have to take Brooklyn shopping for her purity dress, without at least discussing it with me? Brooklyn's my daughter and this is one of the most important events in her life, an event every mother wants to share with her daughter. Never mind that I couldn't go shopping if my life depended on it.

The insecurities I've battled all my life now return with a vengeance. Although I know Mercedes has done nothing but what I've asked of her, I feel threatened. She does things so much better than I ever did. Honestly, I never knew anyone could cook so wonderfully while maintaining a perfect house, keeping up with the laundry, entertaining me, running errands, picking up the kids, helping with homework, laughing, joking, and gossiping with the twins. To top it all off, she looks like the hot tamale I so desperately want to be.

Okay, so maybe she isn't that perfect but that's how it feels to me.

The most difficult thing for me has been the change in my status with the twins. Before Mercedes came into the picture, I was their friend and confidant. I'll never forget the first time I overheard one of Brooklyn's friends say, "Wow! Your mom's so cool!" My heart actually stopped for a single instant but I nearly keeled over when Brooklyn nonchalantly responded, "Yeah, I guess I'll keep her." But, alas, all of that has changed and I'm fearful that I'm being replaced by Mercedes.

Even as I wallow in self-pity, I hate what I've become— what my daddy used to call a 'whiner.' Instead of being thankful that Brooklyn has bonded with Mercedes, I'm eaten up with jealousy. Instead of looking at the stars, I've got my head stuck in the mud. I don't want to feel this way but I can't seem to help myself. Overcome with frustration, I fling the remote control across the room and bury my face in my pillow, sobbing piteously.

I haven't lost control like this since before the accident and it scares me, really scares me. I've been to that dark place and I don't ever want to go there again. Determinedly, I struggle to get control of my emotions knowing that if I don't there's no telling where this downward spiral will end. I force myself to breathe deeply and little by little the hammering of my heart slows. After several minutes, my nearly hysterical weeping subsides into ragged sobs and on an impulse I reach for my cell phone to call my mother. I don't know why I choose to call her instead of one of The Babes but I do. Maybe the frightened child inside of me needs the tender loving care only a mother can give.

In my ear the cell phone rings once, twice, three times. "Hello. This is Pastor Thompson."

Expecting my mother's voice, I hit the end button but not before a gut-wrenching sob escapes my throat. I can't believe this. Not even my mother is there for me. Self-pity again, my only comforter but a dangerous comforter she is, wooing me toward that dark place.

Almost instantly, my cell phone chirps and I check the caller ID. It is an out of area number, and I suspect it is Keith Thompson calling me back. I want to answer it, but I don't; something holds me back. I'm torn with indecision. I want the comfort of another human voice, any voice, but I cannot bear the thought of anyone seeing me in this condition. Finally, it goes to voice mail and I berate myself for the sniveling coward I've become.

After a moment, it chirps again and this time I force myself to answer it.

"Rebecca, this is Keith. Are you okay?"

"Yes...er...no...."

"What is it, Rebecca, what's happened?" His voice is gentle but firm.

Without intending to, I find myself sobbing out my complaint. "It's Mercedes," I wail. "I've been replaced."

Kindly he asks, "Help me to understand what you mean when you say you've been replaced."

I can hear the concern in his voice and I find myself trusting him even though it makes no sense to do so. He's the man who has taken my mother from me, the one who will be taking my father's place on December 30th when he and my mother marry. Loyalty to my father's memory requires me to resent him, or at least that's how I feel, but I can't and over the next few minutes I pour out my heart to him.

I tell him that Mercedes is not annoying, controlling, or obsessive. That she's not bossy, cloying, smothering, or possessive. That she has not come into my house and changed things to suit her preferences: such as rearranging the kitchen or trying to get us to eat on a set schedule. That she doesn't fight with the kids, boss them around, or gripe about their habitual snacking.

When I finally run down he says, "She sounds pretty amazing."

"She is," I reply, hating myself for my pettiness. "And yet, it is these very qualities that I find myself resenting. Does this make any sense to you?"

"Rebecca," he says, pausing to collect his thoughts, "it's not really Mercedes you resent but your situation."

When I don't respond he continues, "You resent the fact that your body has betrayed you. You can no longer do the things you once did—make a home for your husband and children, work in the church, attend Rob's football games, shop for Brooklyn's purity dress, or be the wife you once were to Thomas—that's what you resent. And on an even deeper level you probably resent God. You've always served Him and it feels like He's let you down. First your father dies and then you are stricken with an incurable disease."

Though his tone is gentle and his voice filled with kindness, it feels like he is ripping a scab off my soul. In the deepest part of my being his words resonate with truth but I don't want to hear it. I don't want to admit that I feel betrayed by God and that when push comes to shove I don't think I can trust Him. I don't want to admit that I blame God for Daddy's heart attack or for the illness that has stolen my life from me. I don't want to admit it but I know it's true.

I'm sobbing softly now, shamed by what I consider the failure of my faith. How could I doubt God? How could I question His sovereignty and His goodness? But in my heart of hearts I know I do. If the truth be told, I'm angry at God. Yet I feel guilty too, and ashamed of myself.

Keith's voice comes to me through the cell phone pressed to my ear, a voice of comfort and of hope, a ray of light in a very dark place. "It's okay, Rebecca. Even Jesus questioned Father God. At the darkest moment of His life He cried, 'My

God, my God, why have You forsaken me?' But He didn't get stuck there. A little later He prayed, 'Father, into Your hands I commit My spirit.' Without ever receiving an answer He moved from questioning God to trusting Him."

He pauses, giving me a chance to respond but whatever words I might have are lost somewhere in the confusion inside of me.

Finally he continues, "As Jesus showed us, the way to true faith is often through the valley of suffering where we are forced to confront our deepest doubts and our greatest fears. To move from fear to faith, we have to be honest with ourselves and with God. We can't commit our spirits to Father God until first we give Him our questions, no matter how blasphemous they may seem."

At last, I find my voice. "How could God do this to me? How could He take both my daddy and my health?"

I don't expect him to have an answer and he doesn't but he says something that rocks me to the core of my being. "Becca, sometimes the only way we can get beyond our hurt and anger is to forgive God."

"Forgive God?" I snort. "What kind of insanity is that? Whoever heard of a mere mortal forgiving God?"

"Hear me out," he says, refusing to take offense. "Theologically, I know that sounds insane. Who are we to forgive God? Who are we to presume that God needs forgiving?"

"It's insane all right," I say not even trying to hide my skepticism.

He continues as if I haven't interrupted him. "We are not forgiving God because He has done something wrong, for He hasn't. Rather, we are forgiving Him in the sense that we have blamed Him, that is, held Him responsible for the things that have happened to us. When we 'forgive' Him, we let go of those feelings—all the hurt and anger, all of the bitterness and distrust."

What he's saying makes sense to me. Not necessarily theological sense (whatever that is) but life sense. It squares with the things I've experienced. I've blamed God and my feelings have alienated me from Him just when I need Him most. But I can't go on this way, not if I ever hope to escape this black hole and become the kind of person I long to be.

Tentatively, I ask, "If I were to accept what you're saying—I'm not saying I do, mind you—but if I did, how would I go about forgiving God?"

He hesitates for just a moment before responding. "When my wife died I became terribly depressed. Nothing I did seemed to help. Somehow I did what was expected of me but I wasn't living. I was just going through the motions. My wife suffered terribly before she died and I blamed God. To my way of thinking, He could have spared her and just taken her home but He didn't and that hurt me deeply. What good, I wondered, did it do to serve God if in the end we died like that.

"One evening when I was at my lowest point, I went to the cemetery and sat on a bench by her grave. Without even realizing it, I found myself railing at God. The depth of my feelings shocked me. I told Him how heartlessly cruel I thought He was to let her suffer so and how unfair to take her from me. At one point, I remember thinking He might strike me dead but I didn't care. I had nothing to live for. Finally, I exhausted my anger and for the first time in months I felt a glimmer of hope. Looking up at the now dark sky, I told God I forgave Him, that I wasn't going to hold it against Him anymore.

"My grief didn't end that night, nor for a long time thereafter, but I no longer felt alone. Whatever had been separating me from God was gone and with His help I was able to move on.

"I can't tell you how to do it, Becca, but that's what I did."

We sit in silence for two or three minutes. Finally, he says, "The real strength of Christianity is not that it makes us immune to life's difficulties but that it enables us to live with purpose and even joy under the most adverse circumstances."

"Thanks, Keith," I manage to say, feeling somehow hopeful.

"Before you go," he says, "there's something I would like to ask you."

"Sure," I reply, a little flutter in my stomach.

"What made you decide to call me?"

Laughing with relief I say, "It was an accident. I meant to call my mother."

Without hesitation, he replies, "It was no accident, Becca. It was divine providence. Proverbs 19:21 says, 'Many are the plans in a man's heart, but it is the Lord's purpose that prevails.' God was looking out for you tonight."

CHAPTER

FORTY-TWO

Staring at the bedroom ceiling, I watch as the scientific clock keeps precise track of the time, its results beamed in ruby red upon the intentionally cracked and aged plaster ceiling of our recently redecorated bedroom. I watch as first one, two, then three numbers flash, the march of time continuing despite my stillness.

The conversation I had with Keith a few days ago continues to play in my head, snatches of it, the most important parts, repeating time and again. Just knowing that others have struggled with the same kind of feelings I'm having is enormously encouraging. I'm not yet ready to "confront"

God but I'm closer than I've ever been. *Soon*, I think, *soon I'll be able to deal with all my stuff.*

I still can't believe I called his number instead of Mom's. It's weird, I mean really weird. Maybe God truly did have a hand in it. That's what Keith thinks. How did he put it: "If you look closely, Becca, you'll see God's fingerprints all over your life."

Having spent the better part of the last two weeks confined to my bedroom recovering from my latest "flare," I decide to venture forth. I'm weak as a kitten but by being careful I manage to get out of bed on my own. Thomas is out of town on a business trip, Robert is at football practice, and Mercedes and Brooklyn have returned to the mall for the third time looking for the perfect purity dress for my little sweetheart. That means, I'm alone in the house and a rare treat it is. I feel like a kid let loose in a candy store and I head straight for the kitchen and my hidden stash of those wonderfully, wholly unhealthy, sinfully delicious, hot fudge-iced Pop-Tarts. I know there're bad for you...yada, yada, yada. Yeah, well, sometimes, a girl just needs the comfort that only chocolate can give.

Opening the spice cabinet, I pause long enough to read the scripture Mercedes has posted inside the cabinet door. "Do not be anxious about anything, but in everything, by prayer and petition, with thanksgiving, present your requests to God. And the peace of God, which transcends all understanding, will guard your hearts and your minds in Christ Jesus" (Philippians 4:7-8).

One morning after devotions, we each wrote some of our favorite verses on post-it notes and pasted them in places readily available to us in our time of need. On more than one occasion, I've stumbled onto one of those verses and been enormously blessed. It's kind of like getting a post card from heaven. Mercedes posted several of hers in the kitchen and as a result, I feel like each kitchen cabinet is a Christmas present just waiting to be opened. Maybe I should have tried something like this years ago. I might have actually been inspired to cook!

Soon the kitchen is filled with the wondrous aroma of fudge wafting up from the slats of my Black and Decker toaster. Inhaling deeply, I savor the scent, my mouth watering with anticipation, my mind imagining the Pop Tarts to be a chocolate soufflé, light and fluffy, served with a piping hot espresso. *My imagination drifts. I am sitting at a table for two with Thomas, in Paris, at one of the multitudes of romantic, outdoor cafés. The sun has set, turning a stunning tie-dyed sky to one of dark licorice, the perfect backdrop for the Eiffel Tower looking as if it were draped in champagne diamonds.*

I'm still in Paris when the doorbell rings and I float toward the entryway on a waft of chocolate soufflés and romantic cafés. Slowly, I spin, my feet moving magically to the music in my mind. My waltzing stops just shy of the front door and for an instant I am deflated like my one and only attempt at creating that delectable French delight I was just dreaming about.

Reaching the door, I stand on tiptoe to peer through the peephole, ever the vigilant girl. Seeing my best friend Jessica, I smile with delight, Paris forgotten.

Throwing the door open, I ask, "What are you doing here?!"

Eyes twinkling with mischief, Jess replies, "I brought sustenance." Stepping into the foyer, she presents me with a large Papa John's pizza and a shopping bag containing a two-liter bottle of Dr. Pepper, a tube of chocolate chip cookie dough, and a special treat just for me—a large container of candy-coated sprinkles.

"For *me?*" I squeal, throwing my good arm around her neck.

"Who else?" she replies with a laugh, blowing the hair out of her eyes only to have it get stuck in her lip gloss. Heading for the kitchen, she calls over her shoulder, "You are so gonna owe me after all of this."

"Yeah, yeah, yeah," I reply, as she sits the box of pizza on the counter and opens the dishwasher in search of plates. "What, no plates?" she exclaims, staring in amazement at the empty dishwasher.

"Mercedes," I say and point at the cupboard.

Getting plates, glasses, and flatware, she arranges them on the bar. Knowing that we usually eat out of the box, not bothering with either plates or napkins or even manners for that matter, I ask, "What's the occasion?"

"Mercedes," she says and we both laugh; remembering how aghast Mercedes was the first time she saw The Bunko

Babes devouring pizza, talking with their mouths full, cheese stringing down their chins. Later, we learned that in Argentina people eat pizza with a knife and fork.

Jessica brushes the few remaining strands of hair from her forehead before putting a slice of pizza on each of our plates. Putting ice in the glasses, she pours the Dr. Pepper.

"The limes are in the crisper."

Stunned, Jessica retorts, "You have limes?"

"Mercedes," I sing her name, all the answer my friend requires.

The preparations finally complete, Jessica joins me at the bar. "Whattya say we devour this feast before the pizza gets cold and the cookie dough thaws?"

Picking up her knife and fork, Jessica proceeds to cut a bite of pizza. With the fork still positioned upside down in her left hand, she stabs the bite of pizza and daintily places it in her mouth. "Who do I remind you of? "

"Mercedes," I reply without a moment's hesitation and we both laugh.

"Oh," Jessica adds, "I have one more surprise."

Reaching into her purse, which she has haphazardly tossed onto one of the barstools, Jess pulls out a DVD. I can't see the title but it must be a good one. She's grinning and clasping it tightly to her chest. Finally, she holds it up.

"Beaches!" I squeal with delight. "Our favorite!"

Once we've finished our pizza, Jessica loads the dishwasher and wipes off the counter before we head for the theater room, cookie dough and sprinkles in hand. I can't help thinking what a wonderful surprise this is. I get to spend the evening pigging out on my favorite junk foods, engrossed in one of my all-time favorite chick flicks, with my bestest sister chick.

Unfortunately, things don't work out the way I thought they would. Halfway through the movie, I'm caught off guard by a flood of emotions and I feel myself slipping back into that dark place. Sneaking a peek in Jessica's direction, I see that she's completely engrossed in the movie and totally oblivious to the effect it is having on me. Giving myself a pep talk, I decide to stick it out. I'm not willing to take a chance on hurting her feelings, no matter the cost to my fragile spirit.

By the time CC joins Hillary (who is dying) and her six-year-old daughter Victoria Essex for the summer, I'm a basket case. For me, it is like watching two movies at once—the one on the screen and the one in my mind. "Beaches" is eerily autobiographical, reflecting my own struggles with jealousy and the ever looming possibility of my own death. I cringe with physical pain as I watch Victoria Essex and CC bond while Hillary slips ever closer to death. Most painful of all is Hillary's jealousy, which serves as a mirror reflecting my own ambiguous feelings for Mercedes as I've watched her relationship with Brooklyn develop. Hillary wants CC to become a surrogate mother to Victoria but when she sees it happening it rips her heart out and she begins picking fights with CC. She hates herself for feeling that way, for choosing her own needs over Victoria's, but she can't seem to help herself. *How much like her I am,* I think, cringing at the thought.

Barely able to contain my tears I tiptoe toward the door, trying to be as inconspicuous as possible. "Be right back," I croak, praying Jess will assume I'm headed to the bathroom.

"Do you want me to pause it?" she calls after me.

"No," I throw over my shoulder, not trusting myself to say more.

Fleeing down the stairs, I pass through the kitchen and into the living room where I collapse onto the couch, the pain in my chest cruelly reminding me of my broken ribs.

I concentrate on controlling my erratic breathing, thrusting all thoughts of the movie and the painful images it birthed in me from my mind. Slowly, ever so slowly, I regain my equilibrium and as I do, something Pastor Keith said a few days ago comes to mind: "Feelings are real but they're not necessarily accurate."

My feelings are real—I'm afraid I'm going to die and never see my children grow up, graduate from college, marry and have children of their own. But my feelings are not necessarily accurate. The truth is, before the "flare"...I was making progress, regaining my strength, and the future looked promising. The truth is, I was having a pretty good day until I started watching "Beaches." So what changed? Not my condition, just my feelings. Imaginary images on a screen fed my fears causing me to panic. The good news is, if frightful images can feed my fears, then positive images can feed my faith.

I'm walking a thin line here. I know I dare not repress my fearful feelings or they will poison my soul but I can't entertain them either. Therefore, I must replace them. In my mind, I see a yellow sticky stuck on my makeup mirror. Slowly, I begin to speak the words repetition has imprinted upon my mind. "I am the Lord, your God, who takes hold of your right hand and says to you, Do not fear; I will help you."

As my confidence begins to return, I'm reminded of something else Pastor Keith said. Thinking about it now I can almost hear his voice, his earnest tone, and kindly counsel echoing in my memory. "It's easier to act yourself into right feelings than to think yourself into right actions."

Exercising the sternest self-disciple I can muster, I force myself to take action. Deliberately, I begin thanking my Heavenly Father for Mercedes—her grace and beauty, her health and happiness, her culinary skills and obsessive cleanliness, her willingness to help, and most of all the wonderful connection she has with Brooklyn and Robert. On a feeling level, these things threaten me, tempt me with jealousy, but with God 's help I will not give in to them. I will act myself into the right feelings. I will.

The touch of Jessica's hand, so cool upon my forehead, startles me, and my eyes fly open in surprise.

"There you are," she whispers, "I got worried when you didn't return." Kneeling beside the sofa, she asks, "Are you okay?"

Her face is full of feeling and I am warmed by her concern.

"I am now," I huskily reply before pulling her to me for a hug that is both comforting and strengthening.

Harbored from the storm, I feel safe enough to share my greatest fear; knowing that fear, like temptation, flourishes in the secret but loses its power when exposed to the light. Daring to put a face on my fear, I whisper, "I don't want to die, Jess."

"I know."

In the same small voice, I confess, "I just got scared. Watching Hillary die and leave her daughter, hit a little too close to home." I scrunch up my face and bite hard on my bottom lip, determined not to cry.

"Oh, Becca," she says, "I'm so sorry. I don't know what I was thinking—remembering how much fun we had the first time we saw "Beaches" with The Bonko Babes the summer after our freshman year in college, I guess. More likely, I wasn't thinking. Being in a mood to celebrate, I just picked it up at Wal-Mart on my way to check out."

"Celebrate?" I ask, suddenly eager to focus on something other than myself. "Did you say celebrate?"

"Did I say celebrate?" she teases, looking at me with a sparkle in her eye.

"Don't play coy with me, Jessica Montrose Goldstein. Out with it—what are we celebrating?"

A huge smile plastered on her face, she announces, "I'm pregnant, Becca. God has answered our prayers. I'm going to be a mom just like you said."

I'm stunned. I can't speak. How can this be? Finally, I manage to ask, "Are you positive?"

"Absolutely," she says, smiling through tears of joy. "I've just come from my OBGYN's office. He confirmed what three positive home pregnancy tests had already told me. I'm pregnant!"

Bursting into laughter, I throw both arms around her neck, oblivious to my injured collarbone. "Are you sure?" I keep asking, "Are you sure?"

"Yes," Jessica screams, unable to contain her joy. "Absolutely, positively, supercalifragilisticexpialidociously, Yes!"

Now we're both screaming and clapping our hands and I can't help but smile even wider at her use of our secret Bonko Babe Club phrase that was our way of saying, "Cross my heart, hope to die, stick a needle in my eye." We're talkin' big time stuff here.

Taking Jessica's shoulders in my hands, I look straight into her eyes and say, "This is a God thing, Jessica. You're going to be a great mom."

"Just a little bit of faith," she softly returns. "It just takes a little bit of faith."

CHAPTER
FORTY-THREE

I'm on a spiritual high! Physically, I'm tired and still recovering from the injuries I suffered in an automobile accident nearly two months ago, but not even the precarious condition of my health can dim the rush Jessica's news has given me. After being told that her fallopian tubes were ruined and that she could never have children, she's pregnant. Like Mercedes' engagement ring story, Jessica's pregnancy is the kind of thing I thought only happened in the Bible. Boy, was I wrong. Now, I'm an eyewitness to a miracle—okay, not literally, but I do get to watch as the baby grows.

Moments ago, I heard Brooklyn and Mercedes come in. From the sound of things, I believe they struck gold this time and I thank the Lord, yet again, for Mercedes and all the help she's provided. I simply did not have the strength to follow Brooklyn from store to store while she nitpicked every dress to death. She's the most picky person I know, except maybe my mother. I guess that particular gene skipped a generation.

Setting aside my book, I ease off of the chaise lounge and pad down the hall towards Brooklyn's room. Pausing at the door, I knock lightly before opening it and peeking my head into what Robert has labeled "The Diva Domain."

"May I come in?"

Glancing over her shoulder, Brooklyn replies, "Sure, Mom."

I make my way to a leopard fur love seat strewn with assorted hot pink and purple decorator pillows. Tossing a few of them aside, I make room for my expanding backside. Brooklyn stands before the full-length mirror in one corner of her room holding a lovely white gown. The hanger is draped over the back of her neck giving her the freedom to sway and shift, the full skirt held high in one hand.

In the mirror, I see her reflection. Her porcelain face bears a tender smile, a blend of ambient light and shadows shifting constantly from the glow of the revolving chandelier above us. I feel a knot in my throat and my heart begins to wilt. My little girl is growing up. Soon, that will be a wedding dress she holds and more than anything I wish to slow the relentless march of time.

"What now, Mom?" interrupts Brooklyn having caught my wistful look in the mirror.

"Just thinking about how fast you're growing up. It seems like it was just yesterday that you and Robert were crawling around, getting into things, driving me insane." I smile, shaking my head at the memories. "Especially you, young lady."

Purity dress forgotten, Brooklyn drapes it over the free-standing mirror before coming over and plopping on her bed. Rolling onto her stomach, she rests her youthful chin in her hands. Finally, she says, "Can I ask you something, Mom?"

"Sure, Honey, anything you want," I respond, suddenly concerned by the seriousness of her tone.

Tearfully, she asks, "Are you going to die?"

The fear in her voice and the forlorn look on her face nearly break my heart. Easing off the love seat, I cross the room and lie down on the bed beside her. When I do, she rolls over and snuggles against me in a way she hasn't done in years. I want to assure her that I'm not going to die, but I must not lie to her either.

She's crying now, sobbing softly into my shoulder where she has buried her face. Remembering my own fear and desolation at my father's death, I can only imagine what she's going through. I was an adult, thirty-six years old, with children of my own and yet, Daddy's death was a blow I've not yet fully recovered from. She's just a child, barely thirteen years old, and ill-equipped to deal with the possibility of my death.

Am I going to die? That's a tough question, one for which I have no definitive answer. When my lupus "flares" plunge me back into the bowels of this dreaded disease's torment, I feel sure I will never live to see my babies graduate from high school. But when I start to feel better again, hope returns and I convince myself I can beat this thing. So, what do I tell my frightened baby girl?

Her sobbing has subsided into an occasional whimper and I hold her close, providing what comfort I can. Finally, I tell her, "Systemic lupus is an incurable disease but many people who have it live relatively normal lives for many, many years. Once the doctors get my symptoms under control, I should be almost as good as new."

If she hears my explanation, she gives no indication and belatedly I realize that the reassurance she seeks will not be found in my words but in the comfort of my presence. She's so strong-willed, so fiercely independent, that it's easy for me to forget how young she is and how sensitive, especially given all I've been dealing with. As we continue to snuggle, I make a vow to myself that in the future I will be there for her with a listening ear, a quick hug, or even a word of motherly advice—whatever she needs.

Holding her, I let my mind return to an earlier time when she was just a child, not yet in kindergarten. Even then, she was fiercely competitive and terribly outspoken. She never saw herself as the damsel in distress and in all her childhood games she insisted on being the masculine hero. This concerned my mother to no end. She was sure Brooklyn was going to grow up confused about her sexual identity. I'll never forget the day I overheard Brooklyn tell her, "It's just pretend, Mimi. It's not real."

Having never had a son, I was sure my daddy would be tempted to favor Robert. Boy, was I wrong. If anything, it was the other way around. From day one, Brooklyn latched onto Daddy and never let go. Anytime Robert got near him, Brooklyn would shove him away. "My papa," she would say, "My papa."

Robert loved video games from the time he was big enough to hold the controls but Brooklyn couldn't have cared less. She had eyes only for her papa and early on, she conned him into telling her stories. If he was around at bedtime, she refused to go to sleep until he had told her a "Prince Phillip" story. Of course, daddy was more than happy to comply. Thinking about it now, I can't help but be a little jealous. Never once, did he tell me a bedtime story. Of course, he was usually in the garage restoring a classic car when Mommy put me to bed.

Nudging Brooklyn, I ask, "Do you remember the time Papa was too tired to tell you a Prince Phillip story?"

"Not really. How old was I?"

"You were probably five years old. Anyway, when he told you he was too tired, you immediately jumped out of bed and ran into his office. Getting several sheets of paper from his printer, you stapled them together down one side to make a book. Next, you used a felt-tipped marker to make squiggly lines on the back and front of each page. Returning to the bedroom, you handed them to Papa saying, 'I know you're too tired to tell me a story so I wrote one. All you have to do is read it to me.'"

Laughing, Brooklyn says, "That was cool."

"Yeah, but here's the best part. Taking your 'book' he pretended to read it to you. About ten minutes into that night's episode of 'Prince Phillip', you reached over and tugged on Papa's sleeve. Looking him in the eye, you said, 'Papa, I can't read but I can sure write good stories.'"

We're both laughing now and if the earlier angst has not been banished it at least huddles in the farthest corner unacknowledged. On an impulse, Brooklyn gives me a squeeze. "I love you, Mom. You're the best."

We must have fallen asleep amid the disarray of pillows and "Build-A-Bear" stuffed animals because the next thing I hear is Robert. "I found 'em, Dad," he yells, leaning against the door jamb, his dark hair still damp from his after practice shower. "They're taking a nap in Brooklyn's room."

Stepping into the doorway, Thomas says, "Hey, sleepy-heads, it's time to wake up."

Rolling over, Brooklyn buries her face in a pillow mumbling, "Do we have to?"

"Only if you want dinner."

"I'm not hungry."

"Are you sure? I brought your favorite."

"You brought sushi?" Brooklyn asks excitedly, suddenly awake.

"That I did," Thomas affirms.

Letting out a high-pitched squeal, she crawls over me and gives her father a hug and a kiss on the cheek. Heading for the kitchen, she calls over her shoulder, "I hope you remembered that I like my rolls wrapped in soy paper. Last time you forgot."

Looking at me, Thomas shakes his head and asks, "Are you coming?"

"In a minute," I say. "Go ahead and start without me. I'll be along shortly."

After he has gone, I ease myself into a sitting position on the edge of the bed, trying to wake up. Other than being tired, I feel surprisingly good. Jessica's news and the special time Brooklyn and I shared serve as a boost to my weary soul. I know the battle is not over, but it feels like the tide has turned.

FORTY-FOUR

The December sun is high in the sky, bright but without much warmth. Still, I'm comfortable enough sitting in my sunroom, wrapped in a thick robe, watching two cardinals at the backyard bird feeder. My once hectic life has settled into a contented routine, my overdeveloped need to always be in control having finally yielded to the limits imposed by my fragile health. It wasn't easy but I've learned to accept things as they are. Initially, I raged at God, at the injustice I had suffered, and even at my family and friends. But for all my anger nothing changed. Then, I decided to simply grit my teeth and bear it, which was not one whit better. Soon, I found myself in a dark place, battling not only my disease but depression, as well. Eventually, I was able to accept what I could not change.

I'm not talking about giving up and resigning myself to whatever will be; but acceptance, whereby I continue to believe for a miracle, even as I accept the painful reality of my present condition. I no longer demand a predetermined conclusion; rather, I am now willing to leave the nature of the miracle to the wisdom of God. It may come as a miracle of healing or it may come as daily grace, enabling me to experience peace and fulfillment while living with pain and sickness.

An unexpected benefit of this difficult time has been what I can only describe as the nearness of God, howbeit His presence was seldom easy to discern. In fact, it was often only in retrospect that I realized God was with me, even when I was sure He was nowhere to be found. I'm a different person now, better I hope. Some have suggested that suffering has refined me, but I hardly think so. If there's been any refining, it was God's doing. The most suffering did was to put me in a place where God could do His redemptive work. I pray I never have to go through anything like this again, but I also realize, it may be impossible to experience the fullness of God's grace except in times of greatest need, for that is when God reveals Himself in life-changing ways. At least, that has been my experience.

Temporarily freed from the hectic rush of living, I've had the opportunity to reflect on life. And I can only conclude that no one escapes unscathed no matter how charmed a life they seem to live. Of course, my "research" has been mostly limited to The Bunko Babes and their families, but none of us have been spared life's vicissitudes. If ever a person seemed to have a charmed life, it was Madison, but she now finds herself divorced and a single mom of two preschool age children; however, only part time. In what has to be considered a classic example of juristic high-handedness, the judge granted Michael joint custody. Never mind that the children will be spending half their time in daycare, given the fact that both Michael and Lori work outside the home.

Madison was devastated, as you might imagine, and the first time she had to pack the children's things, it nearly killed her. When Michael came to pick them up, she put on a brave front for their sake, telling them how much fun they would have at Daddy's new house. But once the front door closed, she collapsed in a sobbing heap. They're hardly a month into the joint custody thing and already Michael is tiring of it. Twice, he has brought the children home early and last week, he didn't pick them up at all. Image has always been important to him and, as far as I'm concerned, the only reason he filed for joint custody was to make himself look good. He's never been a devoted father, but he sure wants others to see him that way. I can't help thinking that while Madison is willing to lay her life down for her children, Michael seems only too ready to sacrifice their well-being to preserve his image. All of this has taken a terrible toll on Madison and the children, enabling me to better understand why God hates divorce.

I hear Mercedes banging around in the kitchen and I can't help smiling. Soon, she will call me to lunch or bring a tray and join me here in the sunroom. She's truly a godsend and once I came to grips with my irrational jealousy, I've been able to fully appreciate her for the treasure she is. Hopefully, being here has been beneficial for her, as well. She assures me it has, but given my insecurities, I can't help wondering. Truthfully, I don't know how she would have managed alone considering the distressing news coming out of Iraq on an almost daily basis.

It's bad enough seeing it on the news, but it somehow remains impersonal and far removed from us, no matter how gruesome the footage. But when Douglas sends an email, our defenses crumble, and the tragedy of war, no matter how justified, becomes a reality we can't escape. My heart goes out to Mercedes and I can't help thinking that knowing Douglas' life is constantly at risk, must be like living with a gun to her head. Without the strength that God provides, I don't know how she could bear it. Sometimes I hear her praying as she does laundry or dusts the living room. If she has received a particularly disturbing email, like the one she got a few days ago, I may hear her praying late into the night. Always, her prayers have an urgency, an intensity that I find both inspiring and intimidating.

Douglas is stationed at Fire Base Red, located in Iraq's "Triangle of Death" about fifteen miles southeast of Baghdad. This is one of the most dangerous places in Iraq and the Base has come under attack several times. Some days, he mans a "sniper's nest" on the rooftop of Fire Base Red, keeping a close eye on the palm groves and fields in front of him looking for any hint of movement. At other times, he goes out on patrol, usually in a Humvee that lacks the heavy armor necessary to protect it from roadside bombs, but on occasion he patrols on foot.

That's where he was, the day his best friend was killed, leaving behind a wife and three children in Spanaway, Washington. Thankfully, Douglas was at the rear of the column and thus escaped injury, when a roadside bomb—what the Army refers to as an IED (improvised explosive device)—exploded, hurling deadly shrapnel into those closest to it. By the time Douglas reached him, he was already dead. "When he died," Douglas said, "something died in me, as well. You can't lose a friend without losing a part of yourself."

Mercedes was sobbing when she read me his email. She kept saying over and over, "That could have been my Douglas. That could have been my Douglas."

I did my best to comfort her, reminding her of the promises of Psalm 91:

> *You will not fear the terror of night,*
> *nor the arrow that flies by day,*
> *nor the pestilence that stalks in the darkness,*
> *nor the plague that destroys at midday.*
> *A thousand may fall at your side,*
> *ten thousand at your right hand,*
> *but it will not come near you.*

Yet, even as I quoted Scripture to her, I couldn't help wondering what would have happened if that grieving widow in Spanaway, Washington, had prayed these very verses or some just like them, trusting God to protect her husband and bring him home safe. I don't mean to be cynical but if the last year has taught me anything, it has taught me that while the Bible is a source of great comfort and strength, it is not a magic wand to ward off all tragedies. Still, as I have also learned, God is greater than any tragedy that may befall us and His grace will sustain us no matter what happens.

According to Douglas, one of the worst things about war is what it does to the soldier himself. "Let a couple of your buddies die," he wrote in one email, "and you turn into a killer. The enemy is no longer a human being that Jesus died to redeem, but vermin to be wiped off the face of the earth. One of the most shameful experiences, I've ever had was the night I realized that the 'beast' that drove the insurgents to kill and maim, also lived in me."

To restore his humanity, he began spending many of his off-duty hours volunteering at the U.S. Military Hospital. There, he rediscovered his humanity. In the children's ward, he made friends with a terrified little Iraqi girl whose entire family had been killed by the insurgents. For some reason, she took an immediate liking to the American GI with the bright red hair and infectious smile. Night after night, he would hold her trembling body until she at last fell asleep. Only then would he leave the hospital to get some much needed rest himself.

He credited her with saving him from the "beast" within. Holding her in his arms, he determined he would not become a monster in order to destroy the monster of terrorism. With that decision, his hatred of the insurgents slowly began to turn to compassion, though he could not help thinking how different things might be if the United States had spent the same amount of money on missions as it spent on war.

As November eased into December, I had the privilege of seeing my children take their purity vows, pledging to God and to themselves that they would remain sexually pure, saving themselves for marriage. Sitting beside Thomas on the third row in the center section, I wept unashamedly. There was something so innocent, so pure, about their commitment that I couldn't help myself. That was also the night I tried to strike a bargain with God, promising I would do anything He wanted if He would just let me live until I saw my children marry.

Jessica hasn't yet gone public with the news about her pregnancy but it won't be long now. Her doctor says her pregnancy is textbook perfect and there appears to be no danger of losing the baby, besides she's starting to show. How she's kept the news to herself for this long is beyond me. I would have been shouting it from the rooftops! Of course, I've never been known for my restraint. I've got what my daddy affectionately called "a big personality."

Speaking of Daddy, I'm finally coming to grips with his death, whatever that means. For the longest time, when I thought of him, all I could see was the image of the paramedics wheeling him toward the ambulance or the way he looked in the casket. All I could remember was the way he died, but in recent days, I've begun to remember the life he lived. My pastor says God is doing His healing work, moving me from grief to gratefulness. He calls it a journey of hope. I still grieve and there are times when I can't think of my father without weeping but more and more, I'm remembering the special times we shared and I catch myself smiling or even chuckling at some of the things we did.

Keith has become something of a spiritual mentor to me. Given my initial resentment and animosity toward him, I find it nothing short of amazing. Thomas just shakes his head and laughs. "It must be a God thing," he teases. "No one but God can get you to change your mind once it's made up."

Obviously, God was at work, but Keith has also had a hand in winning me over. It seems he was always there, at the right time, with a scripture, a word of counsel, or a life-changing insight. No matter how much I wanted to dislike him, I couldn't. How do you dislike someone who is so concerned about you and has your best interest at heart? It took some time, but I'm firmly in his corner now.

When they came for Thanksgiving, Mom brought trays and trays of colored slides and Daddy's old slide projector. We spent a couple of evenings looking at them and reliving my childhood. Jessica joined us for the second evening and although Thomas and Jason headed for the theater room to catch a football game, Keith watched every single slide. I worried, thinking all the family pictures might make him uncomfortable, especially the pictures of Dad, but he seemed to enjoy them and the memories they brought back, as much as the rest of us.

I got a chance to ask him about it on Saturday morning, when he joined me in the sunroom, for coffee. "Becca," he said, "your mother and daddy had almost forty years together. If I tried to take away your mother's history, I would destroy an irreplaceable part of the woman I love. Without her past, she wouldn't be who she is today. The same thing is true for me. I'm not going to forget my first wife or pretend I have no history before your mother came into my life. When your mother and I marry, we aren't rewriting our histories; we're simply adding a few more chapters."

I feel so much better now. It's good to know that we won't have to watch every word or pretend we had no life before Keith came into the family. I'm even looking forward to meeting his children and his grandchildren. Being an only child, I've always hungered for family, especially since the twins were born. One of my secret fantasies has always been of three generational holiday gatherings with brothers and sisters and nieces and nephews. Maybe now, my lifelong dream will come true.

Thankfully, since coming off of the steroids, I'm almost down to my pre-lupus weight and hope to be by the wedding. For that reason, I had planned on waiting until just before the big day to look for my dress. But on an impulse, I asked Mom if she would like to help me pick one out and was rewarded with such a joyous response, I thought my heart would burst. To see how such a simple gesture could give my mother such pleasure, made me realize how much she longed for a relationship with me.

Even before Daddy's death, we were prickly with each other, but his presence provided the salve that made our relationship work. After he died, we just seemed to drift apart, especially after she moved to Texas; then, I got sick and she fell in love with Keith. I've always blamed her for what I sometimes call "our cold war" but in recent weeks, I've come to see that the fault was at least partially mine, maybe mostly mine. The fact that she was so good at things in which I had only a passing interest—homemaking for instance, especially the cooking and cleaning part—generated no little resentment in me. Anytime she tried to lend a hand, I felt like I was being judged and found wanting. Only now am I beginning to realize that she wasn't judging me. She was simply giving me the gifts that meant the most to her, gifts that came naturally to her—an orderly home and well cooked meals.

Of course, I couldn't have picked a worse time to shop; the day after Thanksgiving crowds were horrendous, but for once I didn't mind. When I grew weary, we found a little restaurant just off Utica Square, where we shared a quiche and fresh fruit. Of course, she talked about the things she always talks about—recipes, my aunt Linda, what it was like growing up in the sixties, people I never knew—but this time, I listened, or at least I tried to listen and was rewarded with a feeling of closeness we had seldom shared. It made my heart hurt to realize how selfish I had been, never showing an interest in the things or the people who populated her life.

I'm only now, beginning to realize how full of myself I've always been, especially around my mother. Painful as it was, I welcomed this insight, realizing it was just another step, in the holy thing God was doing in me.

We didn't find a dress but I returned home thinking it was a day well spent. Like always, I was only too glad to let Mom prepare the evening meal, but this time, I sat in the kitchen and talked with her rather than parking myself in front of the TV. Mercedes joined us, lending Mom a hand, and I felt a deep contentment knowing that piece of misplaced furniture, which had long stood between my mother and me in the soul of our relationship was gone. We would always be different, I think we both knew that, but it was okay. For the first time ever, I think I accepted my mother for who she was, not needing her to be anything more or less.

With the wedding barely two weeks away, I'm beginning to get excited. Even though I'm gaining strength day by day, I'm still not up to making a trip to Fort Worth, so Keith and Mom have decided to have the wedding here. Originally, they had planned to be married in the Church of the Comforter in Cleburne, Texas, where Keith serves as pastor, but when it became apparent that I wouldn't be able to attend, he graciously consented to move the wedding to Tulsa.

Now, Mom calls almost every day concerned about some detail, and I am beginning to feel like the mother of the bride. Thank God for Jessica and Madison who are handling all the details in my stead. They're so much better than I am at things like that. Unbeknownst to my mother, they are determined to make her wedding extra special. They've ordered flowers and a wedding cake, secured the services of a caterer, hired a photographer, and rented a wedding chapel. Boy, will she be surprised.

CHAPTER

FORTY-FIVE

Standing at the window, I can see cars turning off of 241st East Ave., their headlights piercing the darkness as they make their way toward the Arrow Springs Wedding Chapel. Eight inches of snow has fallen and it continues to come down, harder now if anything, turning the chapel grounds into a sparkling wonderland. Although a winter storm of this magnitude usually brings Tulsa to its knees, it doesn't appear to have dissuaded the guests who have been invited to see my mother and the Reverend Keith Thompson united in holy matrimony. Already, the chapel is comfortably full and the wedding isn't scheduled to begin for another twenty minutes.

As I continue to stare into the darkness, my breath fogging the cold window, I am overcome with gratefulness once more for Jessica and Madison. Without their help, I could've never pulled this off. I prepared and mailed the invitations but they made all the other arrangements, giving careful attention to the details and colors that my mother had selected. Mom arrived in Tulsa thinking she was going to be married in a private ceremony at my house only to discover that Jessica and Madison wouldn't hear of it, nor would I. They also insisted on helping with the added expenses, knowing Thomas and I would be hard-pressed to cover them, given my medical bills.

Turning from the window, I watch as Jessica puts the finishing touches on my mother's makeup. That's something I would normally do, but it has taken all of my strength just to get myself dressed and assist Brooklyn with the stubborn zipper on her emerald green dress.

Although Mom is nearing sixty, you would never know it and it's not hard to see why Keith is attracted to her. Her skin is flawless, her face unlined, and she colors and highlights her dark hair, effectively hiding the grey that has crept in since Daddy's death. Coming up behind her, I bend down and give her a hug. "Mother, you look stunning. I'm so happy for you."

Looking at the two of us in the mirror, I see her eyes glisten. Laughing shakily, she says, "I'm not going to cry. It would ruin my makeup and we don't have time to redo it."

Excusing myself, I slip out to take a peek at the chapel. It is ablaze with candles and decorated with flowers of the deepest hues. With her artist's eye, Jessica has selected bouquets of stunning beauty. I recognize some of the more common species—Roses, Bells of Ireland, Cali Lilies and Irises, but I have no idea what some of the others are. Still, it is the colors that are unforgettable—blood red, deep copper, burnt orange, dark purple, and a stunning teal green. That those colors could be used in combination, would have never entered my mind.

Surveying the guests, I see several familiar faces, mostly friends of my parents from the church they attended, but there are a number I don't recognize, as well. Parishioners from the Church of the Comforter, I assume. I'm impressed that they would come all the way from Texas, especially in this kind of weather. That they love their pastor and his bride to be is apparent. Of course, Aunt Linda, Mom's only sister, is in attendance, as are all The Bunko Babes.

Returning to the dressing room, I note that Jessica has put the final touches on Mother's hair. She's pulled it into a simple chignon with wispy tendrils framing her face and festooned it with flowers in vibrant red, copper, and purple.

I can't help but notice the special bond between them and, maybe for the first time ever, I take joy in it, without even a hint of jealousy. *Thank You, Jesus.*

Jessica has always been stunningly, beautiful, but now she radiates an inner beauty that shines like an incandescent light and her joy is contagious. She's one of those women who seems to blossom during pregnancy, but it's more than that. For her, being pregnant is a spiritual experience; irrefutable proof that she has been forgiven and a manifestation of grace as tangible as the Eucharist.

Glancing at the clock, I see it is almost time to go so I make my way to the full-length mirror to check my appearance one last time. Although I'm not a natural beauty, I'm good with clothes maximizing the assets I do have and I can't remember ever having a dress that made me look better. The rich, magenta color is perfect for my skin tone, giving me a look of healthy vitality I haven't had in months. The crinkled taffeta wraps snugly around my bodice, before tying in a large bow at my waist, just above my left hip. The stiffness of the taffeta adds flare to the knee length, godet skirt. Of course, no dress would be complete without the perfect shoes. Mine are black patent leather with an enclosed toe, four inch, two-tone heels, featuring a wide ankle strap and an oversized gold buckle. I do look good if I say so myself.

Madison, who is serving as the wedding coordinator, opens the door. "Five minutes," she calls. Jessica gives Mom a hug and squeezes my hand before slipping out to be seated.

Now, Mom and I are alone for the first time today and she takes both of my hands in hers. "Thank you," she whispers, her face beaming. "You have no idea how much this means to me."

All my life, I've prided myself on my outrageous humor and sarcastic wit but in recent weeks I've become overly sentimental, even maudlin, and now I find myself teary-eyed and at a loss for words. Holding her hands in mine, I can't help thinking that I hardly know this woman. Although she nourished me in her womb for nine months, birthed me, breastfed me, gave me birthday parties, and nursed me through a series of childhood illnesses, she's hardly more than an acquaintance to me. Because we've always been so different, I've never taken time to get to know her, not as a person anyway.

Suddenly, I am seized with a frightening thought. *What if Brooklyn thinks of me in the same way; as her mom, but not as a person in my own right not as someone she would like to know?* The thought distresses me in ways I can't even put into words. And now, I understand the look I've seen in my mother's eyes; a look reflecting a secret sorrow she would never share with anyone less it cast me in a negative light. I may have hurt her but she would still die for me. It shames me to admit it but I have often taken her for granted and frequently, treated her with no more courtesy than I would extend to a stranger. And I've been only too happy to see her go when her visit was over.

How many times has she asked me if there was anything I would like to know about her life? I feel my face burning with shame as I remember my impatient words. "Mother, you've told me the same stories more times than I can remember. I don't think there's anything about you I don't know." She would laugh then, nervously, to hide her hurt and say, "You might be surprised, Becca. You might be surprised."

I *am* surprised and it pains me to realize how much I've underestimated my mother. Since Daddy's death, she's blossomed in spite of her grief, which has been as painful as an abscessed tooth. She's changed her hairstyle and updated her wardrobe and I'm only now beginning to realize to what extent she allowed Daddy to suppress her tastes and her personality. She allowed it because he loved her and she loved him? Not once did she appear to resent his domineering ways.

Through the door, we can hear the murmur of conversation and the shuffling of feet, as the last of the guests are seated. Releasing my hands, she removes a ruby ring from her finger. Instantly, I'm choked up. Not once in my thirty-seven years can I ever remember my mother dressing up without wearing that ring. It's a family heirloom that's been passed down through at least three generations and one of her most prized possessions. I've always hoped that it would be mine someday but given our prickly relationship, I thought my mother might give it to Brooklyn considering how close they are.

In a voice rich with feeling, she says, "Other than the wedding band your father gave me, this is my most treasured piece of jewelry. It was left to me by your grandmother, who inherited it from her mother. At one time, it was supposed to have belonged to a Russian princess who fled her country during the Revolution and made her way to the United States. I can't vouch for that. All I know is that it has been in our family for nearly a hundred years."

Taking my right hand, she slides it on my finger. "I want you to have it as a token of my love. There hasn't been a single day since you were born when I haven't thought of you. I hope you will think of me when you wear it and remember how much I have always loved you."

Before I can say anything, she is pushing me out the door, "Now, get out of here before I start crying and ruin my makeup."

Madison is motioning for me to join her and Brooklyn at the door to the chapel as it is almost time for us to make our entrance. Keith's oldest son, the Reverend Kent Thompson, is officiating. He and the groomsman are already in place. The music begins and Brooklyn follows me down the aisle. Keith enters from the side, resplendent in his tux and then the guests rise for the bride's entrance.

A hush falls over the small chapel as mother comes down the aisle on the arm of her handsome grandson. Seeing Robert decked out in the black suit he wore to the purity ceremony, I get choked up and quickly turn my attention back to the bride. Mother's gown is the color of champagne, the sheen of the satin picking up the candlelight and reflecting it back in refractions of light. The underlay is a sheath of floor length satin—simple, elegant. The overlay, created from handmade lace encrusted with pearls and sequins, has long, bell-shaped sleeves and attaches at the waist with a simple bow.

Never has my mother looked more strikingly elegant and I risk a glance at the groom who is staring at her with unabashed ardor. Turning my gaze back to my mother, I see that she has eyes only for Keith. Looking at him, her face floods with love and joy, a tender smile gracing her lips.

As the ceremony begins, I find myself thinking of my own wedding. How little, Thomas and I knew of love or the demands marriage would place upon us. The vows we took that afternoon so long ago were just words. We thought we understood the promises we were making to each other and to God but it took life to make them real to us. "In sickness and in health," was just part of the ceremony, until systemic lupus invaded my body, making suffering and the possibility of death unwelcome guests in our home. A less honorable man might have broken under the stress, but Thomas has been a tower of strength, never wavering in his commitment to me and the children.

Although my back is to the chapel, in my mind I can see The Bunko Babes, faithful friends every one. Only God knows how I would have made it this last year if it hadn't been for them. The sisters—Jessica and Kathleen—are sitting with their husbands near the front. Kathleen is seven-and-one half months pregnant and in the language of Scripture, "great with child," while Jessica is just beginning to show. Autumn and her brood of eight take up an entire pew, attracting no little attention from some of Keith's parishioners who have likely never seen a family with eight children, nor a mother so unselfconsciously breast-feeding her youngest.

Karen and her husband are sitting close together his arm on the back of the pew around her shoulders. Enjoying a rare evening away from their three preschool age children, they look like they could be on a date. Michelle does have a date and she looks happier than I've ever seen her, except maybe when we presented her with a check for $3,127.35 to cover her expenses to the national Bunko tournament in Las Vegas. My little "mud-sucker" is undoubtedly dreaming of her own wedding. I hope her beau knows what he's in for. Once she makes up her mind, look out!

Mercedes' parents are here from Argentina and she is sitting with them and Madison near the back. My heart goes out to both of them. I can't imagine how hard this must be for Madison given her recent divorce. I encouraged her not to come but she wouldn't hear of it. Of course, with Douglas still in Iraq, the entire Christmas season has been difficult for Mercedes. Not as hard as it would have been if her parents hadn't been able to come. But still hard enough.

The Bunko Babes—my comrades in arms, a band of sisters, loving and laughing, taking on whatever life throws at us. Sure, we like Bunko, especially the rituals that surround it and the good food but the thing that continues to bring us together, week after week, is the camaraderie. For a few hours, we can be ourselves without fear of being judged or rejected. Maybe this is what Jesus had in mind when He told us to love one another.

Our lives are rich indeed and yet not without their challenges. Still, as I have learned since Daddy's death, many of life's greatest opportunities come to us disguised as challenges or even tragedies. Daddy's untimely death was an unspeakable tragedy and my ongoing battle with systemic lupus remains the greatest challenge I've ever faced. And yet, both have afforded me an opportunity for meaningful personal growth and a profound strengthening of my faith that I might not have experienced any other way. Given a choice, I would have no doubt chosen an easier way but I wouldn't trade anything for the experiences and understanding of life I've gained.

The minister's words call my attention back to the wedding and I focus as he says, "I now pronounce you husband and wife. Dad, you may kiss your bride."

As Keith takes my mother in his arms and kisses her, The Bunko Babes erupt into cheers. Tears of joy slide down my cheeks and I can't help thinking that somewhere up there Daddy is watching, peering down through a peephole. And if he is, I know he's smiling. Because nothing was ever more important to Dad than Mom's happiness and not even death can change that.

THE END

ACKNOWLEDGMENTS

I can't believe I finally got it right! After years of trying a list of countless other occupations, I decided to give up, relinquish the reigns completely, turn them over to God, and do what comes most naturally to me...write. Close on the heels of this colossal decision, I had a story line, a catchy title, and a book contract. Life flew by in a rush of commotion as I juggled life with lupus, a five and six year old, a shift working husband, and a rapidly approaching deadline. Yet, rather surprisingly, I found that on this roller-coaster ride, I could throw my hands up in the air and shout with joy instead of hanging on for dear life, mute in the face of my own fears. Thank you, Heavenly Father and my Savior Jesus Christ, for sticking with me even when I was too stubborn to see how trustworthy You are. I can't wait to see what's over the next hill. WOOHOO!!

None of this would have been possible without the love and support of my husband, Douglas Lloyd Baker. My consummate cheerleader, you have stood beside me no matter what dream I chose to pursue next. Having you behind me gave me the courage to give wings to my imaginings. In my heart and mind, there are few greater gifts than that. Douglas, I love you more than all my yesterdays and a thousand times more with each tomorrow.

Alexandria Starr and Deuce, my doodlebugs, y'all have put up with a lot in order to accommodate my deadline not to mention my own battle with Systemic Lupus and God's continued healing. I can never express how much I love and admire the two of you, even if there are times when I want to pull out my hair from the stress of it all. In our few short years together, y'all have given me a lifetime of love and a wealth of material. (Yes, I admit it! That's the price you pay for being my kids. Sorry.)

I owe an extra special, "You're the man," kind of thing to my editor, Richard Exley. Without you, this book would have only been a skeleton. I had the frame but with your insistence and guidance, I was able to form the muscles, mold the skin, and finally, finish with the wardrobe. Thank you for taking me down one of the most painful processes of my life, but like you said from the very beginning, "Nobody ever said giving birth was easy." You weren't kidding. I don't know about you, but I'm ready to see this baby walk!

Now, onto my dad, if you hadn't kept pushing and insisting that I had a gift, I might never have dared to dream this dream and I know without a doubt that if you hadn't tutored me for three crazy weeks at your "cabin" on Beaver Lake, I wouldn't be near the writer I am today. Thanks for believing in me. Thanks for instilling in me a deep love for literature, language, novels, the written Word and mostly, yes, most of all, sharing with me the gift of salvation. Your life is and has always been a shining example for me to follow and a proud legacy to carry on. I love you a bushel and a peck and a hug around the neck.

Mom, you give and give and give until there is nothing left and then, you give some more. These past three years would have been impossible without your help around the house, with the kids, and assisting in my own care. I can never express how much your sacrifice has meant to me. Thanks for being there any and every time I call and thanks for loving me. I love you this much!!

Last, but not least, a huge "thank you" to all the people at Emerald Pointe Books for taking a chance on a no-name chick from T-town and helping her make her dreams come true. Debbie, Keith, Amanda, Susannah, and the entire sales team: thanks for putting legs on my baby and teaching her to walk. I look forward to a lasting relationship as we journey on with Christ.

And to all the folks at Phenix and Phenix, Inc. in Austin, Texas, "Big hugs and kisses to one and all, I'm so proud to be joining your team."

READING GROUP DISCUSSION QUESTIONS

1. Early on, we discover that Jessica is infertile due to irreparable damage done to her fallopian tubes during a botched abortion she had when she was sixteen. We also learn that she has never shared the fact of her abortion with her husband, Jason. Do you think that Jessica should tell Jason the truth behind her infertility? Or should she keep the past in the past? Why or why not?

2. Becca places people's attitudes into two categories: Star Seekers and Mud-suckers. She believes that our outlook has a lot to do with how we handle life's heartaches and whether or not we will ever find happiness. Do you agree with her philosophy? If so, which category do you honestly think you fall into? How has it affected your life?

3. Jealousy is an ugly green monster that can creep up at anytime within any one of us. Becca is open and honest about her insecurities and bouts with this feeling that can often destroy any or all of our relationships. She got it under control by admitting it, at least to herself and the reader. What other things did she do to keep this monster firmly within her grasp? What are some ideas that you have when dealing with envy? Share them with the group.

4. At first, it is difficult for Becca to admit to both herself and her friends that she is seriously ill. As a result, she finds herself isolated in a world of pain and uncertainty. Have you ever found yourself faced with a problem so overwhelming that you found it easier to hide from it than to face it head-on and deal with it? How did you finally come to grips with it?

5. As a lifetime Christian, it is quite obvious that Becca loves God and has dedicated her entire life to serving Him. Yet, during this crisis she often finds that she is horribly angry with God for allowing her to become ill. How does her reaction make you feel? Do you personally believe that God is big enough to handle our anger? Have you ever experienced feelings of rage toward the Heavenly Father? How did you handle those feelings?

6. Out of *"The Bunko Babes,"* who is most like you? Give reasons behind your answers. Afterwards take time to share with different people in your group, what you admire about them personally and why you feel that way. God made each and every one of us just the way we are and we need to celebrate our differences. So, get busy building each other's confidence.

7. Bunko night is one example of a way to connect with other women in your community, but it is certainly not the only way. Share with the group some of the ways that you have managed to find the time and the creative outlets, which have opened doors for you to

meet new friends or to get together consistently with the familiar ones.

8. In the high-powered, overstressed world we live in we as women are expected to bring home the bacon, fry it up in a pan, keep the house perfect, keep ourselves perfect, and never ever let our husbands forget they're our man. Let's face it! We can't do it. Divorce, depression, suicide, eating disorders, debt, heart attacks, strokes, and lupus; all of these things are at an all-time high and continue to climb at alarming rates. This is our society. Do you think God expects us to be perfect? If not, what do you think His priorities are for your life at this time?

9. *The Bunko Babes* are extremely blessed to have each other to lean on in times of struggle. Who in your life do you have to depend upon? When did you realize that this person was someone you could trust with your life if the need arose? Do you feel that same way about God the Father, His Son, and the Holy Spirit? Why or why not?

10. Several times throughout the book, God gave a word to one woman or another and that particular Scripture verse became a lifeline for her to cling to during her struggle. Is there a particular time in your life when God has done this for you? What is the Scripture passage? Does it still hold great significance for you? Take comfort knowing that God doesn't just answer prayers in a fairy tale, but He does it consistently in real life.

AN INTERVIEW
WITH THE AUTHOR
LEAH STARR BAKER

1. **When did you first realize that you wanted to be a writer? Was there anything in your childhood that influenced you to become a writer?**

    I've always loved the English language, whether listening to a song, reading a poem, or losing myself in a book or movie. The power of words and their uncanny ability to express emotions have long since fascinated me, moved me...called to me, I guess you could say. I didn't discover writing. It discovered me.

    As for a childhood influence? That's easy. My father sitting at his desk, kerosene lamp at his shoulder, preparing his Sunday sermon and me across the room watching, absorbing, Rod McKuen singing softly in the background.

2. **Which writers have influenced your writing and in what ways?**

    Sophie Kinsella comes to mind as one most recently. She really helped me to hone my humor, to sharpen my wit.

    John Grisham taught me the importance of writing out of your own expertise and experiences.

    Margaret Mitchell, what can you say about a woman who wrote only one novel in her lifetime and yet it is one of the greatest in all of history? From Margaret, I hope I gleaned a little about creating unforgettable characters.

And last, but certainly not least, author Richard Exley whose patient tutelage has stretched me, twisted me, turned me upside down, and in the end has helped me to find my "voice" and become the writer that you read today.

3. **Why did you write** The Bunko Babes, **rather than some other story?**

Wow, great question! "The Bunko Babes" chose me, I guess you could say, not the other way around. My husband Douglas came up with the title one night as we were relaxing in our hot tub (he was relaxing, I was trying to ease my pain). He thought it would make a great story about an illegal drug ring being run by these suburban housewives. You know, that sort of thing. That could be intense and quite a twist on a rather common story line, I told him in so many words, as we continued to bounce ideas off one another.

*But God had other plans for this book and as my lupus continued to escalate and the battle in both my mind and body raged on, a different story emerged. Becca and **The Bunko Babes** were born and like any birth, it was messy, it was painful, but I like to think that the final outcome was beautiful.*

4. **Your characters are engaging and very realistic. When reading you become attached to these women and the friendships they share. What inspired the development of**

these characters in your story? Are they based upon people you already know?

Thanks for the kind words. I too, have fallen in love with each of these women and by the end of the novel, though elated by my accomplishment, I was sad to let them go.

But in answer to your question, I'd have to say, "Yes!" These characters are a compilation of the many wonderful, amazing women who have touched my life throughout the years. Past and present, I wove them together to try to create for you, the reader, a feeling of just how much these friends have enriched my life. Even more than that, by drawing upon an actual pool of people, I tried to strike a chord within each of you, a memory, great or small, of someone in your life who may be just like that.

5. How do you develop your plot and your characters?

Okay, here goes. I feel like I should put in some sort of warning here or an escape clause! Something to the effect of: The following is not intended or recommended as a guideline for new or experienced novelists.

You see, I broke all the rules with this book and honestly, it made my life (and that of my editors) more difficult. When I started this book, I only knew that it was going to be about eight women who played Bunko together. That's it. I didn't create an outline, time line, list of characters. I didn't know my characters' names, ages, physical characteristics, personalities, nothing. I simply turned off

Jewelry Television, sat up in bed, put my computer on my lap, and started typing. Crazy, huh?

6. **How would you describe your writing style—not your literary style—but the actual writing itself? What kind of techniques do you use?**

   My writing style? I'd have to say, "Quirky, very unusual." They (I'm not sure who "they" actually are) say that my style of writing is quite tricky to do as well, but it comes very naturally to me. I write as if I am sitting on the couch, sharing a cup of coffee and chatting it up with one of my girlfriends and it works. I like to think of the reader as a "participant" in the story, instead of an "observer." Possibly that right there is the technique that is the most different or unique to me. My readers are my friends and I want them to feel that way from the opening paragraph to the ending phrase.

7. **There's obviously more to a novel than just an entertaining read. What do you want the reader to take away from** *The Bunko Babes?*

   First and foremost, a sense of hope and encouragement, the realization that no matter how dark the day seems, there is always the dawn of God's love waiting just around the corner. We just need to dare to open our eyes enabling us to catch sight of it. Also, I want my readers to go away with an understanding that nothing and no one is perfect. Life is not perfect and God doesn't expect us to be perfect, He just wants us to be real, to learn to depend upon Him for all our needs.

8. **We've talked about the authors who have most influenced your writing. Now on a more personal level, as an adult, what one person has been most influential in your life?**

That's tough. I've been blessed with so many that it's hard to choose. I'd have to say my husband Douglas. He's always been there for me through thick and thin. And no matter how many career paths I've wandered down or how sick I've become, he has been my greatest cheerleader and has given me the strength to carry on. I like to say that: Behind every successful dreamer is a supportive doer. Douglas is that for me and so much more.

9. **In conclusion, tell us something personal about Leah Starr Baker that most people may not know.**

I'm a closet tomboy. Seriously, looking at me, you would never guess that beneath the makeup, fashion forward clothes, high heels, and love of jewelry beats the heart of an action movie fanatic, suspense novel addict, professional boxing's youngest female supporter (Cassius Clay aka Muhammad Ali Rules), Houston Rocket's lifetime lover (miss you, Rudy T. & Hakeem the Dream), and last but never least, the biggest Denver Bronco's Diehard Defender ever to grace this earth (John Elway for President!). Yep, I guess that's what happens when you're the only child of a sports junky.

ABOUT THE AUTHOR

 **Leah Starr Baker:** a Christian, a wife, a mother, a born storyteller. The daughter of a minister/author, Leah wasn't born with a silver spoon in her mouth. No, instead, she was teethed on the Gospel. Living in the hill country of western Colorado until age ten, she spent many a night listening to the early beginnings of her father's writings. It was there that she learned the true beauty of the English language and the power of the pen. From Colorado, her family moved to Tulsa, Oklahoma, and though the life of a preacher's kid was challenging at times, Leah wore the mantle of "role model" well.

Leah had big dreams and a multitude of talents. In 1994, she found her soul mate, Douglas Baker, and they were married later that year. He, like Leah, was a dreamer and a huge supporter of her dreams. With his help, she went on to be crowned Mrs. Oklahoma 1995 and to record an album in Nashville, Tennessee, before turning her sights entirely upon the joys of being a wife and mother.

But the birth of two children in less than eighteen months took a toll on her body and she was stricken by an unexplainable illness. After months of testing it was discovered that she had Systemic Lupus, a chronic disease that affects the immune system. Trapped at home in a body that refused to cooperate, she turned to her forgotten love...writing. Without a doubt, Leah has a promising career as a novelist ahead of her and we look forward with great anticipation to additional stories from this shooting STARR.

For more information on Leah and her upcoming events, please visit her at: www.thebunkobabes.biz where you can sign-up for her weekly blog and get fun ideas for your own bunko group.

OTHER GREAT READS FROM
EMERALD POINTE BOOKS

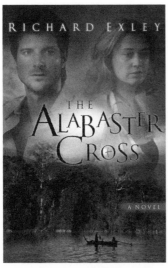

0-9785-370-3

Trapped in a world of anger, twenty-nine-year-old Bryan Whittaker cannot move on with his life until he takes a journey into his past...a dangerous journey that will lead him into the heart of the Amazon Rain Forest. Instead of the revenge he seeks, Bryan finds Diana and through her love he is able to make peace with his past and find redemption.

If you've ever struggled to restore a broken relationship, you will identify with Bryan's journey as he strives to make peace with his past.

0-98751-371-1

Luke Hatcher is the pride of Magnolia Springs, Louisiana. The perfect kid, he's the star of the high school baseball team and is on his way to LSU after graduation on a full scholarship—destined for the big leagues. Little did he know that a simple dare from his high school sweetheart would change his whole life.

A riveting novel that celebrates the God who gives second chances. If you've ever looked back on your life, feeling you threw away a golden moment, you will walk away from this passionate story cheering and with a renewed outlook on your own life.

Additional copies of this book and other titles by
Emerald Pointe Books are available
from your local bookstore.

If you have enjoyed this book,
or if it has impacted your life,
we would like to hear from you:

Please contact us at:

Emerald Pointe Books
Attention: Editorial Department
P.O. Box 35327
Tulsa, Oklahoma 74153

Emerald Pointe Books